SHIPWRECKED DREAMS

SET IN EARLY 20TH CENTURY NORTH PACIFIC, MYSTERY AND ADVENTURE

HARPER STANWICK, SR.

CONTENTS

CHAPTER ONE.

The liner's smoke streamed smoothly behind, staining the soft blue sky, as she glided through the north pacific's gentle waves, her engines purring steadily. Beneath her lofty bows, foam ignited with phosphorescent flames, streaming green and gold flashes down her ivory-white hull, which gleamed in the half-moon light. The foam boiled up again in fiery splendor in the wake of her twin screws. Tall yellow funnels and mastheads cut through the sky with a measured swing, the long deck slanted gently, its spotless whiteness darkened by the dew. The draught from the boat created faint harmonies like elfin harps strumming from wire shrouds and guys.

Sometimes the melodies rose clearly, sometimes they were lost in the roar of the parted swell. A glow of electric light poured from the saloon and the smoking-room; the skylights of the saloon were open, and the notes of a piano combined with a girl's voice drifted aft. Jimmy Farquhar, second mate, dressed in a crisp white uniform beneath a swung-up boat, smiled at the refrain of the old love song. He was in an unusually impressionable mood, and he sensed the danger of losing his head as his eyes admirably rested on his companion, charmed by the blue and silver splendor of the night.

Ruth Osborne leaned on the rail, looking forward, her face bathed in moonlight. She was young and delicately pretty, with a slender figure and a warm coloring that hinted at an enthusiastic temperament. In the daylight, her hair carried ruddy gleams in its warm brown, and her eyes sparkled with a curious golden sheen. But now, her hair formed a dusky mass above the pallid oval of her face, and her look was thoughtful. She had developed a habit of meeting Jimmy when he was off watch, and the mate felt a sense of pride from her honest preference for his company. He suspected that several of the passengers envied him, and that miss Osborne was a notable lady back home.

She was known as the only daughter of an american merchant who had secured the two best deck rooms, which might explain her somewhat commanding demeanor. Miss Osborne did as she pleased and made it seem perfectly natural; and it was clear that she enjoyed conversing with Jimmy.

"this trip has been delightful," she remarked.

"yes," Jimmy agreed, "the best i can remember. I wanted you to have a smooth voyage, and i'm glad it turned out well."

"that was kind of you," she said with a smile. "i couldn't help but enjoy it. The ship is comfortable, and everyone on board has been pleasant. We should see Vancouver island by late tomorrow, right?"

"it'll be dark when we spot the lights, but we'll dock in Victoria early the next morning. I believe you're leaving us there?"

The girl was quiet for a few moments, and there was a hint of regret in her eyes that stirred something deep within Jimmy. They had spent a considerable amount of time together during the voyage, and it stung him to think that their companionship would likely end soon. But he dared to hope that she might share his sentiments, even if just a little.

"in a way, i'm sorry we're almost home," ruth admitted frankly. Then, smiling, she added, "i'm starting to realize i love the sea."

Jimmy took note of her words. He was a handsome young english-man with a humble nature, not one to chase after wealth, but he had been teased by the other crew members. It wasn't entirely unheard of for a wealthy young woman to fall for a ship's officer during a pleasant long voyage. However, miss Osborne had only displayed a friendly affection toward him, and with their parting imminent, he knew it wouldn't be sensible to make a fool of himself at the last moment.

"the sea isn't always like this," he replied. "it can be very unforgiving, and not all ships are as comfortable as this."

"i suppose not. You mean life is tougher on other ships?"

Jimmy laughed.

Jimmy had always been a conway kid, but right after graduating from the legendary old ship, he lost a guardian who had provided the support and connections he'd relied on. Orphaned of influence, he found himself apprenticed to a stingy firm and began his career on an ill-equipped, undermanned iron sailing vessel. Onboard, he endured hunger, dampness, and cold, often pushed to the brink of exhaus-tion. Pride kept him from deserting, and after four grueling years, he emerged tough and lean, only to start another arduous journey in steam cargo tramps. But a twist of fate changed everything when he met an ailing merchant on one of these ships. The merchant vouched for him to the directors of a mail company, and from then on, life eased up for Jimmy. His progress was swift, and after all he had endured, his current environment seemed almost luxurious.

"steam is making things better," he said. "but there are still trades out there where mates and sailors have to push beyond what any human should."

"and you've experienced this firsthand?" ruth asked.

"more than enough," Jimmy replied.

"tell me about it," ruth urged, curious.

Jimmy chuckled. "well, on my first trip around cape horn, we left the mersey short-staffed and lost three crew members before we even got past the falkland islands. Two of them were thrown from the royal yard when rotten gear broke. That made a huge difference. We faced vile weather—gales head-on, snow, bitter cold. The galley fire was out half the time, the deckhouse constantly flooded. We didn't have a dry stitch of clothing for weeks, and warm food was a rarity. It was a blessed relief when the gale intensified, and we hove to, icy seas crashing over the weather bow while we slept like logs in our soaking bunks. But moments like that were few and far between."

Every shift in the wind or sudden storm forced us back out onto the yards, our bodies frozen and drenched, to free the stiffened canvas. Inevitably, just an hour later, we'd be ordered aloft to secure it tightly again. Each encounter with that flailing sail was a perilous fight for survival. Our hands became raw, the cuts refused to heal, and the relentless waves soaked our supplies, rendering them useless. Often, we subsisted on soggy biscuits, but the demand for brutal labor never lessened. By the time we caught a fair wind northward, we were mere shadows of ourselves.

"wow!" ruth exclaimed. "that must have been brutal. Didn't it make you despise the sea?"

"i despised the ship, the captain, the owners, and especially the cunning clerk who calculated how cheaply the vessel could be operated down to the last penny; but that was different. The sea casts a spell that ensnares you, and it never really lets go."

"yes," ruth agreed. "i've felt that too, although only from the safety of a liner's deck in good weather." she paused, deep in thought, before continuing. "i'll never forget this journey, heading home over sparkling waters, the wind at our back, smoke rising serenely, warm decks, everything shimmering in the sunlight, and the glow of the moon and sea fire around the hull at night."

Jimmy felt tempted to say that this voyage would live on in his memory even longer, but he held back, wary of letting his feelings spill out too freely.

"were you entranced by Japan?" he asked, steering the conversation to safer ground. Ruth welcomed the topic shift, her eyes lighting up with excitement.

"oh, absolutely!"

The cherry blossoms were in full bloom, transforming the landscape into a magical realm, more enchanting and curious than anything i had ever imagined.

"you must have traveled to many fascinating places," Jimmy remarked.

"no," she replied, her expression growing slightly serious. "i don't even know much about my own country."

"most americans i've met seem to love traveling."

"the wealthy ones do," she admitted candidly. "but until recently, we were not well off. During the klondike gold rush, my father finally struck it rich, and for many years i scarcely saw him. When my mother passed away, i was sent to live with elderly relatives in a small, insular new england town. They were good-hearted but very narrow-minded, and my world was limited to the mundane and provincial. Then i attended a very strict, elite school and stayed there far longer than most girls." ruth paused, then smiled wistfully. "by the time i joined my father, it felt like i had woken up in an entirely different universe. I felt the same way when i first saw Japan."

"but you'll be glad to get home, won't you?"

"yes," she said slowly, "but there's a part of me that will regret leaving. We've been very happy since our departure; my father has been more carefree, and i've had him all to myself. At home, he's often worried and always busy. I have friends and many acquaintances, but there are moments when i feel quite alone."

Jimmy watched her thoughtfully, appreciating her candidness without any trace of naivety. She was untainted by her newfound fortune and had none of the airs of a flirt. He wondered if she was aware of her own charm or if her apparent indifference to admiration stemmed from pride. Though he was not well-versed in understanding young women, he sensed she was proud and possessed a strong character.

"if you're ever near tacoma, you must come visit us," ruth said warmly. Jimmy thanked her and soon after excused himself to resume his watch on the bridge.

As they cruised beyond the sight of land, Jimmy found himself alone except for the quartermaster at the wheel in the glass-enclosed pilothouse. The vast expanse of ocean stretched out endlessly, unmarred by any sail or plume of smoke. The boat rolled gently from side to side, slicing through a deserted sea that shimmered in dusky blue, except where a broad belt of moonlight turned the water into glittering silver. Gradually, the sounds of voices and laughter from the decks below faded away; the glow of lights dimmed, while the rhythmic throb of the engines and the roar of churned water grew louder.

A faint breeze had picked up, causing the smoke to stretch out in a long, black smear over the starboard quarter. As Jimmy paced back and forth, he occasionally paused to sweep his gaze across a different segment of the horizon. On his last scan, he halted abruptly—the smoke had shifted forward. For a moment, he thought the wind had changed, but a quick glance at the white-streaked wake revealed the vessel was turning. He rushed to the pilothouse and peered in through the open door to see the quartermaster leaning slackly against the small brass wheel, his face pale in the moonlight and his forehead damp with sweat.

"what's going on, evans?" Jimmy demanded. The quartermaster, jolted into awareness, glanced at the compass in panic.

"sorry, sir," he mumbled, spinning the wheel. "the ship drifted off course. Something came over me, but i'm alright now."

"it might come over you one time too many. This isn't the first instance," Jimmy reminded him sternly. A shadow moving across the moonlight caught his eye, and Jimmy turned to see the captain standing in the doorway. The skipper took a moment to inspect the compass and study the quartermaster's face before signaling Jimmy to step outside. The captain's approach had been utterly silent, his soft slippers making no noise. Jimmy felt a keen sense of unease, wondering how long the captain had been observing them.

Jimmy had never really gotten along with his captain.

"evans had his helm hard over; was she much off course?" the captain asked with a foreboding calm.

"about thirty degrees, sir."

"how long has it been since you checked his steering?"

Jimmy answered him.

"do you think that's often enough?"

"i was keeping an eye on the smoke, sir."

"the smoke? you realize a light breeze can change directions often?"

"yes, sir," Jimmy replied. "she couldn't veer off much without me noticing it."

"it seems unlikely after what i found out. But i hear evans had an episode like this on your previous watch."

"yes, sir," Jimmy repeated stubbornly.

"didn't it occur to you that you should report it? you knew evans has a heart condition that could strike at any moment. If it happened while we were entering a crowded harbor or crossing another ship's path, the consequences could be catastrophic. By not reporting it, you assumed a responsibility i can't allow my officers to take. Do you have anything to say for yourself?"

Jimmy knew he had no valid excuse. In today's world, where a ship's course is charted meticulously, accurate steering is crucial. He had acted out of misplaced sympathy. Evans was a reliable man with a family back in england, and he had once saved the second mate from being injured by a heavy cargo sling through quick action.

"perhaps the best way to handle this situation," the captain said briskly, "would be for you to voluntarily leave the ship at Vancouver. You can let me know your decision when you come off watch."

Jimmy sullenly returned to his duties, believing his mistake was minor, but there was no room for appeal. He'd lose his chance to serve his current employers, and getting another job on a mailboat wouldn't be easy. He kept his watch and later went to sleep with a heavy heart. The next evening, he was brooding on the saloon deck when he saw miss Osborne approaching.

Jimmy stood in the shadow of the boat, trying to escape the weight of his thoughts. He had no energy to feign cheerfulness, especially when the girl was kind to him. In those moments, he always had to exercise restraint, and now it felt impossible.

"i've been looking for you," she said, her voice cutting through the din of the night. "with everyone so busy tomorrow morning, i might not see you. But you seem a bit down!"

Jimmy balked at the idea of telling her he'd just been dismissed. That was only a small part of his troubles. Her voice was gentle, her eyes filled with a sympathy that quickened his heartbeat. He wished he were a wealthy man or anyone other than a soon-to-be-unemployed steamboat officer.

"well," he began, "the end of a voyage is often bittersweet. After spending weeks with good people, it's hard to say goodbye, knowing everyone will scatter and you'll part from friends you've come to like." A slight blush touched ruth's cheeks, but she smiled warmly.

"that doesn't mean they're forgotten," she replied. "and there's always a chance of meeting again. We might see you in tacoma; it's not far from Vancouver."

Jimmy wasn't one to overstep, and the lead she gave him made him taste regret—it was bitter. Despite his optimism, experience had taught him not to entertain such thoughts. His current situation wasn't conducive to romancing her. Realistically, it would only complicate things.

"i might be on a different route soon," he said. She examined him briefly, her eyes careful but keen. The moonlight highlighted his white uniform, showcasing his sturdy yet refined stature and the clean tan of his skin.

He had light hair and steady, dark blue eyes, though at that moment, they showed a trace of unease.

"well," she replied, "you know what's best; but regardless of what you decide, my father and i owe you a great deal. You've really made this voyage enjoyable." she extended her hand, and he held it briefly. "and now, since this is what you want, goodbye."

As she walked away, Jimmy leaned against the rail, watching her stroll quietly up the long deck. He was tormented by a barrage of confused thoughts and pointless regrets. Still, he had made the right choice: it wasn't wise for a dismissed steamboat officer to entertain the enticing dreams he had forcefully pushed out of his mind.

CHAPTER TWO.

The sun had just slipped behind a jagged black ridge topped with ragged pines when Jimmy, clad in brown overalls and a seaman's jersey, sat cooking dinner on the rocky shore of Vancouver island. In front of him, the enclosed sea stretched out, gleaming with a steel-like shimmer, into the east. Behind him, where the inlet met the hills, stood the city of the springs. Back then, it was little more than a shuttered sawmill, a row of run-down wooden houses, and two shabby hotels. The site, shadowed by rising pine woods and sheltered by rocky terrain, was as picturesque as any in the romantic province of british columbia, despite the human touch that marred its forest charm with rusty iron chimneys, charred fir stumps, and unsightly mounds of sawdust.

Yet, the ancient, untamed forest loomed close by, and ahead lay the pristine sea. The air was uniquely invigorating, the balsamic scent of the firs blending with the sharp odors of drying seaweed, tar, and the cedar shavings scattered around the camp. Jimmy, bent over his frying pan, took a deep breath, reveling in these aromas of the sea and wilderness. He had recently turned his back on the comforts of civilization, embarking on an adventure that thrilled him deeply.

Nearby, a man with a rugged, weather-beaten face was fitting a plank into the bilge of a hauled-up sloop. She was a small but elegant vessel, about forty feet long, crafted following a design favored by a prestigious yacht club on the Atlantic coast. Jimmy could see her potential speed, though she had fallen to lesser purposes and suffered from neglect. He never discovered her full history and always held some suspicion about whether the man they bought her from had the rightful claim to sell her. Moran, once a lobster fisherman from nova scotia, had moved to british columbia to try his hand at the new halibut fisheries, which had ultimately disappointed him.

Bethune, sprawled on the rocky beach with clothes well past their prime, was a "remittance man" known for his endless optimism and unshakeable good humor. It had been a while since he'd tackled any demanding job, so after a day spent sawing wood, he was taking a well-earned break, throwing playful jabs at moran. Jimmy had met both of them in a rundown boarding house in Vancouver, where he'd ended up after striking out on finding a ship and taking odd jobs on the docks. He could have worked as a deckhand, but he realized that once he sought a position on a liner, explaining his past voyages would be challenging, especially if he served as an able seaman. When there were no shipments to unload, he toiled away at the vast hastings mill, soon realizing that this path wouldn't make him wealthy. The relentless and grueling work, driven by relentless foremen, began to wear him down. Had he just come from a sailing ship, he might have handled it, but he freely admitted that it was tough for a former mailboat officer. Despite this, he had some savings. So when Bethune presented a business proposition that also involved moran, Jimmy agreed.

"hank," Bethune drawled, after watching moran wrestle with the task for several minutes, "you folks from the maritime provinces are a stubborn bunch, but you're not going to get that plank in place if you keep on like this until tomorrow."

Moran paused, wiping the sweat from his brow.

"i hate being beaten," he confessed. "i can get it to bend up just fine lengthways, but getting the edges to curve into the frame is impossible."

"exactly. This isn't some fishing dory or lobster punt."

"take your plane and hollow out the plank down the center," said Bethune.

Moran followed the instructions, finding it much easier to fit the plank into place afterward.

"why didn't you tell me that before?" moran asked, slightly exasperated.

Bethune grinned. "i've known you long enough to realize that some people have to try the hard way before they appreciate the easy one. It's not their fault; you can't blame a man for his nature. Trust me, i know—my temperament has often been my downfall."

"how do you know so much about bending planks, anyway? you never mentioned being a boatbuilder."

"do you really expect a man to reveal all his talents? here's another tip—don't nail that plank down just yet. Leave it supported until morning. With a couple of wedges, you'll get a perfect fit by then. Now, let's see if Jimmy hasn't charred our supper."

The meal was far from gourmet, but moran admitted he had eaten worse. Afterward, they sprawled out on the shingle, lighting up their pipes. As usual, Bethune was the first to break the silence.

"the lumber and canvas Jimmy starts working on tomorrow have drained our funds," he remarked. "if we take on any more costs, we'll probably come up short. But hey, that just makes the job more interesting. Prudence is a dull virtue for anyone with spirit. Helping yourself is fine, but doing it all the time often makes it tougher to help others."

"when you're done pontificating, let's get down to business," Jimmy interjected, somewhat impatiently. "i'm in on this venture, but i still know very little about this wreck you're leading us to. Try being practical for a change."

"moran's practical enough for all three of us," Bethune replied with a chuckle.

I'll let him tell the story, but i'll start off by saying that when he discovered that halibut fishing wasn't as profitable as people said, he sailed up the northwest coast with a partner to trade furs with the natives. That's when he discovered the ship.

"the reef," moran began, "is exposed to the southwest. I found seven fathoms next to it at low tide. A mile offshore, near a low island, there's a sandbank extending into the water, and the back half of the wreck is perched on its edge, buried deep in the sand. At low tide, you can see a couple of timbers sticking out of the choppy waters."

"is it always rough water?" Jimmy cut in.

"pretty much," moran replied. "even though the island beach rises and falls, the current was steady to the northeast at around two miles an hour the whole week we were holed up in the cove, and the swell from the open sea created choppy waves on the shoals."

"doesn't sound like a great spot for a dive. How did you get down there?"

"i stripped and swam down. One day, when it was unexpectedly calm for a few hours and jake was busy fixing the sail, i rowed the dory out. I needed to figure out what those timbers were from, and i knew i had to do it then because the ice was coming, and we needed to leave with the first favorable wind. I tied the dory's line to a timber and dove down twice. I saw the bottom at about three fathoms, the water was fairly clear. The sand was packed against her bilge, but she was still intact. When i swam around to her open end, there wasn't much in the way, just the orlop beams."

I could have walked right aft under decks if i'd had a diving suit, but i'd been in the water long enough, and a sea fog was creeping in.

Moran didn't seem to think much of his feat, but Jimmy could grasp the grit he'd shown. The wreck lay far up the northern coast, chilled by polar currents, and moran had ventured down to her when the ice was closing in. Jimmy imagined the tiny dory, pitching over the broken waves, and the half-frozen man carefully crawling aboard to avoid capsizing, while the fog that could have stranded him thickened around. It was an adventure demanding exceptional strength and courage.

"why didn't you take your partner with you?" Jimmy asked.

"i'd seen jake pull some shady moves when we traded for the few furs we managed, and i suspected he wasn't playing fair. Anyhow, he said he didn't care much about wrecks, and when he saw i'd come back empty, he never asked me about it."

"but if she was on the reef, how did she end up a mile away on the bank?"

"i can't explain that exactly, but i guess she shook her engines out after snapping her spine, then slipped into deeper waters. The currents and the surging sea might've dragged her along the seabed."

"it turned out she only had a little rock ballast," Bethune added. "maybe it wasn't enough to hold her down, but what matters is that the strong-room at the aft is intact, according to hank."

Jimmy nodded.

"how about you tell me everything you know about this?" he said. It was typical of both that when they first brought up the venture, one had been satisfied with a rough outline, and the other hadn't pressed for details. The idea had captured their imaginations, and once they committed, the required preparations consumed all their focus.

Bethune leaned back against a boulder, refilling and lighting his pipe. His clothes were well-worn and tar-stained, yet his diction was crisp, and his face exuded intelligence and refinement.

"alright," he began, "when Hank mentioned his find, i saw a chance i'd been waiting for. So, i dug around for details about the vessel. She was an old wooden propeller ship that had sailed around cape horn many years ago. When she couldn't keep up with modern steamships, they reinforced her for whaling in the polar sea. But she guzzled too much coal and didn't fare well under sail. It seemed like she was doomed to failure in any trade. Then came the klondike gold rush, and someone bought her on the cheap, running her up to juneau, alaska, and then to nome. Other boats were better, but packed to the brim, and the gold- seekers heading north weren't picky; they just wanted to reach the goldfields fast. She managed a few trips alright, though her owners struggled when stricter u.s. Passenger regulations kicked in. Likely due to a lack of available vessels, a small mining syndicate—apparently quite successful—shipped a quantity of gold south on her. Along with the gold, the ship carried a bunch of miners, each hoping for fortune. After a day or two at sea, something went wrong with the engines. They rigged sails and she rode south before a strong gale until she hit a reef on a foggy night. The impact broke her back, and the aft hold flooded within minutes."

The vault was submerged beneath the waves; there was no time to dig down to it. They managed to get the lifeboats launched, and once they had rescued the crew and passengers, a salvage company from san francisco deemed it worthwhile to try and recover the gold. By the time their tugboat arrived, the ice had forced them off the reef. The seas were perpetually rough, and after a few weeks of battling the elements, they abandoned the mission. The insurers covered all the losses, and that seemed to be the end of it.

But then, the stern half of the wreck drifted into shallower waters, offering us a slim glimmer of hope. Now, i think you understand the situation as well as i do."

Jimmy sat in contemplative silence, coming to grips with the precarious nature of the adventure he had embarked on. The wreck lay in rarely navigated waters, plagued by fierce currents that brought in chunks of ice, lashed by sudden squalls, and often cloaked in fog. The equipment they were able to scrounge up was bargain-basement at best, and the journey in their small sloop would be perilous. But Jimmy was desperate—his financial situation called for a bold gamble, and he wasn't easily cowed by the daunting challenges ahead.

"well," he said, "i guess we stand a chance. But i still don't quite get why you were so eager to dive into this."

"it's simple," Bethune replied, lazily tossing a pebble into the water. "Victoria is a beautiful city, no denying that. It has splendid views. But when you can't find steady work and have spent years idling away at the waterfront and in dingy bars, the place starts to lose its allure."

"you could've left. Didn't i meet you in Vancouver?"

"sure," Bethune said with a slight grin. "i could leave for up to thirty days at a stretch. But, barring sundays and a few holidays, i had to report to a lawyer's office on the first of each month."

I had just enough money to get by for the next four weeks with strict budgeting; however, if i missed a single deadline, the funds would be cut off permanently. This system might benefit those footing the bill back in the old country since it ensures my stay here, but it's a significant hassle for me. How can someone secure and keep a job outside the town when they must return on a fixed schedule every month? when i was in Vancouver, a large part of my allowance was spent just to collect it.

"and now, by heading north, you're leaving that behind?"

"exactly," replied Bethune. "i should have done this sooner, but without ever having been taught how to work or skip a meal, the decision required some real courage. It's sink or swim now."

Jimmy nodded in agreement. All his money had been tied up in the expedition, and to recover it, he needed to succeed where a well-funded salvage mission had already failed. Though the wreck had shifted position, the outlook wasn't promising.

"well," he said, "we'll give it our best shot, but i wish we had a better supply of provisions."

"Hank can fish," Bethune said with a grin. "in fact, he'll have no choice but to fish whenever there's a catch. Fortunately, fish is both wholesome and sustaining. Anyway, we have a big day ahead tomorrow; we should get some rest."

Jimmy lingered a bit longer, smoking as the others returned to the sloop. Night was falling, but a band of pure green still glowed along the crest of the dark ridge to the west. The air was cold and utterly still, and wisps of gray wood smoke hung like gauzy ribbons above the town's roofs. The tall pines were fading into the twilight, but their sharp, sweet scent lingered over the beach, and the gentle swell lapped the shingle with a soothing murmur.

Jimmy had always felt a profound connection to the sea, and now, with anticipation coursing through his veins, he was set to embark again. This time, it would be aboard his own ship, free from the constraints that had previously bound him—except the crucial one of ensuring the journey was profitable. It wouldn't be a walk in the park;

challenges lay ahead, but the adventure held a particular allure that filled his heart with excitement and determination.

CHAPTER THREE.

That evening, as the last glimpse of Vancouver island faded from sight, Jimmy found himself in the cockpit of the cetacea, a chart of the north pacific spread out before him on the cabin hatch. The map detailed the maze-like straits, dotted with islands of every size, through which they had skillfully navigated over the past week. Despite head-scratching winds and rushing tides, they had miraculously avoided running aground. Jimmy, experienced navigator that he was, couldn't help but marvel at their accomplishment.

He had now charted their course north along the jagged coastline of british columbia. Rolling up the chart, Jimmy stood and took in their surroundings. It was nine o'clock, but daylight lingered. A long, slate-green swell, speckled with ripples, rolled up from the south. To the northwest, the horizon was marked by an ominous stripe of glowing saffron, where the sea tops cut sharply against the sky. The east, in contrast, was immersed in a hard, cold blue, with shadowy mountains faintly visible high up against the sky and a few rocky islets emerging, blurred by blue haze, from the heaving sea.

The sloop rolled lazily, its boom groaning, while the tall white mainsail billowed and collapsed with a harsh slap of canvas and a loud clatter of blocks. Above, the topsail arced wide across the sky. Silky trails of water trailed off the stern, accompanied by a soft gurgle at the bow. By Jimmy's calculations, they were moving at about three miles an hour.

"what do you think of the weather?" Bethune asked, lounging at the steering wheel.

"it's not looking good," Jimmy replied. "if we weren't in a hurry, i'd suggest taking down the topsail. There'll be wind before morning."

"i'm with you on that," Bethune agreed. "but time is a luxury we can't afford. Every day out here costs us. We need to make her move."

"have you figured out what we're shelling out to that ship-chandler for the cables and diving gear each week?"

"no, i haven't. His rates were intimidating enough in total without breaking them down. Have you looked into it?"

Bethune chuckled.

"i've logged the expense of everything in my notebook. Honestly, i was a bit surprised at myself for bothering. If i had done some simple calculations and acted on them back home, chances are i wouldn't be here now." Bethune grimaced. "boiled halibut and fried halibut are starting to wear on me, but it's still better than my digs in Vancouver, which were worlds better than what i had in Victoria. I suppose it made sense to cling to those few dollars a month for as long as i could, but i'll never forget that hotel. I never quite got used to the two damp public towels next to the row of grimy wash-basins, or the gramophone blaring in the grimy dining room. And worst of all was the long, dull evening dragged out in the lounge. You've probably seen the tough guys lounging back, feet up on the radiator pipes by the windows, the piles of dead flies that seldom get swept up, the bleak, dreary squalor. Imagine three or four hours of that every night, with only last week's colonist newspaper to kill time!"

"i'd think a railroad or logging camp might be better than that."

"much better, though they're no luxury resorts. The problem was i couldn't get to Victoria and keep my job. Once or twice, when payday was approaching, it got pretty tight. I vividly remember walking seventy miles in two days along a freshly made wagon trail."

The softer parts of the ground were littered with jagged stones from the hillside, while the drier patches were so deeply rutted that getting my boots off felt like a surgical operation.

"it might have been wiser to just give up your allowance," Jimmy remarked.

"you're probably right," Bethune replied. "i can see that now, but i had one grueling experience after another—clearing land, laying railroad tracks. Hauling forty-foot rails through melting snow, choking on the fumes of blasting powder hanging in the air. It was brutal. Even worse was handspiking giant logs up skids in relentless rain. The logs would slip back and crush a tenderfoot's ribs. I guess that ordeal turned me into a coward of sorts; and in truth, the allowance felt more like a right than a favor. That money had been in the family for ages; i'm the eldest son. Sure, i wasn't a paragon of virtue, but i didn't have any serious vices or crimes to my name. So, if my family decided to send me away, it seemed only fair that they should pay for it."

Jimmy nodded, seeing the logic in his friend's perspective.

"but now, i stand on my own," Bethune continued with a carefree laugh. "i can't predict how this journey will end, but right now, this works for me. Is there anything better than commanding a sturdy boat of your own?"

Jimmy agreed, his eyes scanning their surroundings. Seated to windward, he could see the gently rounded deck stretching forward to the curved bows, topped by the tall, billowing jib. The arched cab-in-top flowed gracefully into the deck, and though there were patches here and there on the wood and canvas, everything his eyes touched was in perfect harmony. The Resolute was small and low in the water, but she was swift and reliable, and Jimmy had already developed a fondness for her.

Their success hinged on the boat's seaworthiness, and he believed she wouldn't let them down.

"i like the boat, but i've been fixing gear all day. It's my turn to rest," he said, exhaustion seeping into his voice. The cramped cabin, stretch-ing from the cockpit to the bow, was cluttered with disassembled diving pumps and equipment. Despite the chaos, there were lockers on either side where one could lie down. The air reeked of stale tobacco smoke, tarred hemp, and fish – but Jimmy had endured worse in the merchant navy. He lay down fully dressed on a locker, glancing across the cabin at moran, wrapped in old oilskins on the opposite locker. As the Resolute swayed with a rhythmic motion, moran's shadowy form rose and fell above Jimmy's level. The water lapped noisily against the hull, interrupted by the occasional groaning of timbers and the sharp clatter of blocks. Jimmy, lulled by the motion, soon drifted off to sleep.

Suddenly, he was jolted awake by a heavy blow, finding him-self sprawled on the floor, having struck one of the pump castings. Half-dazed and shaken, it took him a few moments to get to his knees; standing was impossible in the low- ceilinged cabin. It was pitch dark, and Jimmy couldn't see the hatch. It felt as though the Resolute had rolled over onto her side. Above him, the cacophony of heavy water pounding the deck mixed with the wild flapping of loose canvas and the fierce howl of the wind. Bethune's voice, faint and strained, cut through the chaos, calling for help.

Knowing it was time for action, Jimmy pulled himself together and struggled toward the cockpit. When he first emerged, he was momentarily blinded by the spray driving across the boat and into his face. He squinted through the stinging water and saw the Resolute was pressed down, with most of her lee deck submerged. White torrents swept her windward side and cascaded into the cockpit, a grim testament to the storm's fury.

The tall mainsail stabbed into the thick darkness, though it was no longer flailing wildly. Jimmy sensed a frantic speed as the half-seen waves raced alongside them.

"ease her! let her come up!" he yelled to the shadowy figure hunched over the wheel. Bethune's reply hinted at losing the mast unless the others could quickly reduce the sail's area. Jimmy rushed forward, battling through the surging water, and released the peak halyard. The sail's head dropped and billowed out to leeward with a dangerous thrashing; beneath it, the partially lowered topsail dangled, complicating things further. Moran was already working to swap the jib for a smaller one, and Jimmy hurried to help him. Although the sail wasn't attached to a masthead stay, it wouldn't run in; when Bethune turned the boat into the wind, the loose canvas swept across the bow, bulging like a balloon and then collapsing with a force that threatened to snap the straining mast.

Jimmy and moran, drenched and barely able to see, knew something had to be done quickly. Awakened abruptly from sleep, they struggled with the heavy gear in the water. Their boat was large enough to make the equipment burdensome but not so large as to lessen the urgency when hit by such a harsh squall. Despite their exhaustion, Jimmy and moran took a brief moment to catch their breath. The jib still needed to come down, and with a rough shout to moran, Jimmy lowered himself from the bowsprit until his feet found the wire bobstay. The Resolute dove into the waves, drenching him to the waist, but he pushed forward, the canvas battering his head, until he grabbed an iron ring. It took a determined effort to wrench it free so it could run in, and as the sail finally whipped behind him, he felt the warmth of blood seeping from his injured hand.

He clambered back on board, and once he and moran had hoisted a smaller jib, it was clear they needed to reef the mainsail urgently. They took a moment to gather their strength for the daunting task ahead. The sloop was heeled over hard, waves crashing over her side and sending froth streaming under the boom. Jimmy couldn't fathom why Bethune hadn't adjusted the wheel. The foam washed so high it nearly reached the cabin top, and it seemed like they were on the verge of capsizing. They felt powerless and overwhelmed, struggling against the sails that threatened to submerge the boat. But the battle couldn't be avoided. Steeling themselves, they reached for the halyards.

Through labored breaths and burning muscles, they tugged the mainsail down, its head lowering slowly. Jimmy, leaning precariously over the edge with foam up to his knees and his chest pressed against the boom, managed to knot the reef- points. Finally, it was done. The sloop righted itself slightly, shedding some of the water. Moran turned to Bethune, slumped in exhaustion at the helm, and questioned why he hadn't luffed the boat, which would have made their job easier. Bethune, soaked and dripping, pointed out the problem—the dinghy they carried on deck had been knocked against the wheel, rendering it immovable.

They repositioned the dinghy, and once Bethune regained control of the sloop, he recounted what had occurred, his voice disjointed and breathless.

"the wind picked up but i held course. Then a squall hit, and i let the topsail go, thinking the breeze would ease. Instead, it whipped around head-on, howling, and i called for you."

Talking was tough over the din of the roaring sea, with spray stinging their faces and snatching their words away, but Jimmy shouted to be heard.

"where's the compass?"

"in the cockpit, or it went overboard—the dinghy broke it off."

Moran felt around in the water sloshing around their feet, grabbed something, and crawled into the cabin, where a faint light flickered to life.

It disappeared in a couple of minutes, and he returned.

"the binnacle lamp's broken," he reported. "she's pointing roughly east."

"towards shore," Jimmy noted. "once you're set, we'll try turning her around."

But the boat wouldn't budge. Overpowered by the wind and waves, she stalled for a moment and then veered back onto her original course. They tried twice, each time hesitating to turn her the opposite way; eventually, they retreated to the slight protection of the coaming, realizing there was nothing more they could do.

"she might stay off the beach until daylight," Jimmy said hopefully. "then we'll see exactly where we are."

Jimmy's glance forward revealed little. The long swell had transformed into crashing waves that pounded the struggling sloop relentlessly from the darkness. As she heaved over them, the small patch of storm jib surged up, unveiling the sharply tilted strip of mainsail; the rest of her disappeared in the spray and furious foam. Sailing fast and close-hauled, she raced toward the shore. Jimmy could feel her shudder as she plunged into the waves. The morning felt an eternity away; but finally, the darkness began to lighten. The foam brightened, and the dark mass of the rollers became more defined and imposing as they rose, enormous and menacing, from the gloom. Then the sky began to pale in the east, and the exhausted men turned their eyes towards the shore, shivering in the biting cold of dawn. Gradually, as the horizon steadily pulled back, a gray, misty blur appeared to starboard. Now that they could see the waves, they managed to turn the Resolute around. As she headed offshore, a red glow spread across the sky, and rocks and pines took shape in the east. Then a break in the coastline revealed shining water instead of foam, indicating an island; cautiously, they turned her back toward shore, as she could gain no ground against the steep, white waves offshore.

The sloop surged forward, her lee deck skimming the water as she veered away, revealing the sound. The crew watched as waves crashed onto a rocky shore, rolling in perfect, majestic ranks. As they met the shallows, the waves erupted into frothy cascades, a spectacle that made their vessel seem minuscule in comparison. Still, she pressed on, and Jimmy, clutching the wheel, stared resolutely ahead.

"we'll have to take a risk on finding deeper water; the lead line isn't reliable here," he said. "if anything shows up in the sound, it will be a sharp rock."

The sloop plunged past the point, rolling and drenched in spray with only two scraps of soaked canvas set. As Jimmy steered her into the island's lee, everything changed. The water calmed into a steady swell, glittering with tiny ripples; the tilted mast straightened; and the sloop glided toward a sloping beach, threading through unpredictable gusts. Then, as she slowed and the sails flapped, the anchor splashed overboard, and the clattering chain sent a flock of birds swirling above the rocks. Within half an hour, the crew was busy cooking breakfast, and soon after, they were fast asleep. The night's wind had altered more than just their course; it had forged a new dynamic among them. Their endurance had been harshly tested and had withstood the trial. From that point on, they were bound not just by shared interests, but by a deeper, more elusive connection. They were comrades forged by mutual respect and trust.

CHAPTER FOUR.

O n a gray afternoon, with fog hanging over the leaden water, they finally spotted the island where the wreck lay. The wind, though barely strong enough to ruffle the long swells trailing the sloop, nudged them astern. Jimmy calculated the tide was at half-flood, a fact confirmed by a blur on their port side that quickly became a reef, with the sea crashing over it in snowy turbulence. As the gray ridge behind the reef emerged from the fog, Jimmy could make out a few dark patches that looked like scrub pines or willows. As the coastline came into view, he noticed a strip of beach littered with seaweed-covered boulders and the bare slopes of sand and stones beyond.

This island was starkly different from the ones they had visited on their journey. Unlike those, thickly covered in ragged firs and tangled undergrowth of brush and wild fruit vines, this had a desolate, forbidding appearance, as if only the toughest plants could survive the cold, fierce winds that swept across it. The men, worn from the long and arduous voyage, sported clothes stiff with salt from repeated soakings. Two of them were nursing raw sores on their wrists and elbows from the chafing of their coarse garments. Their food supply had been neither plentiful nor varied, and they all had grown to detest the monotonous diet of fish.

"i've seen more cheerful places," Bethune remarked, peering through the binoculars Jimmy handed him. "i suppose we anchor under its eastern end?"

Moran nodded. "pretty good shelter in the cove, about two fathoms deep. Keep an eye to starboard—the reef will show you where she is."

Jimmy turned his eyes in that direction but saw nothing immediately. Then, as the haze lifted slightly, he caught sight of something glinting faintly in the dim afternoon light.

Then the waves, rolling gently behind them like slick oil, suddenly erupted into a frothing white explosion, sending a cloud of fine mist into the air like a geyser.

"it's no wonder the old steamboat broke in half," he remarked. "where did she go down?"

"not far ahead, but with how high the tide is right now, we won't see anything of her for the next nine hours."

"and it'll be dark by then," Bethune said grimly. Jimmy shared his friend's despondency. After spotting land, they had been filled with tense anticipation. It was entirely possible the wreck had disintegrated or disappeared into the sand since moran last saw her. They had braved countless hardships and risks to get here, and if the wreck had vanished, they'd have to return empty-handed. The crucial question would remain unanswered until the next day.

"couldn't we anchor here and search for her with the dory when the tide goes out?" Jimmy suggested.

"that wouldn't be smart. When you drop anchor in the bay, you're pretty secure; but out there, two cables wouldn't hold her when the sea gets rough, and it blows here more often than anywhere else i know."

"then let's bring her in. This trip hasn't exactly been lucky for us; we're two weeks behind schedule. It'll be something just to feel solid ground under our feet."

They navigated into a basin flanked by gray rocks and stones on the landward side, and a shoal where the surf pounded on the seaward side. After anchoring, they rowed ashore. The island stretched about two miles long with only sparse patches of scrub growing in the hollows of its central ridge. However, as moran pointed out, it did have two springs of fresh water. Birds screeched above the surf and waded along the shore, a seal lounged on the stony beach; these were the only signs of life. The raw air echoed with the lonely sound of the sea.

As the sun set, they returned to the boat. Under the warm glow of the lamp, the cramped cabin felt welcoming in contrast to the barren landscape outside. Conversation dwindled to almost nothing; the men were restless and a bit downcast. Come daylight, they'd learn if their hard work was for naught, the uncertainty gnawing at their patience.

"first thing in the morning, we'll see if she's still resting on the bank," moran said, arranging their blankets on the lockers. "then, let's get out the net and all the lines we brought. We might as well keep the diving pump stashed in a hole on the beach."

"yeah, we'll need to fish and save our supplies. Even the worst beef out of chicago would be a real treat right now," Jimmy agreed. "but why put the pump ashore?"

Moran wasn't known for his humor, but he managed a smile.

"well," he started, "we don't have any legal claim on the wreck, and if folks find out where she's lying, we'd soon see a steamboat coming up from portland or Vancouver equipped with proper salvage gear. This island's off the main route to the alaska ports, but in my experience, unexpected visitors tend to show up just when you least want them."

"he's right," Bethune chimed in. "we shouldn't make our objective obvious to anyone who might come by. I'm no expert on salvage laws, but i bet the underwriters would be fair if we brought back the gold. And if not, the courts would likely give us a decent award. But we need to be cautious; without any official standing, we can't afford to be questioned on why we didn't report the find instead of trying to get what we could quietly."

After that, they soon drifted off to sleep. When they awoke a few hours later, dawn was already breaking. In these northern waters free from ice, the night is fleeting.

A thin fog blanketed the land, revealing only a narrow strip of wet beach. There was still no wind, a fact moran found rather unusual. As the tide receded, Jimmy suggested they should launch the dory and row out immediately to scout for the wreck. Moran, however, objected.

"it's a long haul, and we can't afford to waste time," he said. "suppose we find her? we couldn't operate the pump from the boat, and we'd have to come back for the sloop. It's not often calm here, and we need to take advantage of it while we can."

The others agreed. After a hurried breakfast, they hauled up the anchor and set off, with moran sculling the Resolute and Jimmy and Bethune towing her from the dory. Towing proved arduous; the stream and swell worked against them, causing the light boat to jerk back as it crested steep waves. Despite their efforts, the line would untangle and slide along the boat's side as it veered, posing a risk of pulling them under. Though the air was chilly, they were drenched in sweat before covering even half a mile. Bethune paused to cool his blistered hands in the water.

"this is tough when you're not used to it," he complained. Jimmy was grateful for the brief rest, but moran's urgent shout interrupted them. "watch out! where do you think you're going?"

Looking around, they saw the cetacea's bowsprit looming above them as it lurched toward them on a smooth swell. Pulling hard against the dragging rope, they managed to rotate the dory, then rowed steadily, breath short, sweat dripping. It was grueling work, but Bethune reminded them they weren't on a pleasure cruise. Finally, moran dropped the anchor. Once aboard the sloop, the men spent an hour in tense anticipation, watching the sea.

The island had faded into a faint, dark blur, surrounded by an unbroken wall of mist resting on the calm, gently shifting waves. None of them had anything to say; they smoked in anxious silence, their eyes fixed on the glassy water, which betrayed nothing of what lay beneath. Bethune jumped up impatiently.

"this is too tedious for me!" he exclaimed. "can't we use the dory to sweep for the wreck with a line?"

"you need to stay sharp," moran warned him. "if the wreck's there, it'll show up soon."

They waited, with Jimmy occasionally glancing at his watch. Finally, moran extended a pointing hand.

"what's that, to starboard?" he asked. For a few tense moments, during which the anticipation strained their nerves, the others saw nothing. Then, a faint ripple disturbed the glassy surface of the water. It smoothed out, and the long swell passed undisturbed across the spot; then the ripple appeared again, with a dark streak in its center.

"seaweed!" shouted Bethune. "it must be growing on something!"

"probably," said moran. "it's probably caught on a piece of the ship's timber."

Five minutes later, the timber's head was visible, and with keen but silent excitement, they secured a line to it and brought the sloop close. The diving pumps were already set up, and after they had lowered and lashed a ladder, moran coolly donned the heavy canvas suit. He claimed that, as he had led the expedition, he would be the first to descend.

His companions watched with grave concern as they screwed on the copper helmet and attached the lead weights. Neither of them had any real experience with diving, aside from what they had learned from a pamphlet published by a diving apparatus manufacturer. They had studied and debated its content on the voyage up, but there was a nagging fear that the pamphlet might omit some crucial detail, and even a minor oversight could lead to disastrous consequences.

As the copper helmet slipped beneath the water's surface, a cascade of bubbles surged upward, and Jimmy's pulse quickened, his hand growing clammy with sweat. Clutching the signal line, he was well-versed in the code and knew the precise number of strokes per minute needed to supply adequate air. Nonetheless, his mistrust in the pumps lingered. Despite the hefty deposit and exorbitant rental fee, the equipment's age was apparent. The bubbles advanced steadily, drifting toward the weed-encrusted timber below. Suddenly, the line jerked sharply, and Bethune's gaze snapped to Jimmy.

"more air!" he shouted. "give it a few more cranks. He's fine for now."

Relief washed over them as the bubbles gradually approached the ladder once more. When the diver finally clambered back onto the deck, they hurriedly unscrewed the helmet. Moran took a few deep breaths and wiped his face before addressing them.

"it's rough for the first minute or two," he admitted, sparing no further detail on his experience. "as far as i can tell, there's no accessible entry from the deck. The poop's wrecked, and you'd definitely snag the pipe or line in the mangled beams. But the hold looks relatively clear. We'll need to break through the aft bulkhead; it's clogged with sand and a load of debris. Bethune, you're certain about the strong room's location?"

"i made sure to verify it. Apparently, it's beneath the poop cabin. I couldn't get my hands on a plan of the ship, though."

"we'll focus on the bulkhead." moran turned to Jimmy. "you're up next. Grab the shovel and see if you can clear some of that sand."

Jimmy wasn't a man easily spooked, but as his comrades strapped the heavy suit and helmet onto him, unease gnawed at him. The equipment felt unbearably cumbersome as he trudged to the ladder. His grip tightened around the rungs as he began his descent. When a green haze enveloped his helmet's glass, an unsettling fear took hold of him.

Struggling with the descent, he was plagued by a pounding headache and an unsettling sense of pressure. His ears throbbed, his breathing felt labored, and he paused, uncertain, at the bottom of the ladder. The visibility was murky, as if peering through a grimy, greenish lens. The flickering light created disorienting reflections. He watched air bubbles rush to the surface and the shadow of the sloop's hull sway back and forth. His gaze fixed on a poorly defined dark shape, which he assumed was the wreck.

Reluctantly releasing the ladder, he experienced an unexpected change. Instead of feeling crushed by a heavy burden, he now felt absurdly light. Despite his weighted boots, maintaining his balance was a challenge. His feet didn't land where he intended, and his arm movements were erratic when he tried to wield the shovel he carried. It seemed like a strong current might sweep him away completely, but he steeled himself. He hadn't spent all his savings and embarked on this dangerous journey to be deterred by a few strange sensations. He was determined to break into the wreck, and he cautiously approached it.

Stopping where the aft section had broken off, he saw before him a dark cavern, bordered by jagged planks and splintered timbers, adorned with long tendrils of seaweed that undulated with the wash of the ocean. Jimmy felt a strong reluctance to venture inside. The darkness could conceal strange and dangerous creatures. For a few moments, his imagination ran wild like that of a frightened child. But he forced those thoughts aside. Jimmy reminded himself that he had an electric lamp. Clumsily fumbling with the switch, a trembling beam of light pierced through the water, and he cautiously entered the hold. Sand had filled the gaps among the stone ballast, with only a broken orlop beam obstructing his path.

Jimmy felt a bit more at ease, realizing he wasn't too far below the surface, though he wished he had more seasoned hands at the pumps. He moved aft along the shaft tunnel and reached a mound of sand piled against the shattered deck. The bulkhead sealing off the lazaret had to be behind it. He picked up the shovel and got to work. It was tough going; a powerful shove threw him off balance, and he pondered whether his weight and the pressure were suited for this depth. There was only one way to find out, and Jimmy was wary of conducting a test here and now. Steeling himself, he managed to shift a few shovelfuls of sand before a sharp pain shot through his head. He drove the shovel deeper and lurched forward. Instead of hitting the deck, he flailed in a comical dance before regaining his footing.

Checking the signal line to steady his nerves, Jimmy found it tighter than it should be. Wasting no time, he grabbed the shovel and started retreating. If the line was caught on something, it might snag the air pipe — a prospect that was anything but comforting. Emerging from the hull, he had a strong urge to kick off his leaden boots and swim for it, but he dismissed the thought and climbed the ladder instead. Relief washed over him as the helmet's glasses were unscrewed and fresh air hit his face. He collapsed onto the cabin top, breathing heavily.

"we'll get the hang of it eventually," he said to Bethune with measured words. "but don't expect to accomplish much right away."

Bethune took his turn, and when he resurfaced, moran asked with dry humor, "how much sand did you shift?"

"three full buckets, which i suspect is more than Jimmy managed," Bethune replied with a grin.

Jimmy's expression turned serious. "since we're dealing with forty or fifty tons, we'll have to step up our game."

"definitely," moran agreed.

Conversation fell away, and Jimmy lit his pipe. Despite the chill in the air, it felt good to lounge on the open deck and breathe air at normal pressure. The stream was calm, the sea was smoother than he expected, and everything seemed to be in their favor. Still, the thought of diving again filled him with reluctance, and he suspected his companions felt the same. It was a relief when the thinning mist suddenly parted, revealing a dark line advancing towards them over the rolling sea.

"a breeze!" Jimmy exclaimed. "we'd better head back while we still can. The channel will be nearly dry at low tide."

Bethune nodded as a gust of cold air brushed his face. While they shortened the cable, small white ripples splashed against the bow. The ripples grew larger and angrier as they hoisted the mainsail, and once the anchor was up, they headed back for the bight, the swell churning and frothing behind them. By the time they reached the sheltered sands, the wind was howling. They spent the rest of the day lounging in the cabin, the sloop tugging at its cable, while the halyards slapped rhythmically against the mast.

CHAPTER FIVE.

For three days, a fierce storm battered the island, whipping up clouds of sand and fine gravel along the shore, and heaving the mighty pacific waves onto the shoals. The air was saturated with the salty tang of the spray, and even below deck, the crew's ears were assaulted by the relentless roar of the ocean. Then, the wind subsided, and as the swell lessened, they resumed their work with renewed vigor and found the task becoming slightly easier. They figured out the optimal pressure for the shallow depths, their lungs adjusted to the extra effort, and none of them hesitated to descend into the dark hold. Despite occasional disruptions from the rising sea, they steadily cleared away the sand. Their biggest challenge was the brief periods they could spend below. The bulkhead remained elusive, and another gale from the east could undo all their hard work, washing the sediment back in. If that happened, they'd have to break through the side of the hull—an undertaking none of them relished, given how tightly packed and thick the timbers of a wooden ship are. For now, only the weather posed a threat. Then came a calm day, with tendrils of mist drifting lazily across the water. Jimmy noticed a wisp of smoke on a clear stretch of horizon.

"someone's farther east than they should be," he remarked, leaning on the pump handle. His gaze was fixed on the spot where bubbles broke the surface. Although he was used to the job, the bubbles still held a strange allure. It was hard to tear his eyes away from them as they traced a milky path through the green water, or paused, expanding into a frothy patch. As long as the bubbles behaved this way, everything was fine with the diver below.

An hour later, as the mist thickened again, Jimmy lay smoking on the deck. He had gone down longer than usual this time, and he felt drained and a bit melancholic.

Recently, he'd been plagued by a relentless headache, likely caused by all the diving. Over the past few days, the sand had become uncommonly tough. The underlying layers had merged into a concrete-like block due to the pounding waves and relentless tides. The work itself was grueling, even when they weren't deep in the wreck. It wasn't easy towing their sloop against the swell during the calms. And when the sea suddenly rose, as it often did, they were forced, if the tide was low, to battle it out and hold their ground until they had enough water to navigate back up the channel. Sometimes they couldn't even attempt the entrance and had to ride it out under storm sails until the weather improved. During those times, they took turns at the wheel, steering the beleaguered vessel through the frothing waves. Then, crammed into the cabin's narrow bunks with wet sails and gear, the wild seas made sleep or any kind of rest impossible.

The Resolute was small and drifted leeward quickly, often requiring hours to fight their way back to the island against the still-raging sea when the wind began to ease. It was an exhausting existence, and Jimmy could feel his nerves fraying. Bethune had gone below, and

Jimmy was working the pump's crank when a deep, throbbing sound resonated from the fog. Moran looked up instantly.

"that darn steamboat is headed this way!" he shouted, diving into the cabin to grab their binoculars. The rhythmic thud of engines was unmistakable, blending with the roar of water being churned up by the bow. Jimmy realized they hadn't heard it earlier because of the noise from the pump.

"she's real close! keep pumping, but bring him up; you've got the line!" moran commanded. Bethune responded to the signal, and as bubbles began surfacing near the sloop, the steamer emerged from the mist.

Her sleek white hull and small cream funnel made it clear she was an auxiliary yacht.

"we've got enough wind to get out of here, and we need to move fast," moran said, signaling to Bethune once more. Finally, when the copper helmet came into view, they hauled Bethune onto the deck and quickly began shortening the anchor cable. The yacht was now visible about a mile away, slowly moving, suggesting they were sounding depths before anchoring. Amidst the land, the sloop would be hard to spot, but they still had to pull in a lot of heavy chain before raising the sail. Jimmy, in his haste, slipped the breast rope holding them to the wreck. They had tied its outer end to a large keg buoy for easy retrieval. As they got underway, heading for the bay, a white gig soon appeared in pursuit.

"they won't stick around long," Bethune said. "either they're after fresh water or just a walk ashore. It's a shame we don't have time to hide the pumps. The best we can do is meet them at the water's edge. Luckily, the big net is right there."

Pulling to shore in their dory, they waited for the yacht's boat, which carried two uniformed seamen and a young man dressed smartly in blue serge with bronze buttons and polished white shoes. He seemed cheerful and greeted them warmly, his eyes catching sight of the net.

"glad to see someone here; i guess you're fishing?" he said. "do you know where we can get water? we're running low, and the engineer's got issues with the salt in the boilers. I'll take some fish if you can spare them."

Bethune laughed.

"take all you want," he said. "anything we keep, we'll have to eat, and we're getting sick of it. There's a good spring behind the ridge; we'll show you where it is."

The man signaled to the seamen, who picked up two brass-ringed water barrels, and the group started up the beach.

When they reached the spring, the crew returned with containers to fill the boat, using it as a makeshift tank for water. Meanwhile, Jimmy led the yachtsman to a hut they had put together from stones nestled between two large rocks. They used this hut as a refuge when wind or fog halted their operations. Jimmy offered the yachtsman a cigar and explained that the yacht was coming back from a northern expedition where they explored several glaciers. He mentioned his amateur interest in ornithology as the reason for coming ashore, though the island's bleak appearance had put off his friends, who were now playing cards.

"have you noticed any rare seabirds around here?" the yachtsman asked.

"there are a few nests further off," Bethune replied. "not sure what species they are, but after trying to eat their eggs, i can't recommend them."

The yachtsman laughed.

"you might have cooked eggs that collectors would pay good money for. Anyway, i'd appreciate it if you could show me the nests. My crew will be busy loading the water for a while."

"i'll take you there shortly," Bethune said, giving Jimmy a telling glance. "do you have that spool of fine thread?" he asked Jimmy. "we need to secure some hooks onto the new line."

Jimmy, realizing that Bethune wanted to speak in private, stepped outside, and Bethune followed.

"well?" Jimmy asked.

"what do you think of the weather?"

Jimmy surveyed their surroundings. The sky was mostly clear with a few streaks of thin clouds, and the mist was gliding in faint trails along the shoreline.

"it'll clear up soon, and we might get a breeze," Jimmy noted.

"exactly. It crossed my mind that it will be after half-tide when our yachting friend departs."

Besides, it would seem unfriendly and maybe even raise questions if we didn't take him to supper," Jimmy said thoughtfully.

"true," replied hank. "the wreck's out in the open now, pumps are in place, and it's a pity we forgot to move our marker buoy."

"exactly! it would be foolish to assume the man's oblivious. If he spots the diving gear and the buoy, he'll undoubtedly put two and two together. Someone on that steamer has surely heard whispers about the wreck in the southern ports. If word spreads, a professional salvage crew could be dispatched. We might finish before they get here, but i'm not confident."

"you're right," Jimmy sighed. "what's our next move?"

"the ideal strategy would be for you and Hank to get the pumps ashore while the fog still provides cover. Then, you can slip the buoy and hide it among the boulders near the wreck. I'll keep our guest away from the water; although, the high ground with the bird nests overlooks the beach and the steamer isn't too far offshore."

Hearing footsteps, Jimmy turned to see the stranger leaving the hut.

"my partner will show you to the bird nests," he said to the man. "i have some tasks to handle on board."

Gesturing to hank, Jimmy walked down to the beach with him, explaining their plan. Hank agreed. If their activities were exposed, it would be pointless to continue the search. They had to be cautious since anyone with a good pair of binoculars on the yacht, which had moved closer to shore, could spot them. Occasionally, they caught clear glimpses of its white hull before it faded back into the mist.

They boarded the sloop and dismantled the pumps. Along with the lead weights and the diving helmet, the small dory was heavily laden. Fortunately, the tide was ebbing, creating a smooth channel between the exposed sandbanks for them to navigate.

They had no trouble in the channel, but when they reached open water, they met a chaotic swell pushing against them. The fog had thickened again, reducing their view to the gray waves emerging from the mist. Rowing became laborious, and they had to stay alert; if a swell curled and broke before they could avoid it, the dory might capsize, plunging them into the icy waters. They labored across a wide shallow, sounding with the oars, until they lost contact with the bottom and had to guess their way to a safe landing spot. Soon it seemed they had lost their bearings, with no sign of the beach, and a rough rattling sound erupted nearby. Moran stopped rowing.

"the tide's carried us offshore," he said. "the yacht skipper's either shortening the cable or breaking out the anchor. Looks like he's drifted into shallower water than he expected."

While they waited, drifting with the tide, the rattling of the windlass grew louder; then it ceased, and a dim, white shape emerged from the fog. It grew larger and more distinct until they could make out the bow's sweeping curve, the trickle of water along the hull, and the low deckhouse just above the rail. Rowing away unnoticed was impossible, but the dory was small and low in the water, providing some concealment.

"they've hove her short, found another fathom. We need to stay hidden; they'll keep a sharp anchor watch," Jimmy said. "best we lie low."

They lay down on the wet floorboards, and Jimmy peeked over the gunwale. They were perilously close to the yacht. He could see silhouettes near the deckhouse. As they drifted closer, the figures sharpened, making it seem unavoidable that they would be noticed. Yet, no one hailed them. They were close enough to hear voices and the soft notes of a piano drifting through the air.

The vessel's tall, white hull loomed above them as they found themselves parallel with the funnel. The ash hoist began to clatter noisily; Jimmy watched dust and steam rise as furnace clinkers splashed into the sea. They continued drifting aft, a gray blotch on the water, nearly aligned with the stern when Jimmy spotted a man leaning on the rail. His head was turned towards their dory, and Jimmy braced himself, expecting a shout. It never came; the sleek curvature of the white hull ended in the swoop of counter above the tip of a propeller blade, and the dory drifted silently into the mist behind.

"we've got her around now!" moran exclaimed, a note of relief in his voice. "we'll have to row."

Navigating the dory, laden with its heavy cargo, to the shore without swamping it was tricky. Nevertheless, they managed to land safely, and after unloading, set off for the wreck. Their buoy was visible some distance out, as the mist thinned and moved seaward. The main challenge was hauling the cumbersome iron keg ashore. They had barely achieved this when the steamer emerged clearly through a break in the fog, and a chill gust of air hit Jimmy's face.

"it's coming," he yelled. "we need to hurry back!"

As they pushed off the beach, the tide began to ripple. The yacht lay exposed, gleaming like ivory on the clear, green water. Visibility was no longer an issue; their sole focus was returning home before the rising wind churned up the sea. Soon, spray flew about the dory and frothy waves chased her from behind. The swells grew steeper as they neared the shoals, and the men struggled to keep her straight with the oars as she surged forward on a crest of foam.

They barely had time to take in their surroundings as the steamer's whistle blared, signaling the recall of her boat. A gasoline launch shot past them, its hull rocking wildly through the deeper waters. Upon entering the channel into the bight, they encountered the same launch coming back more slowly, towing a boat. Someone on board waved a hand in greeting before disappearing behind a projecting bank. Jimmy and moran continued rowing until they reached the sloop.

"they cut it close," Bethune remarked as they climbed aboard. "i guess you saw our 'friend' leave. If they're not careful towing that thing, they'll end up with brackish water in their tank," he added with a smirk, brandishing some silver coins. "at least we earned something this afternoon. The guy insisted on paying for the fish, and i thought it best to accept."

"good call," Jimmy replied. "moran and i did our part; now it's your turn to whip up supper."

While they ate, the sound of a windlass rattled through the air. Looking out through the scuttle, they watched as the yacht steamed off towards the sea.

Chapter Six.

Though it was nearly eleven at night, the light hadn't quite faded and the sea shimmered around the sloop as it rocked gently at its moorings by the wreck. To the north, streaks of ragged cloud marred the sky, while the edge of the sea was harshly clear. To the east, the horizon was cloaked in a cold, blue haze as the tide neared its lowest ebb. Angry white surf crashed along the exposed shoals, breaking the silence with a tremulous roar, and though the swell looked smooth as oil, it was high and steep. The air was still, but Jimmy agreed with moran that a storm was definitely brewing.

In the cabin, a dim light flickered as the men waited for the meal that Bethune was preparing. They felt both exhausted and ravenous. Supper had been delayed to extend their diving hours, and they had submerged far more often than was healthy. The bulkhead they were trying to clear of sand was still hopelessly buried. Frequent bad weather had disrupted their progress, pushing them to make the most of any favorable conditions. This urgency kept them anchored to the wreck instead of moving into the bight, despite the dangerous low tide now approaching. With their provisions dwindling, Bethune was experimenting with some damaged flour that had been forgotten in a flooded locker during a recent gale. The bannocks he flipped in the frying pan exuded a sour, unappetizing smell.

"they might taste better than they look," he said, trying to sound optimistic. "if the sky had looked this rough at mid-tide, i would've insisted we head in. We won't get much done tomorrow."

Moran stretched out wearily on the port locker.

"we should probably tie two reefs in the mainsail just in case, but i'm too beat, and the wind might hold off until morning. What really gets me though is the food situation."

We can't last much longer if this flour is inedible. I don't get how it went moldy in a day or two. Usually, you can leave a flour bag in water for a while, and it's only the outer inch that might get spoiled."

"yeah," Jimmy added. "i think the flour was already bad when we got it. That ship-chandler had a shifty look. But when you rely on someone else's money, you can't be too picky."

"he's pretty secure," Bethune grumbled. "with a lien on the boat for his loan and a hefty markup on everything he supplied, the only risk he faces is us losing the boat—but that's almost happened a couple of times already. Anyway, you might as well try the flour."

Taking the frying pan off the stove, he served a thick, greasy bannock and a tiny piece of pork to each of his companions. The food was too hot to eat. Jimmy, cutting his portion with his knife, watched anxiously as it cooled. If the flour was usable, they could stay at the wreck site a week or two longer, and he believed it wouldn't take many days to reach the strongroom. If not, he'd have to return to the grueling work at the sawmill and the monotonous life in cheap hotels. He thought he'd learned on sailing ships not to be picky, but he sniffed the food with disgust. Resolutely, he cut off a piece and took a bite, then threw down his knife.

"it's foul!" he exclaimed. Moran, reaching up through the hatch, tossed his bannock overboard.

"alright," said Bethune. "that cuts our stay short. We'd better get the pumps down into the cockpit once you've finished with the pork and tea."

Reluctantly, they did so, grumbling all the while, then sprawled on the lockers, smoking and too restless to sleep.

The air thrummed with an unspoken tension, the roar of the surf growing ever more ominous and insistent.

"whether we find the gold or not is anyone's guess, but one thing's for sure: we're in for a lot of hard work," Bethune remarked after a pause. "in a way, hank's got it worse than any of us. He didn't have the luxury of taking it easy when he headed out west."

"the big lobsters were nearly wiped out; making a living with traps was next to impossible," moran explained. "then i stumbled on some pamphlets that made getting rich through fishing in british columbia sound like a walk in the park. Wish i could get my hands on those liars; they deserve to be stuck in a half- swamped dory picking up a trawl."

"i don't think i had much more choice than he did," Jimmy interjected.

"you could've stayed on that liner, all decked out in smart uniforms, living large with a chinese steward at your beck and call, if you'd just shown a bit of tact and respect for authority. When the skipper didn't want a man with a heart condition steering his ship, which he had every right to, you should've agreed with him."

"i'm glad i didn't," Jimmy said stubbornly. "anyway, you're no better off, even if you do practice what you preach."

"that would be asking too much," Bethune laughed. "but i readily admit i'm a fool. If i ever had doubts, they've been pointed out to me plenty of times. It's easy to conform on the surface—all that's really required—and you can do as you please in private. A small concession to popular opinion now and then doesn't cost much."

"if you mean i should've gotten the quartermaster fired after he stopped a ton of cargo from crushing me, i'd rather starve."

"well, you might just end up doing that if you stick to your foolishness. If you had stopped to think, you would have seen it was your duty to side with your skipper."

"mistaken pity is a dangerous thing."

"save the sermon for later," Jimmy snapped, rubbing his temples. "it's making my headache worse! why don't you just light your pipe and relax?"

"hey, let him blow off some steam," moran cut in. "it doesn't matter as long as you don't take him too seriously."

"alright, alright," Bethune said with a lazy sigh. "so, who's on dish duty?"

Moran gathered the dirty plates and shoved them into a locker. "i'm wiped out and homesick. Wish i was back east, fishing the normal way, on top of the water! but it looks like none of us will be making it down to the wreck tomorrow."

Silence settled in, broken only by the crashing waves and the occasional clank of a halyard hitting the mast. The noise grew more frequent as Jimmy began to nod off, but he was used to the weather's warnings. Lying comfortably on the locker, he drifted into sleep. It was as dark as it gets during a northern summer when a violent jolt startled him awake. The sloop seemed to rear up, and moran's rough shouts barely carried over the loud clanging of a chain on deck.

Jimmy scrambled out quickly, seeing the fisherman hunched over where the cable cut across the bits, with a streak of foaming sea ahead. Individual waves rose up, and the sloop lurched over them, her bow slicing through the frothy water before plunging into the troughs.

Jimmy wasted no time assessing the situation; they'd held onto their moorings far too long, and swift action was essential. With Bethune's help, he close-reefed the mainsail and hoisted the shortened canvas. It took all three to break free of the anchor, and Jimmy crouched in the water sweeping the forward deck as he stowed it while the others hoisted a storm-jib.

They drove the sloop before the sea, eyes straining to locate the entrance to the channel.

Even though dawn hadn't arrived yet, it was far from dark. They could make out the foamy crests of the waves rolling up the shoals and, beyond them, a wide, white strip of surf. Soon, a break appeared in the surf, but it was narrow and twisted, making it seem impossible for the sloop to navigate through. After another couple of minutes, moran stood up on deck for a better view.

"there's about two feet of clearance at the bend," he said. "if we don't maneuver perfectly, we'll end up on the shore. The odds are just too risky."

Taking the chance might give them shelter, but refusing meant battling the open sea. Reluctantly, Jimmy agreed with moran's assessment.

"yeah," he said. "we should stay off it. Get ready while i jibe her around."

With that, the sloop swung in front of the oncoming waves as Jimmy turned the helm. A massive wave loomed behind them, and the boom swung out violently, the wet mainsail puffing up like a balloon. Moran and Bethune frantically worked the sheet—it was a race against time for their safety. Jimmy adjusted the wheel slightly, and the sail and heavy spar swung over. The Resolute rounded up and buried her lee deck into the sea. She shook off the water with a fierce jolt, and as moran and Bethune tightened the sheets, she drove upwind, escaping the treacherous shoal. Without the chance to reach the bay, their safest bet was the open water.

When dawn finally broke, casting an ominous red light, the Resolute was hove to with only a small trysail up. She rose and fell in an unsteady rhythm as the long, white-topped waves pounded her weather bow. Though she wasn't taking on any heavy water, she was drifting swiftly to leeward. The island had already faded to a gray smudge on the horizon.

It would take a full day's effort to beat back to the island, assuming the wind would let up—but there was no sign of it easing. By noon, the land was out of sight, and the sea had grown even more menacing.

The sun peeked through a veil of mist for a couple of hours, casting a glowing blue hue over the advancing walls of water. The waves shimmered with an almost incandescent brilliance. Some of the swells curled menacingly, and the trysail flapped weakly as the Resolute plunged into the trough. The vessel lingered there, almost suspended, while the crew watched the next wave rise. Struggling up the slope of the water with a drenched sail and slanted mast, the Resolute looked precariously small. Nonetheless, she managed to crest the waves before they could break over her. Jimmy wasn't sure how much he was aiding her with the helm, but sweat from nervous tension dripped steadily from his face as he twisted the wheel. Sometimes, the boat was agonizingly slow to respond, and when she did, her stern was often buried in a torrent of frothy water. Each time, the water sluiced off, and the sharp plunge into the next trough began again. When moran finally took over, Jimmy felt utterly drained. He'd had only an hour or two of sleep after a grueling day, and breakfast had been a meager piece of cold, stale fish, torn hastily from a pan. There'd been no chance to cook a proper meal.

"i'll try to make some coffee," he announced, heading below deck. Lighting the stove was a challenge. The cabin was damp, almost like a dripping cave. The grate and wood were soaked, and even when the fire began to catch, Jimmy had to kneel on a locker to keep his feet out of the bilge water that sloshed around. There seemed to be quite a bit of it.

"can't you start the pump?" he called out to Bethune.

"i could, but i'm not sure it'll help much. The suction's exposed, and the outflow's underwater half the time."

"then come in and cook while i handle it!"

"oh, fine," Bethune replied with a sour tone, and Jimmy turned his focus back to the kettle, leaving his companion to grumble alone.

Jimmy was familiar with the strange weariness that sometimes grips men in the face of the ocean's wrath. This wasn't just physical exhaustion; it was more of a moral paralysis, a resignation to the futility of any action. It wasn't fear either. The best remedy was sheer determination, and as he heard the pump's rhythmic clatter, he knew Bethune would soon feel more energized. Jimmy brewed some coffee, found a few of moran's rock-hard biscuits, and, with a rare indulgence, opened a can of meat. The meal, a welcome change from their usual fish, was a small luxury. After eating, Jimmy, still soaked, lay down on a locker. He wedged himself between parts of the dismantled diving pump and drifted into a restless sleep.

By midnight, it was his turn at the helm. The sky was moonless, and the sea was shrouded in gray scud. Foam-crested waves rolled relentlessly, and the Resolute heaved heavily. Jimmy stood watching moran work the pump before heading below. Then, mustering his focus, he settled in for his dismal watch. The slow lightening of the east brought no relief. Dawn arrived, and they spent yet another grueling day lying hove to. While the sloop posed little trouble and they managed to pump out the water she took on, their anxiety grew by evening. The gale had intensified. They must have drifted significantly and might be nearing land. If that were the case, the sloop wouldn't have enough sail to steer clear, and disaster loomed if they were blown ashore.

At dawn the next morning, Jimmy was back on deck, but all he could see was a narrow circle of churning waves and the scud that obscured the horizon. By noon, however, the skies started to clear. He trained the binoculars on the horizon, waiting hopefully through sporadic bursts of sunshine. The wind seemed to be easing, and the haze was thinning. Gradually, it lifted, revealing a towering, gray mass about four or five miles away.

Moran shouted as he spotted it first, but Jimmy kept his focus, scanning the horizon through his binoculars.

"that's the headland, alright!" he confirmed. "if the weather hadn't cleared up, we would've been wrecked on the shore hours ago. Now we have to make a plan. She might handle a triple-reefed mainsail."

"it would take us a week to beat back to the island, and we'd be out of supplies by the time we got there," Bethune cautioned. "i'm not thrilled about battling the wind for that long."

"with this breeze on our quarter, we could reach comox in no time," moran proposed. "we might find someone at a store willing to spot us some provisions."

"not likely, considering she's under bond," Jimmy replied. They let the boat drift as they stared gloomily toward the island. To reach it would mean a grueling fight against the wind, a vast expanse of churning sea between them and the wreck. Exhausted and disheartened, neither of moran's companions objected when he abruptly stood and loosened the mainsheet.

"i reckon we'll head where we can find a meal," he declared. "you can set a course for the straits while i hoist the mainsail."

Relief washed over Jimmy as he adjusted the helm, and the Resolute swiftly turned south with the wind at her back. Steering was tense work, and Jimmy suggested keeping the mainsail furled, but the worst was over. Ahead lay rest and shelter, a respite much needed.

CHAPTER SEVEN.

A light breeze faintly disturbed the sheltered waters as the Resolute glided into her anchorage near a small lumber port along the eastern coast of Vancouver island. A massive boom of logs was tethered near the dock, and towering stacks of freshly hewn lumber and unsightly sawdust piles lined the shoreline. Beyond them, tall iron chimneys, clusters of wooden houses, and rows of charred stumps stood guard, while steep, pine-covered hills enclosed the town like sentinels. Though a couple of steamers were anchored nearby and there were signs of life in the streets, the place had an unfinished, raw feel. Still, the crew of the Resolute welcomed it.

Cramped in their tight quarters on the ship, they relished the freedom to roam. The resinous scent hanging in the air was a pleasant change from the sharp tang of the sea spray. But their visit was not for pleasure; they were here on business, and soon Bethune stopped a passerby.

"where's the best and biggest general store in town?" he asked.

"jefferson's, three blocks from here. He's been around since the mills started."

"do we really need to go to the best store?" Jimmy asked as they continued walking. Bethune chuckled.

"not really. Now that we know where it is, we can look elsewhere. I've got a feeling that a prosperous dealer, who can pick his customers, won't be much interested in our business. It's the struggling ones who are more willing to take a risk."

"we trust your judgment," Jimmy said confidently. Bethune had handled their trade dealings with savvy and tact, recognizing that securing supplies without upfront cash wasn't easy. After wandering through the town, they entered a modest wooden store with a sign that read, "t. Jaques: shipping supplied." inside, they found the proprietor leaning casually on the counter. He was a young man with an energetic demeanor, but despite his polished appearance, Bethune sensed he hadn't yet attained success. In fact, he thought he detected signs of worry etched into the man's keen features. Taking out his notebook, Bethune began listing the supplies they needed and examined the samples on offer.

The provisions were decent; the store was tidy and fairly well stocked. Jimmy leaned on the counter, scanning the surroundings. He noticed that the goods had been arranged smartly to give the impression of abundance, which hinted that the dealer likely had limited reserves. While the shopkeeper chatted with Bethune, Jimmy saw a woman approach a glass door at the back and pause, evidently intrigued by the interaction. This all suggested that Bethune had chosen the right place for their business. While the provisions weren't their main focus, they needed ropes, chains, and marine supplies that would come with a heftier bill.

"i can send the small items over whenever you need, but the other stuff has to wait until the Vancouver shipment arrives, which will take four days," Jaques said, his eagerness evident. "can you wait?"

"oh, yes. I figure we won't be leaving for at least a week."

"good. I'll wire in the order. You'll pay upon delivery?"

Bethune smiled and said, "we should discuss that. I can give you ten dollars upfront."

The dealer's face fell, and he pondered.

"well," he said slowly, "i'd really like this order. What's your offer?"

"i don't have a specific offer yet. Maybe i should explain our situation, and you can suggest a solution."

"let's talk in the back and have a smoke," Jaques invited. They followed him into a room that doubled as a warehouse, living room, and kitchen. A young woman was busy at the stove. She looked up and smiled in welcome, then returned to her cooking. However, Jimmy felt the intensity of her scrutiny.

Jaques fetched some chairs and placed a few cigars on the table.

"alright," he said to Bethune, "you may proceed."

"first, i need your word that you'll keep this between us," Bethune said, glancing discreetly at the woman.

"you've got it, and you can trust mrs. Jaques. Susie keeps her business to herself, and she's invested quite a bit of her own money in this store. That's why i invited you in; she's sometimes got a sharper eye than i do."

Bethune nodded towards mrs. Jaques, and to Jimmy's surprise, began openly detailing their financial troubles and their plans for salvage. As he recounted their efforts at the wreck, his story grew rather compelling, and mrs. Jaques listened intently, a greasy fork suspended in mid-air. Jimmy couldn't help but wonder if Bethune was wise in revealing so much. The storekeeper leaned on the table, deep in thought, while moran sat motionless, his weathered face unreadable. Apart from Bethune's voice, the small, sparsely furnished room was silent. Jimmy suspected that the deal on the table was of significant importance to the people in the room. It certainly was crucial to his own group, as they could not carry on without supplies.

"there's already a bond on your boat," Jaques pointed out when Bethune paused.

"for about half its value. If it came to it, we could force a public sale if the boat were seized; the remaining funds would clear your debt."

"it's tough to get a good price for a vessel of her size, one that doesn't fit into regular trade operations."

"you actually got her for a bargain?" Jimmy asked.

"yeah, a gamble we had to take," Bethune replied nonchalantly.

Their conversation was cut short by a knock on the door. Jaques stepped into the store, reappearing a few minutes later.

"it was nolan, the river-jack," he explained. "needed gumboots. Figured i should give them to him, even though he still owes for the last pair."

Bethune couldn't help but chuckle. "exactly proves my point."

Jaques exchanged a knowing glance with his wife, who acknowledged with a subtle nod.

"dinner's almost ready. You should stay," he suggested. "it's simple food, but susie's biscuits and waffles are the best in the province. Plus, it'll give us more time to mull things over."

Gratefully accepting the invitation, they let the topic of business drop as they enjoyed the delicious, well-prepared meal. Jimmy found himself increasingly impressed by their hostess. Susie, with her sharp mind and warm demeanor, managed the table in a charmingly simple dress. Jimmy did his best to keep pace with Bethune's entertaining banter, noticing Jaques's approving silence. As for moran, he focused on savoring every bite.

"if we keep getting meals like this, ma'am, we might not want to leave your town," moran commented between mouthfuls.

Mrs. Jaques laughed and replied, "then my husband will miss out on his order." despite her playful tone, Jimmy sensed a deeper undertone.

After dinner, once the table was cleared, Jaques lit a cigar, smirking slightly when Jimmy inquired about business.

"could be better," he admitted. "that's partly why i'm interested in making a deal. Running a store isn't as profitable as people think. I've been here two years, and most of my customers are either late payers or won't pay at all. The better customers go to my competitor."

"where were you before?" Jimmy asked.

"toronto."

But the wages i was making in a department store weren't enough to get married on. With the little money susie had saved and what i'd managed to put aside, we thought we might barely get started. But there wasn't much opportunity left for the small guy in the eastern cities, so we headed out west. It's been tough, but we'd make some progress if those darn bush settlers would just pay their bills."

Jimmy felt a surge of sympathy. The man looked like he was having a hard time.

"have you got your business sorted out?" mrs. Jaques asked, stepping in from an adjoining room.

"not yet," Bethune answered. "i suspect your husband was waiting for you; and i couldn't blame him, hoping you might put in a good word for us."

Mrs. Jaques scrutinized him carefully. He was a handsome man with elegant manners, and she thought him honest. It was hard to reconcile deceit with Jimmy's open expression.

"well," she promised, "i'll do what i can."

"then let's get to the point." Jaques turned to his guests. "you're confident you'll find the gold when you get back?"

"no," Jimmy admitted honestly. "we're hopeful, but we can't even be sure we'll locate the wreck. The storm might have shattered it and buried it in the sand."

"then, if your plan fails, i don't get paid."

"that's assuming a lot. We'd still have something left if we had to sell the boat, and we can earn more than our keep working on the docks or in the mills. Your debt would be our first priority."

"it would take you a long time to pay it off on what you'd save from two dollars a day."

"that's true," Bethune conceded. "let's be clear, though—i suppose you believe we'd make an effort?"

"we'll take it that you intend to deal honestly with me. Anyway, you believe you've got a decent shot at finding the gold?"

"i think it's a reasonable business risk."

To prove our commitment, we'll make the effort if you supply us with what we need. We wouldn't be taking this risk if we didn't believe we had a shot at success."

"alright then. You're not suggesting i loan you the truck and take a partner's share in exchange, are you?"

"no," Bethune replied firmly. "not unless you insist."

Mrs. Jaques nodded approvingly, appreciating both the question and the answer. It showed that the adventurers had enough faith in their plan to want to keep it to themselves.

"i'd prefer my husband stuck to his usual business," she said.

"then," Bethune continued, "here's my proposal: provide us with the supplies, and charge us ten percent interest until they're fully paid off. You'll get the money back, with interest, eventually."

Jaques glanced at his wife, who gave a nod of agreement.

"alright then, it's a deal!"

Half an hour later, as they prepared to leave, Jimmy turned to mrs. Jaques.

"while your husband has been fair with us," he said, "we owe you thanks, and it's a matter of honor to prove you weren't mistaken in trusting us."

He noticed now the early signs of worry lines forming around her eyes and the work-worn calluses on her hands, but she smiled warmly at him.

"running a store teaches you that a customer's character can be as important as their bank balance."

"that's the nicest thing anyone has said to me since i arrived in british columbia!" Bethune declared cheerfully. Mrs. Jaques smiled.

"if you find the evenings dull before you set sail, feel free to drop by for a chat," she offered. When they stepped outside, Bethune admitted something.

"i was seriously tempted to take our business elsewhere."

"they're good people, and it seems they've had a tough time making ends meet."

"whatever happens, they must be paid," Jimmy insisted firmly.

"absolutely," agreed moran, who rarely voiced his thoughts unless it involved nautical matters. "that's a given!"

"how about inviting them for a picnic on one of the islands?" Bethune suggested. "it'd be a nice afternoon outing, and the water's usually calm here. I doubt mrs. Jaques gets many breaks."

The others liked the idea, and once the sloop was refitted and ready for sea, Bethune made it happen. His guests were delighted to join, and with a gentle breeze rippling the blue waters, they sailed up the straits under a brilliant sun. Jimmy placed a cushion for mrs. Jaques near the wheel, and her pale face brightened as he asked if she'd like to steer. He could tell she knew her way around the wheel by the confident grip on the spokes.

"this is wonderful!" she exclaimed as they glided swiftly through the water. "i used to sail occasionally back in toronto, but ever since we moved here, i haven't been on the water once."

She glanced wistfully at the sparkling sea. Gentle surf created a snowy fringe along the pebble beach, and beyond that, dark pinewoods stretched back into the rocky landscape towards blue, distant peaks. Overhead, the tall, white topsail swayed rhythmically in the cloudless sky. Silken threads of ripples streamed back from the bow, and along the cetacea's side there was a soothing gurgle and lapping of water.

"you're lucky to be able to sail away like this," mrs. Jaques murmured.

Jaques let out a sigh that was almost wistful. "still, it's not all smooth sailing up north."

"definitely not," Jimmy agreed. "there have been plenty of times i'd have gladly swapped the sloop for your back room, or even a few dry feet of land."

She laughed. "i can imagine. You've got gales and fog to deal with, while we struggle against jefferson and try to keep our bills paid. I'm not sure which is worse."

Jimmy felt a pang of sympathy. She was young, but a weary look in her eyes hinted at the hardships she faced in the rustic wooden town. Her life seemed to be a grind of work and worries, and it was touching to see how much she cherished her rare breaks. Late in the afternoon, they anchored in a rock-walled cove with a beach of white pebbles where sparkling wavelets danced. Dark firs climbed the rugged slopes above, their scent wafting over the clear green water. Bethune, who had been busy cooking, emerged with an unexpectedly fancy meal, setting it out on the cabin top with the best glassware and china he could borrow. Despite his efforts, he looked anxious as he served the first course.

"i've done my best here. I used to think i was a decent cook, but after that dinner mrs. Jaques made for us, my confidence is shaken," he confessed. "it's easy to get a swelled head when you don't have anything to compare your work to and your critics are kind. Jimmy's been very patient with me, and i'd say moran would eat anything remotely edible."

"i've had to," moran shot back. "but honestly, i've seen you cook worse than this."

No one had any complaints, and the hearty appetites were flattering. They joked and chatted in high spirits, until moran pointed to the lengthening shadow of the mast moving across the deck.

"it's peculiar, but we've spent an hour over supper, and there's still food left."

"i guess i never spent more than ten minutes on a meal before," mused Bethune as he took a bottle from an ice-filled locker and poured drinks into the borrowed glasses.

"to our next happy reunion!" he proclaimed, raising his glass. "our guests, who made this journey possible, won't be forgotten while we're away."

They clinked glasses, drained them, and refilled once more. Mrs. Jaques then turned to their hosts with a warm smile.

"may you achieve the success you truly deserve!" she responded. A few minutes later, Bethune signaled moran and went forward to hoist the anchor.

As the light began to fade, they maneuvered the Resolute close to the wharf, where a waiting boat approached. Amid heartfelt goodbyes and well wishes, Mr. And mrs. Jaques disembarked, and the sloop set sail toward the desolate north.

Chapter Eight.

B right sunlight poured into the clearing on the edge of puget sound, where henry Osborne made his home. The quaint wooden house, adorned with a wide veranda and intricate scrollwork, nestled perfectly amid tall pines. The resinous scent from the conifers seeped through the rooms, while the expansive lawn, dotted with vibrant flower beds, stretched down to the pebble-strewn beach.

Rocky islets, crowned with dark firs, dotted the sparkling waters, and beyond them, ascending woods and hills, painted in varying shades of blue, dissolved into the distance. A faint gleam of snow capped the scene. The hush of the afternoon was punctuated only by the gentle splash of waves on the shore and the rhythmic patter of water from automatic sprinklers casting shimmering arcs over the thirsty grass.

Caroline dexter, recently arrived from a small new england town, sat in the shade of a cedar tree. She was elderly, exuding a stern demeanor. Her plain, ill-fitted gray dress accentuated her lean frame, and her homely face bore an air of austerity. Yet, her gaze was direct, and those familiar with her knew that beneath her stern exterior lay a warm heart. As she surveyed the house and garden, her expression was one of disapproval.

Everything she saw suggested prosperity and taste, but while she didn't dismiss wealth out of hand, she fervently hoped henry Osborne had acquired his honestly. She'd never fully trusted him, and hadn't been pleased when he married her younger sister. She deemed him lax and worldly; but after his wife's untimely death—a profound loss for caroline—she had taken his child under her wing and cared for her with great affection. She believed she had shaped ruth Osborne's character and won her affections. The girl could have ended up in worse hands, for despite her rigid outlook, caroline dexter was unwaveringly upright.

Seated stiffly in the garden chair, she turned to her niece, who lounged with casual elegance in a canvas chair nearby.

Caroline sighed, brushing off the indulgence she saw in the younger generation. Yet, despite her stern outlook, she recognized ruth's underlying commendable traits. Ruth was undeniably pretty, and though caroline believed appearance was deceptive, she hoped the rigorous upbringing she provided had kept ruth grounded.

"this place is lovely," caroline observed. "it's clear your father's fortunes have improved. It's a pity your mother isn't here to see this."

Her provincial attire accentuated her austere demeanor, yet there was an air of distinction about her, with a crispness in her accent that set her apart. Ruth met her gaze with a thoughtful expression, tinged with regret.

"i often think about the struggles she must have faced," ruth said quietly. "even though i was quite young, i remember the run-down boardinghouses we lived in and my mother's worried face whenever she and my father talked in the evenings. He rarely mentions those times, but i know he hasn't forgotten."

"it's admirable he never remarried," caroline said bluntly, but without harshness. "he truly loved your mother, and that's something that deserves respect."

"but does he really have much to be forgiven for? men do remarry sometimes," ruth responded.

"and sometimes more than twice! but those men are for women who'll have them. The love of a true man or woman outlasts even death," caroline said, her voice unexpectedly warm.

Ruth looked at her, half-mocking, half-curious. "you seem to speak with passion," she remarked.

A flicker of unease crossed miss dexter's eyes as she stared blankly at a seabird hovering above the water. Quickly, though, she turned to her niece with her usual composed demeanor.

"we were discussing your father's finances," she said. "i see some wasteful spending: servants you don't need, a gasoline launch, and two cars."

Ruth chuckled.

"father needs to get to town quickly, and cars can break down; besides, i think he can afford them. Sometimes, aunt caroline, i think you're a bit too harsh on him."

"i admit i've often wondered how he made his money so fast. You can't make a fortune quickly without facing many temptations. Did you know your uncle charles had to lend him a thousand dollars not long after you were born, and he just repaid it a few years ago? has your father ever talked to you about his business?"

"i never thought to ask," ruth replied, a bit heatedly. "he's always been very kind to me, and i trust whatever he does is right."

"that's a good attitude to have," her aunt acknowledged. "no doubt, he's not worse than others; but men's morals are quite lax these days."

Ruth felt more amused than offended. Though loyal to her father, she suspected her aunt mistrusted all who made fast fortunes rather than her brother-in-law specifically. Caroline dexter's frugal, old-fashioned disdain for modern luxury was clear, but she had piqued ruth's curiosity about her father's past struggles.

A billowing cloud of dust rose among the firs where the winding road cut across the hillside, and a sleek gray car flashed through a gap in the trees. Ruth recognized the vehicle instantly; there was only one person she knew who would navigate that treacherous dip at such a reckless speed.

"it's Aynsley," she said, her face lighting up. "i'll bring him over."

"and who is Aynsley?"

"oh, i forgot you don't know him," she admitted.

Aynsley Clay was the son of my father's old partner and made frequent appearances at our home whenever he was around.

As i turned back toward the house, a young man emerged onto the veranda. Clad in white flannel, with a straw hat and a blue serge jacket, his pleasant face bore the bronze of sea adventures.

"i came straight through," he said, extending a hand. "it's particularly nice of you to get up to greet me."

"i'm happy to see you back, Aynsley," ruth replied warmly. "did you have a good trip? when did you get home?"

"docked the yacht at portland yesterday and came right over. Found the old man out of town, so i figured i'd stop at martin's place. I'm supposed to be there tonight."

"but that's twenty miles out, over the mountains. This isn't the closest route," she remarked, puzzled.

Clay chuckled, though there was a trace of shyness in his smile. "what's twenty miles on a hill road when you're eager to see friends?"

He watched her as intently as he dared, looking for any sign of her feelings, but her demeanor remained enigmatic.

"you know that isn't a proper road," she teased. "someday, you'll end up arriving here in pieces."

"would that bother you?" he asked, his tone lighter but curious.

"you ought to know by now," she said with a playful glance. "come on in, my aunt is eager to meet you."

As he was introduced, miss dexter regarded him with candid scrutiny. While Aynsley exhibited a certain elegance and an easygoing nature—qualities she didn't highly regard in young men—his face bore an earnestness that she liked, and his gaze was frank. If he was among the leisure class, she thought, he was a rather pleasing example.

"what are your pursuits?" she asked directly after they conversed a bit.

"it's hard to pin down because i have various interests and talents. I dabble in naturalism, enjoy yachting, and i must say, i'm quite adept at handling a troublesome automobile."

When i was younger, i dreamed of taming a wild stallion, but now my days are filled with tinkering with valves and cams. Times change, though it's hard to say if they're getting any better."

"so, you don't really do anything?"

"you've got my father's practical viewpoint, but we might disagree on what counts as hard work. For example, today i spent two hours lying under the car, wrestling with awkward bolts. Then i drove fifty miles on a miserable road littered with rocks and fallen trees. I've got another twenty miles to go, and if you ask me, i'll have done enough for any ordinary person by the end of it."

"and how's that benefiting anyone?"

"well, at least nobody's worse off because of it. Though, i've seen the community suffer when they didn't move out of the way fast enough."

She shook her head in disapproval, but there was a twinkle in miss dexter's eyes.

"i guess you're a product of your time, shaped by your surroundings. There are more dangerous hobbies than cars and yachts. Enjoy them while you can; it might prepare you for something tougher later. And i see a look in your eyes that makes me think that day will come."

Half an hour later, ruth and Aynsley walked through a grove of pines by the water's edge.

"what did you think of my aunt?" she asked.

"i think miss dexter is an impressive woman. And i see something in you that reminds me of her. Do you know that you two aren't so different?"

Ruth smiled. Her aunt had harsh features and dressed poorly, but she knew it wasn't her appearance that had impressed him.

"the feeling seems mutual," she said, "and to be honest, that surprised me a bit."

"she definitely doesn't go easy on slackers."

"i knew she'd judge me by my clothes, so i went along with her assumptions. It's funny how people respond when you play into their stereotypes. Speaking of slackers, before i left, the old man was getting on my case about wasting my talents; said it was high time i did something worthwhile. He even offered to cover the losses i'd make in the first couple of years if i took over the canadian mill he just bought. I pointed out it might cost him more than my usual indulgences in boats and cars, and he joked it off, saying he'd consider it the price of his parenting methods. Anyway, let's not dwell on that. It's too beautiful a day."

True to character, ruth found his lightheartedness amusing. He was always so carefree and spontaneous, and though she had known him for ages, she appreciated his easygoing nature. It was odd, perhaps, that she had never wondered about his feelings for her; she simply accepted their uncomplicated friendship. On the rare occasions he did get sentimental, she had no trouble steering the conversation away from dangerous waters.

"so," she prodded, "you haven't said a word about your trip. Surely you must have encountered something interesting, maybe had a bit of excitement?"

"best policy is to steer clear of adventures when you can, and we stuck to that. But the most intriguing part was meeting three men fishing on a remote island way up north."

"fishing? that doesn't exactly scream excitement," she replied skeptically.

They settled down where a gap in the pines revealed a breathtaking vista of sun- dappled forests descending to the sparkling sound below. Aynsley took a moment to light a cigarette before continuing.

"it sure looked like fishing, but i've had my doubts since. If they did catch anything, they were far from any market, and though they looked rough enough, two of them didn't seem like your typical fishermen."

One fellow was the kind you'd find at a sporting club, while the other had the unmistakable mark of a navy or first-class mailboat officer. He was english.

Ruth looked up quickly. Jimmy had often crossed her mind since their last meeting, though he hadn't taken her up on her invitation, so she hadn't asked about him. However, Osborne had visited Vancouver and, seeing the ship at the dock, inquired about Farquhar, learning he had left on the previous voyage. Ruth resented his silence but couldn't forget him.

"what did the man look like?" she asked.

"which one?"

"the navy man," she clarified, feeling slightly embarrassed by the directness of her question. Aynsley gave her an incisive look.

"as i recall, he had light hair and darker blue eyes, which isn't so common. He was about my age, definitely a sailor, but with a sharp look and an air of command. Do you know someone like that?"

Ruth hesitated, uncharacteristically reserved. She was fairly certain this was the second mate she'd spent many evenings with on the liner's saloon deck.

"oh, we've met a few steamboat officers; they're mostly similar types," she replied nonchalantly. Aynsley noted her guarded response. He knew girls often had a soft spot for mailboat officers, who were typically well-mannered and good-looking. Nevertheless, he kept his thoughts private, knowing he wouldn't get far by pushing his feelings too vigorously.

"anyway," he said, "they were pleasant enough and seemed to have it rough. Between the ice, gales, and fog, it's not exactly an easy posting."

"wasn't it on one of those islands where my father was wrecked and lost the gold he was transporting?"

"somewhere around there."

"islands are common up north." Aynsley paused and chuckled. "still, given my father's interest in the gold, i doubt he lost much. Losing things isn't exactly his style. I think he even had a stake in the ship."

"but it sank."

"doesn't matter. The insurers probably ended up paying more than it was worth. It's funny, considering my background, that i have no head for business."

"our fathers have been partners for a long time, haven't they?"

"they've supported each other for years. Seems like we're meant to be friends too, but sometimes i think you don't realize how much your friendship means to me."

"of course we're good friends," ruth said nonchalantly, "but you have plenty of other friends."

"i have lots of acquaintances; but you're different. It might not sound original, but it's true. There's something about you—something unique and timeless. It's like a quality you don't find in our bustling cities, more like something from the quaint corners of new england. It's a refined elegance that isn't born overnight."

"both my father's and mother's families lived simply in a small eastern town."

"that just proves my point. I can imagine the kind of place: a 'sleepy hollow' where life moves at its own pace, untouched by the westward expansion. Your mother's family was likely steeped in tradition, holding on to the ways of yesteryears. That's where you get your poise, your character, and a kindness i've never found in anyone else."

Ruth stood up with a gentle smile of reproach and purposefully changed the subject.

"yes, i know," Aynsley said with a sigh. "i'm not supposed to talk like that."

When i act like the friendly fool, people applaud, but the moment i speak honestly, they quickly shut me down."

"you're never foolish," ruth smiled. "but if you want to get over those hills before dark, we should get you something to eat."

He turned to her, looking both resigned and frustrated.

"oh, well! if the car crashes through a bushman's bridge or tumbles into a ravine, you'll regret dismissing me."

"we won't expect anything that drastic," ruth replied. Then, with a sharp shift in her tone, she added, "take that job at your father's mill, Aynsley; you really should."

He regarded her for a moment and then nodded.

"alright! i'll do it," he said. An hour later, she watched him start the car, then settled among the pines to think. There were questions needing answers. Aynsley was very likable, but she didn't delve deeper. Her thoughts drifted to Farquhar, and she wondered why his disappearance bothered her so much. She knew little about him, apart from the evenings they spent leaning on the rails together as their ship sailed under the moonlit sky. Now, believing he was the man Aynsley had encountered, he was up in the desolate north. She speculated on his activities and the dangers he faced there. It took effort to push him from her mind, but another curiosity gripped her. How had her father spent those years when she was with her aunt, before becoming wealthy? he never spoke of his struggles, but she had to ask. Sometimes he seemed worn out, and she longed to support him with an understanding heart. How had he amassed his fortune so quickly? ruth had complete confidence in her father, despite her aunt's doubts, but she resolved to question him.

CHAPTER NINE.

Osborne sat on his veranda one sweltering evening while ruth lounged in a wicker chair, eyeing him thoughtfully. Lately, she felt she barely knew her father; there was a guardedness about him she couldn't quite penetrate. Since her arrival, he'd indulged her every whim with kindness; before that, there had been a long gap with no contact, and those years had clearly left a mark on him. She felt a mix of compassion and guilt. Until now, she'd basked in his attention, taking everything and giving nothing in return. It was time for that to change.

Osborne was of medium height with a lean build, and he had a slight limp. His overall appearance was agreeable, though he hardly fit ruth's image of a successful businessman. There was a dreamy, imaginative air about him, and his face bore lines and wrinkles that hinted at past troubles. Ruth had heard tales of his headstrong and romantic youth, but now he seemed more philosophical, with a touch of ironic humor. She wondered what hard experiences had snuffed out his youthful fire.

"Aynsley mentioned he's planning to take charge of the canadian mill," she said.

"i imagine you supported his decision. In fact, i wonder if he made it entirely on his own. The last time Clay brought it up, he said the young man couldn't make up his mind."

Ruth felt uneasy under her father's amused gaze. He was shrewd, and she wasn't ready to admit she had influenced Aynsley.

"but don't you think Aynsley's making the right choice?" she asked.

"oh, in a way. We admire industrial initiative, and that's generally a good thing. But sometimes i think our bush ranchers and prospectors, who stay a step ahead of civilized progress while still contributing to it, show sound judgment."

Turning our natural treasures into dollars, and leaving behind eyesores of mining dumps and factory chimneys, is undoubtedly the norm now. Our commercial system has bred a lot of both moral and physical ugliness."

The girl was used to his light jabs and often found herself unsure of his seriousness.

"but you're a businessman," she pointed out.

"that's true. I've paid my dues for it; doesn't mean our way of doing things is perfect just because i've followed it."

"where did you first meet Aynsley's father?" ruth asked, steering the conversation to personal topics she preferred. Osborne's face lit up with a hint of nostalgia.

"in a lonely settlement in arizona quite a few years back. The southern pacific had just hit the coast, and i was heading west without a ticket. When i couldn't avoid it, i walked. But the railroad workers were kinder back then. Most of the journey from omaha, i was clandestinely riding inside or even clinging beneath the freight cars. The space under them was choked with dust in those dry regions."

Ruth glanced from the charming wooden house, furnished without concern for budget, over the sprawling lawn where a diligent gardener was maneuvering a gas- powered mower. The image of her father hitching a ride on a freight train seemed almost surreal. But another thought crossed her mind.

"where was i then?" she asked.

"with your aunt, or maybe just starting school. I can't pin down the exact time," Osborne replied without caution. Ruth was overtaken by a mixed wave of love and gratitude. She knew her school had been pricey and her mother's family wasn't well-off. Yet, despite the small yearly inheritance her father received, it appeared he had funneled it all towards her education while he lived in stark poverty. Impulsively, she moved her chair closer to him and clasped his large hand with her cool, delicate fingers.

"i get it now," she said softly, "why there are lines on your forehead and why you sometimes look so tired."

"your life must have been pretty tough."

Osborne replied with a hint of levity, "oh, it had its moments. Anyway, Clay was also on the move, and i found him quenching his thirst with water from a locomotive tank. We faced the daunting task of crossing about a hundred miles of barren desert with just two dollars between us. Clay tackled the water issue first by crafting a makeshift water-bag from some railroad rubber sheeting he 'borrowed,' while i scoured the settlement for provisions. Managed to get some, though the prices were sky-high. By midnight, we were hiding near the tracks, waiting for a freight train to depart. The brakemen had a habit of checking around the cars before starting off. Though the days were scorching hot, nights were freezing cold, and we huddled behind a cluster of cacti, shivering. At one point, a man almost stepped on us while he ran down the line, but then the engine's bell rang. Clay jumped up, struggling to slide back one of the heavy doors, while i held onto our food and water. The runners were stiff, and as the train began to move, it was a race against time. Clay managed to pry the door open a few inches, and i had to jog alongside the moving train. By the time he could crawl through, it was too late for me to climb in. With a hazy memory of the long journey ahead, i tossed the food and water into the car."

"that's so typical of you!" ruth exclaimed with a proud smile.

"i think it was more absent-minded than anything. Standing between the tracks, watching the train fade into the night, i felt incredibly sorry for myself. It didn't help that of our combined two dollars, only fifty cents was his."

"when did you meet him again?"

"a few years later in san francisco. He seemed to be doing well, while my luck hadn't improved. Thanks to clay, i ended up working for the alaska commercial company."

That was before the klondike rush, back when the a.c.c. Still ruled the frozen north.

"you got your first break in alaska, didn't you? you've never really told me about the mine you found," she said.

Osborne frowned at the memory, but seeing her interest, he decided to indulge her. Despite her idealized view of him, ruth had to admit that Osborne didn't fit the miner stereotype. His summer outfit was impeccably chosen, and there was a refined air to his appearance and manners that clashed with his rugged past.

"well," he began, "it was a cursed mine from the start, and i wasn't even the first to find it. I'd been with the company for years when they sent me out as an agent to one of their outposts. The place was perched on a wind-battered coast, nothing but barren tundra and muskeg stretching out behind it. The climate was brutal. No trees tall enough to shield from the harsh winds, and for six months, the ground was buried under deep snow. A small ship came by once or twice a year, and my job was to trade with the indigenous tribes and russian half-breeds for furs. Winters were bleak, with only a few hours of daylight. I'd get books shipped from san francisco and read them by the red-hot stove while blizzards pounded the factory. Even back then, people suspected there was gold in alaska, but the a.c.c. Discouraged prospecting. The terrain was so unforgiving that few outsiders could navigate it. Still, some prospectors managed to make their way in and likely perished because we rarely saw them again. I remember a few grizzled men who stayed with us for a day or two before disappearing into the wilderness.

"it was late in the fall when one showed up with two aleut indians in a skin canoe."

I never discovered where he hailed from or how he got so far, especially given the limited communication with the north, accessible only via the company's ships. He mentioned his aim was to find a rumored mine and hoped to return before winter's onset. He left with the aleuts and a few provisions he had bought. That was the last we saw of him until the following summer.

I ventured inland to visit a tribe that hadn't brought in any furs. One night, we set up camp among a grove of willows. While gathering wood, i noticed that some larger bushes had been hacked down, clearly the work of a white man. The next morning, we stumbled upon an empty provision can, the kind we used, and later, bits of charred sticks where a fire had been made. This discovery prompted us to follow the creek we had camped by, and soon enough, we found the man who had built that fire.

"dead!" ruth exclaimed.

"he had been dead for months. All that remained was a skeleton, bleached by the snow, and a few ragged pieces of clothing. The most

disturbing detail was that the breastbone had been split – sharply, as
if cleaved by an ax."

"how horrible! do you think the indians killed him?"

"it seemed likely. There might have been a fight over the last of the
provisions, which the aleuts took, as i found very few cans and just
one small empty flour bag. But the tools indicated it was the same man
who had visited the factory."

I had never heard his name, and if he had any friends, they remained
unaware of his fate; yet he died wealthy."

"he found the gold?" ruth's eyes sparkled with excitement.

"yes," replied Osborne. "not far from here, the creek had shifted
its course, and there was a shallow pit, partly filled with ashes. As the
scrubland is three or four miles away, it's easy to picture him hauling
the half-dry brush to keep a large fire burning."

"but why did he need such a big fire?"

"to soften the ground. The soil never thaws more than a couple of
feet deep, and it was clear that early winter had caught him off guard.
He was a stubborn man, determined to hold on until the very end."

"do you think his companions killed him for the treasure?"

"no; back then, the indigenous people didn't care about gold. They
might have killed him for a silver fox's pelt, though; furs were our
currency. If there was any conflict, it likely started because he insisted
on staying when winter was near and food was running low. Despite that, i couldn't find the gold he must have discovered, but there
was plenty in the sediment he left behind—tiny, rounded nuggets
alongside grains. It was a rich alluvial pocket, easy to work with basic
equipment, and i vowed to return to snowy creek someday."

"but you weren't alone! what about your companions?"

"i had two half-breeds with russian ancestry; good trappers, but
with little more intelligence than the animals they hunted. Gold held

no value to them; their greatest aspiration was to own a magazine rifle."

"couldn't you have panned some of the gold?"

"i managed to collect a small amount, but i was under the company's employ and had its business to prioritize. Plus, we only had enough provisions for the journey."

The a.c.c. Found that the fur trade was far more lucrative than mining and wanted to keep their territories secure. No one realized just how wealthy the land truly was. Not long after i returned, i had a dispute with the head manager. Expecting trouble, i kept quiet about my discovery. The company sided with him, so i left the a.c.c. With my secret and a few hundred dollars."

"what did you do after that?"

"to be honest, explaining all my misadventures would get pretty tedious. Sometimes i had a couple hundred bucks, sometimes nothing but a worn-out suit. But whenever things got really tough, a new opportunity always appeared. I wandered around the pacific coast until i ran into Clay again."

"so, you didn't go to him right after leaving the a.c.c.?"

"no; he'd helped me out once, and i didn't want to keep asking for favors." Osborne paused, his expression turning more serious. "besides, we had some differences, and back then i was quite headstrong."

"aren't you still?"

"i've learned that it's smarter sometimes to keep your opinions to yourself," Osborne replied dryly. "it's easiest to be independent when you have nothing because then it doesn't matter who you upset."

"was Clay doing well?" ruth asked.

"he was starting to make a name for himself as someone to take seriously, but he was still strapped for cash and ready to chase any venture that promised a few dollars. Clay never backed down from a risk, but i genuinely think he was happy to see me. In a moment of openness, i told him about the snowy creek mine and the gold waiting for me when i could return."

"ah! i've been waiting for you to circle back to that. I knew it was important."

"it was the mine that made you rich and surrounded me with a luxury i was half afraid of at the beginning, wasn't it?"

Miss dexter approached along the terrace, and Osborne smiled, gesturing subtly towards her.

"your aunt has always been inclined to disapprove of my actions, and i don't suppose she'd be interested in hearing about my prospecting adventures. We'll save those stories for another day."

Ruth nodded in agreement, though she felt a nagging suspicion that her father was relieved by the interruption. As miss dexter joined them, ruth found herself tugged into the flow of general conversation, guided by her father's unspoken cues. Yet, even while engaging in polite chatter, ruth's mind wandered. She struggled to understand why her aunt, someone whose love for her was undeniable, maintained such a critical stance toward her father. Caroline was narrow-minded but principled; it seemed implausible that she could find any genuine fault with him.

However, ruth couldn't shake her discomfort about his association with clay. Clay was neither refined nor principled, and, to his credit, made no pretense of it. Ruth had heard men of varied temperaments speak of clay's business dealings with a mix of indignation and cynical amusement. Skeptics might thrive on blackening the reputations of successful men, but there was a cloud of suspicion around Clay that was hard to ignore. Ruth couldn't help but wish her father had partnered with someone more reputable.

CHAPTER TEN.

R uth had plenty of time to mull over her father's unfinished tale, as a full week passed before she could coax him to pick it up again. Osborne had been away on some business for a few days, and when he returned, his distracted demeanor indicated that he had important matters on his mind. Ruth decided not to press him. Still, the subject intrigued her deeply. She had been too young to grasp more than a vague sense of her father's struggles back in the day and had come to view him as the polished and successful gentleman she had reunited with after a long separation. Now, adjusting to the idea of him as a desperate adventurer taking on risky and morally questionable endeavors was challenging for her. She prided herself on not being overly judgmental, but reconciling these two starkly different images of her father was tough.

Finally, one evening, as they ambled across the lawn at dusk, ruth resolutely led the conversation back to the topic, ignoring the amused smile with which he initially deflected her questions.

"i don't see why you're so eager to hear about the mine," he said, lighting a cigar as they settled on a bench beneath a towering, weather-beaten pine. "honestly, i'd prefer to forget the whole thing. The gold from snowy creek seemed cursed—none of it ever brought good fortune."

He exhaled a cloud of smoke before continuing, "well, it was sometime after the klondike rush began, when gold was being found readily on both american and canadian soil. I went up to alaska to re-open the mine. Clay had already headed north by then, but not as a miner. He claimed it was cheaper to have someone else dig the gold for him. He invested in a share of a wooden steamboat, launched a transport service to several mining camps, and financed prospectors who struck it rich. Everything he touched turned to gold, and he was well-liked in the burgeoning towns where canvas tents sprouted like mushrooms. So, i wasn't surprised when he showed little enthusiasm for my plan."

Eventually, after a lot of coaxing, he agreed to join us, and we set off with two hired carriers and enough supplies to give us a fighting chance at success.

That summer arrived late, and we dragged the sledges two hundred miles through the snow. I won't bore you with the details of the trek, but it certainly was a struggle. One afternoon, we reached the creek, soaked and exhausted, having slogged through thawing snow and sodden muskeg. Our feet were encased in hide moccasins, usually drenched, and mine finally tore under the snowshoe straps. My foot, previously frostbitten during the first trip to the mine, was deeply cut, making the last stretch a supreme test of my endurance. I pushed through because i couldn't face another night without knowing my fate. Everything i had was riding on this venture. If it failed, i'd return to camp with nothing.

"understandably, you were anxious."

"it was tough to stay calm, but fatigue and pain had a way of grounding me. I believe i kept my cool, though i envied the others' composure. I can still picture them: Clay shuffling along in his worn skin coat and ragged boots, the two carriers grumbling about the slush, stooped under their burdens. All around us stretched a desolate wilderness to the horizon; gray soil and rocks streaked with melting snow, out of which straggling patches of withered scrub poked out forlornly. We eventually reached the creek, guided by the compass, near where i thought we would. Soon, i recognized a landmark, and Clay did too."

"clay? but he hadn't been there before!"

"you're observant," Osborne noted. "Clay and i had gone over my plans many times. He knew almost as much about the place as i did."

You couldn't miss the prominent ridge rising in the distance, though it took us a while to get close enough.

"and the mine?" ruth asked eagerly.

"we reached the spot by evening. I got there first, despite the pain in my foot. Sometimes i think Clay held back on purpose to let me pass. I had to muster every ounce of my self-control and, for a few moments, stood there silently, fists clenched. Where i once left a small hole, now there was a large one, and a significant pile of tailings scattered in the creek bed. It was clear—we were too late."

"how awful!" ruth exclaimed. "after everything you endured, it must have been unbearable. What happened then?"

"it's all a blur. Clay spoke first; i can still hear his steady voice, 'looks like someone beat us to it, partner!'"

"but that seems so understated! didn't he react at all?" ruth pressed.

"he just sat down on his pack and lit a cigar; he always kept his cool under pressure. As for me, i vaguely remember grabbing a stick of dynamite, hurling it into the hole, and then frantically digging out bits of dirt and rock until darkness fell. It was futile—i knew, because whoever found the pocket wouldn't have stopped until they'd cleaned it out completely. Eventually, i threw down my tools and lay among the stones, exhausted and trembling, as Clay began to speak."

"but who found the mine?" ruth interrupted.

"i never found out. But Clay handled it with reason. He pointed out that it was only a pocket, a small alluvial deposit. The stream that brought the gold likely deposited more in the slower eddies, and there was still a chance of finding the mother lode, where the gold originated. We had enough provisions to explore the area for a while."

The next morning, we embarked on our mission, following the creek and discovering gold sporadically. However, it became evident that our supplies might run out before we reached the watershed.

"were any of the pockets as rich as the one that was stolen?" ruth inquired.

"no," her father replied cautiously. "we did find some gold, though, and managed to get back to the coast safely. For a while, i assisted clay. He then informed me he had to head south before the ice closed in. We set sail on a vessel that he and some of his friends had purchased. As we rowed toward her on a foggy day through heavy surf, i didn't anticipate a comfortable journey. She was an old wooden steamer, a former whaling ship with tall bulwarks and truncated masts that made her look unstable. The cramped, grimy saloon and part of the 'tween- decks teemed with successful miners and others fortunate enough to afford passage out before winter set in. Nobody among them wished to revisit the north, and no one who had experienced it could blame them. Those who had gold had earned it through sheer toil and relentless endurance. Those without were returning as broken men—frostbitten, accident-prone, and plagued by illness.

We struggled to set sail. Several crew members had deserted, and those that remained were mutinous, forcibly kept on board. They seemed a sloppy and unseamanlike bunch. Adding to our difficulties, a stiff wind was blowing onshore, and the ship strained at her anchor, dipping her bows into the long swells in the exposed anchorage. The rickety windlass chain snapped as we tried to raise the anchor, forcing the miners to help with tackles before we could hoist it to the bow. Eventually, she limped out to sea with half steam. Although the prospects weren't great, i held out hope for a swift voyage.

The young first mate and an engineer seemed competent, but the rest of the crew left much to be desired. The captain himself was lackadaisical and too fond of drink. He was a small, slouched man with unsteady eyes.

"how did such an old ship manage to get passengers, and why didn't they hire a better crew?" ruth asked, curious.

"during the gold rush, passengers weren't picky, and good sailors were in short supply on the pacific coast. Most of the skilled ones had gone off to the goldfields."

"oh! where did they keep the gold on board?"

"in a strong-room beneath the stern cabin floor, at least the gold that was officially shipped. I believe some miners carried as much gold on their person as they could and hid the rest under their bunks. You'd see men keeping watch while the cabin stewards worked. I imagine it was risky to accidentally bunk in the wrong bed at night. I usually struck a match to double-check my number. Most of the passengers seemed trustworthy, though. I had more faith in them than the crew.

"our problems began on the first day out when a pipe burst in the engine room. There was no panic when the ship stopped and steam billowed out of the skylights. Men who had braved the alaskan wilderness and navigated rapids when the ice broke weren't easily rattled.

"'looks like the old boiler's blowing. Guess we'll be delayed another day or two,' one remarked, lighting his pipe nonchalantly.

"'they've got sails up there. She'll make it, given enough time,' replied his companion calmly.

"the ship lay for many hours, rolling violently, making it impossible to stand, while a miner and the second engineer wrapped the pipe with copper wire and brazed the joint. But the next mishap was more serious."

She was plowing through a white-capped sea with both topsails unfurled when a harsh grinding sound preceded the abrupt shutdown of the engines. A collar on the propeller shaft had snapped, the bolts had sheared off, and until we could fix it, there was no way to connect the engines to the screw.

The crew set more sail while the engineers dove into their task; hours later, Clay and i found ourselves in the captain's quarters. Clay seemed unfazed by the mishap, but the captain had a nervous air about him and was tipping back more rum than what was wise. A bottle sat in the rack as Clay poured himself a glass just as a miner entered. He was a burly man, with a rugged, weathered face and piercing eyes that seemed to miss nothing.

"can your engine crew fix this, cap?" he asked.

"they're working on it," the captain replied curtly. "might take a while."

"what's the plan in the meantime?"

"we'll head south under sail." the captain's tone grew sharper. "is there something else you need to know?"

"just this—can you handle her with the men you've got?"

The captain stood, flushed red with anger, and i thought for a moment we'd see a confrontation, but Clay interjected, glancing at the miner and nudging the captain back into his seat.

"you'd better answer him," Clay said.

"if the wind holds, i can keep her on course until the engines are back up. That should suffice for now."

"certainly," the miner said. "if you found the job too big, we'd have rounded up more hands for the shaft or to manage the sails. Anyway, if you need help later, you know where to find me." with that, he walked out, and the captain downed his glass, a habit he indulged too often.

"could the miner really make good on his promises?" ruth asked, breaking into my thoughts.

"quite likely. In fact, i believe we could have found a doctor, an architect, or even a clergyman among the diverse mix on board. The miner certainly managed to locate a couple of mechanics. Once, i even crawled into the shaft tunnel just to see them at work."

Working in such tight quarters was nearly impossible. They huddled uncomfortably in a four-foot-wide iron tube, trying to make cuts in the damaged section. Every swing of the hammer and chisel was a struggle; black oil mixed with saltwater sloshed around their feet from a leaking seal. The smoke and flicker of open lamps above their heads made the cramped space even more stifling. Despite the foul air, they labored in shifts with the ship's engineers for several days. All the while, the weather deteriorated, and the boat pitched angrily through the turbulent sea with its sails up. Waves drenched the deck as massive swells crashed over the rails. It was freezing cold, and a gray mist swallowed the horizon. Since visibility was zero, the captain had to rely on dead reckoning to navigate, an often unreliable method.

"you must have felt anxious with all that gold on board," ruth commented.

Osborne paused briefly, a hesitation ruth didn't notice. "no," he replied. "Clay had the vessel and the gold insured under a floating policy. He had a tough time sorting it out but managed to arrange it through a broker who owed him a favor."

"Clay seems to have a lot of influence," ruth said thoughtfully. "how does he manage that?"

"it's just his knack," Osborne replied with an enigmatic smile. "back to my story, knowing the gold was insured helped because, as a part-owner, i had to sign off on its value. That document went aboard another ship with the bill of lading. Honestly, i was more worried about our safety. The cold, the mist, and the relentless storm were nerve-wracking. Eventually, the gale subsided, but the fog thickened as the sea calmed. One night, i was jolted awake by a crash that hurled me from my bunk."

As i threw on a few clothes, i could feel the ship take another hit. Rushing out on deck, half-dressed, it was painfully clear this would be her last voyage. She lay at a sharp angle, swallowed by the sea, with her aft sinking and the persistent swells crashing over her. You could see the smooth waves emerging from the darkness, turning to foam that engulfed half the deck, while the planking buckled with a dreadful noise as the reef tore into her bilge. Despite the chaos, there was no panic. The miners methodically helped to swing the boats out. Seeing that the ship was holding together for the moment, i joined Clay and two sailors to open the strong-room. It was accessed through a trapdoor in the cabin floor, but broken beams had jammed it shut, so we took to the deck with bars and axes.

The deck was sharply tilted, the stern heaving and creaking as the swells roared around it. A large lamp, still burning, hung at an awkward angle from the bulkhead. I remember a maple sideboard, torn from its place and smashed to pieces, lying in a pool of water on the leeward side. Yet, there was no time to take it all in. We worked furiously, Clay more so than any of us. He was half- dressed, face savage and dripping with sweat, swinging his ax with a relentless fury, oblivious to everything else. His intensity puzzled me later.

"but his gold was down there!" ruth exclaimed.

"it was fully insured," Osborne cut in. "i didn't think Clay would go to such desperate lengths for the sake of the insurance companies; and he certainly wasn't pretending, because when the angle of the floor got steeper and we were urged to get out before the ship slipped off the reef, he recklessly shouted offers of money at the men to push them to keep going."

We might have made it if we'd had just a few more minutes. The strong-room was probably already flooding, but then the lamp fell when a wave hit, plunging us into darkness with water lapping at our ankles. We had no choice but to retreat, and it was clear that she was going down as we stumbled across the after-deck. A lifeboat was waiting under the quarter, but as soon as i dropped into it, a wave swept it away. As we lurched through the swell, a heavy crash echoed behind us. A blue light flickered, revealing other lifeboats and half the wreck, towering black against the spouting foam.

It seemed that everyone had made it off the ship, and we took turns rowing through the pitch-black night. We missed a nearby island and landed two days later on a barren beach of the mainland. We survived there for two weeks, mostly on shellfish, until a canadian sealing schooner arrived at a nearby inlet for water. They took us aboard, and as we filled her, it was a relief when she transferred us to a wooden propeller off the northern end of Vancouver island.

"so, the gold was lost?"

"all of it in the strong-room; most miners saved their personal stash. No one was held responsible for the wreck, the underwriters paid up, and when a salvage expedition turned up nothing, that was the end of it. The gold still lies at the bottom of the sea, and though i'm not usually superstitious, i think that's where it belongs. From the start, it brought nothing but trouble."

"quite a tragic tale," ruth said. "i wonder what would happen if someone managed to retrieve it?"

Osborne laughed. "not likely."

The wreck must have slipped off the reef shortly after we departed, because the salvage crew found both halves of it in deep water. Unfortunately, the strong tides and bad weather kept them from working, and they decided she would be buried in the sand before another attempt could be made."

He turned to her, a smile flickering in his eyes.

"now, young lady," he said, "you know the whole story, and i hope you're satisfied."

"i found it very interesting," ruth replied thoughtfully. "so, it was really the insurance payout that gave you a start?"

"in a way," Osborne said, his tone serious. "but it wasn't a huge amount by today's standards, and sometimes i think i'd be glad to give it back."

"i doubt Clay ever felt that way," ruth remarked.

"probably not. Clay's the type who keeps whatever he gets. He's not the kind to let his imagination get the best of him."

Osborne got up and wandered across the lawn, but ruth remained seated as night began to fall. The story she had just heard was intriguing, and she thought she could understand her father's feelings about the gold. It had brought him nothing but disappointment, permanent injury, and hardship. Still, there was something puzzling about clay's determined efforts to break into the strong-room while the ship was breaking apart. He was insured against all loss and wasn't the type to take unnecessary risks. Ruth's thoughts drifted back to the gold; it held a certain allure for her. Perhaps it wasn't impossible to recover it. Unusually fine weather or a shift in the currents might make another attempt feasible. Treasures had been retrieved from wrecks long after they had sunk. Ruth thought of Jimmy Farquhar, who was involved in some mysterious venture on an island up north. It seemed far-fetched to think he had found the wreck, but it wasn't outside the realm of possibility. It would be quite something if he were to recover what her father had lost from the depths.

Her father always warned that the gold brought nothing but misfortune. The encroaching twilight inched over the lawn, cloaking her in shadows, as she pondered Jimmy Farquhar isolated on that remote northern island, bewildered by his ties to the cursed treasure.

CHAPTER ELEVEN.

O sborne didn't venture into town on saturdays, so he and ruth found themselves lounging in a shady corner of the lawn. It was a hot afternoon, and the quiet was interrupted by a plume of dust swirling up among the fir trees. The rapid pace at which it climbed through the forest was telling for ruth, but it was the sight of the big gray car flashing through an opening that truly caught her attention.

"there's no mistaking Aynsley's trail," Osborne chuckled. "he leaves a path marked by fallen chickens and wandering hogs, but it seems you noticed he wasn't alone."

"i did. I'd have preferred if he'd left his father at home."

"so i figured," Osborne said with a smile. "it seems that's what the older generation is for. But clay's not the type to be content on the sidelines, and, to be fair, you can't blame him. Aynsley may look impressive behind the wheel, but his father's the one who keeps the engine running. So far, Aynsley's achievements have only come when everything was already laid out for him."

"at least he hasn't caused any harm."

"that's quite a lukewarm virtue. Not highly regarded around here."

"i told him not long ago that he ought to work," ruth admitted with a hint of candidness.

"it'll be interesting to see if he heeds your advice. His friends have been urging him for years without much success."

"he plans to take charge of the canadian mill. Though, of course, he might have several reasons for doing so," ruth added quickly. Osborne stayed quiet. Lately, he had begun to wonder where ruth's friendship with Aynsley might lead. It wouldn't have bothered him if she had shown any romantic interest in Aynsley, but he had yet to see evidence of that.

He moved forward to meet his guests, and when they emerged from the house a few minutes later, Aynsley headed straight across the lawn to greet ruth and miss dexter, who had joined her niece. Clay and Osborne took a path winding through the pines. Clay was powerfully built, with dark hair, dark eyes, and a somewhat fleshy face that suggested he enjoyed the finer things in life. However, his sharp expression saved him from looking indulgent. There was a rakish boldness about him, emphasized by his casual attire. Wearing a white panama hat, well-tailored yet carelessly worn clothes, a heavy gold watch-chain, diamond studs, and a black silk sash around his waist, Clay appeared more like an adventurous rogue than a conventional businessman. This impression wasn't entirely misleading; despite his shrewd use of modern methods, he retained habits and traits reminiscent of a romanticized past.

"have you held on to those elk park building lots?" he asked. Osborne nodded. "yes."

"still have an option on the adjoining frontage?"

"i believe so; the offer wasn't fully formalized."

"then wire and close the deal. Do it right now."

"ah! the municipal improvement scheme is going through?"

"absolutely. Got a tip by phone just before i left. Whatcom's been pretty reliable, but there are other players in the game, and the news is bound to spread this evening. We've got a head start by an hour or two. Here, write your message."

Handing Osborne a telegram blank from his pocket, he then tipped his hat with exaggerated gallantry as they unexpectedly came upon the others through a break in the pines. Ruth greeted him with a rather cold nod; his voice had carried enough for her to catch a disconcerting snippet of conversation. She had low expectations of clay, but it appeared her father might be complicit in a scheme to unfairly profit from upcoming civic improvements.

She had no solid grounds to question them; yet her aunt, known for her boldness, confronted the issue head-on as Osborne returned after sending the telegram.

"what's this i hear, henry?" miss dexter asked, not one to mince words.

"i'm not sure. You weren't supposed to hear anything," Osborne answered with a calm demeanor.

"then your friend should lower his voice. Have you been snapping up properties the city requires?"

"it's a fairly common practice. I assume you're not a fan?"

"need you even ask?" miss dexter shot back, her voice full of righteous indignation. "do you think it's morally right to burden the people just because they want a healthier, cleaner town? is this the kind of example you want to set for your daughter?"

Osborne smiled, unruffled.

"i doubt ruth will feel the urge to dabble in real estate. Besides, the tax is optional. People don't have to pay it unless they want to."

"that's a cop-out," miss dexter countered sharply. "they wouldn't pay your exorbitant prices if they had another option."

"jumping to conclusions isn't wise. In fact, there are two better options available in the market."

Miss dexter's brows furrowed in confusion.

"if that's true," she said, "it only makes matters more suspicious. Something isn't adding up."

"i'm afraid that's often the case," Osborne replied with good humor. "while i don't expect you to approve of everything i do, i hope you're not questioning my honesty."

"i have no reason to."

"i beg your pardon, henry," miss dexter replied with a touch of dignity. "i'm pleased to say i've always found you trustworthy."

"well, that's something in my favor." Osborne turned to clay. "my sister-in-law isn't a fan of modern business practices."

"she's right," Clay responded with a chuckle. "i still believe, ma'am, that women are better off away from business."

"why?" miss dexter asked sharply.

"you have a more important role in life. We rely on you to elevate our society, uphold family values, and keep the home in order."

Osborne seemed entertained, and Aynsley smirked, but miss dexter's stern expression suggested she was less amused.

"how exactly are we supposed to do that?" she questioned. "it's pointless to clean up if you men just mess it up again."

"that sounds reasonable," Aynsley interjected. "we probably do need some changes."

"absolutely," miss dexter said dryly, to the surprise of her niece. "idle men are particularly problematic."

"i was thinking of the busy ones. My view is that a man is most dangerous when he's chasing money."

"what's that?" Clay turned to his son, his face hardening.

"did i just hear you side with miss dexter against our business ethics?"

"there's a difference; she's a lady," Clay replied firmly. Aynsley laughed and walked away with ruth, who was deep in thought. What she'd overheard intensified her doubts about Clay and his influence on her father. Although inexperienced, she couldn't help but feel uneasy.

"did you tell your father you'd take over the mill?" she asked Aynsley.

"yes, and i think he was quite pleased, even though he just said it was about time i came to my senses. Still, after mulling it over, i'm having second thoughts."

The old man has enough money for both of us, and personally, i'd say driving a car or sailing a yacht is a lot less risky than outmaneuvering the people you deal with."

"but is that really necessary? can't you run a business without exploiting your competitors and customers?"

"i'm not the best judge, but from what i've heard, it sounds pretty tough. When i take over the mill, i've got to make it successful. It would be devastating for the old man if i lost the money he invested. He'd feel disgraced, and it would really strain his feelings for me. Even though he calls me a fool often enough, he's genuinely fond of me."

"yes," ruth said. "i've noticed that, and i like him for it. You need some sympathy. The situation is complicated."

"that's true. I'm worried i might not be smart enough to handle it. Of course, there's always compromise: you do your best overall, but make small concessions here and there."

"i'm not sure that would work. Isn't there a risk of making too many concessions? it might be safer not to give in at all."

"that does sound pretty extreme. The trouble is, my relatives and friends expect too much of me, and i suspect some of them are pulling in different directions."

Ruth felt sorry for him. Though he had his flaws, he was honest, and she believed he would never stoop to anything deceitful. Now, however, he faced a stern test: he needed to make the sawmill profitable, and Clay wouldn't be satisfied with just a modest gain. Ruth felt some responsibility for convincing him to take on a challenging task; if he wasn't up to it, his problems would multiply. Still, she couldn't shake the belief that it was possible to gain wealth honestly.

"after all," she said, "you have every advantage: the best assistants and the latest machinery."

"that's true."

"they're a liability, you know. Every misstep will be counted against me, and i'll have to show that i've made the most efficient use of them. In some ways, i'd prefer to start with less refined tools."

"that sounds defeatist. It's not like you to be so unsure," ruth replied.

"it's about knowing your limits," Aynsley responded. "besides, i feel a duty to live up to the confidence you and your father have placed in me, despite how reckless it felt."

"i'm sure my faith was well-placed," ruth said softly. Aynsley turned to her sharply. She looked enchanting, her lithe figure framed by the soft summer dress that contrasted against the dark pines. The twilight emphasized her exquisite features, but her face was solemn. There wasn't a trace of the tender shyness he yearned to see, not even a hint of playful flirtation that might encourage him to make a move. Sometimes, he thought ruth was unaware of her own power, not yet fully awakened; but clearly, her words were spoken out of friendly kindness, and he had to accept that.

"thank you," he replied, his voice a bit strained. "i'll pull myself together and see what i can accomplish."

They heard his father calling and turned back to the lawn where Clay was waiting, ready to leave. He explained to miss dexter that he had only stopped by for a word with Osborne, though he found it hard to leave. She listened with a twinkle in her eyes, watching him cross the lawn with his typical jaunty gait. There was something about him that made him seem more romantic than his strikingly handsome son.

"a man of many talents, it seems," she remarked. "makes you wonder if he uses them to their fullest potential."

"that's a matter of perspective, and not really our concern," Osborne commented.

"it certainly isn't mine. How far it might be yours, i can't say, but a man like that never walks alone."

"he drags everyone along in his wake," Osborne said with a chuckle as they heard the car's hum growing distant along the hillside.

"he sets a pretty fast pace," Osborne admitted, "but i suspect his son's at the wheel, indulging his love for speed."

Indeed, Clay was leaning back against the cushions, hat snugly in place, watching Aynsley's sharply defined profile. The car roared along a rough dirt road, kicking up red dust and dry needles, bouncing wildly over the bumps. Above, a canopy of dark foliage loomed, occasionally pierced by shafts of bright sunlight, held aloft by the towering trunks of douglas firs. Deep potholes pocked the uneven road surface, threatening to wreck the car, and the boggy stretches bridged by split logs left gaps where the wheels sank into soft soil. Yet Aynsley never slowed. He maneuvered with precision and nerve, the car swerving, at times perilously close to the fern-brushed embankments, or following the erratic paths carved by wagon wheels. Clay, an astute judge of character, observed his son's calm, bravery, and quick reflexes. Aynsley's daring wasn't reckless; he took necessary risks with a calculated boldness that impressed his father, who watched with a thoughtful unease. Given Aynsley's evident strength of character, Clay found it perplexing that his son hadn't yet made a mark. Perhaps, Clay mused, this was because he saw no venture as significant unless it involved making money.

He believed that a worthwhile vocation which enriched an individual could also contribute to the nation's well-being.

"i got a letter from Vancouver this morning," he said, as they ascended the hill and their pace slowed enough for conversation. "they're installing the new engine and expect to have the mill operational in two weeks."

"i'll be ready then," Aynsley replied. Clay noticed that, despite his lack of enthusiasm, the boy's resolve was evident. If the task wasn't particularly to his liking, he intended to see it through, which was reassuring.

"there's something else i want to discuss. That Osborne girl seems nice, though i think you could do better."

Aynsley turned to look at his father.

"that's a ridiculous statement, sir."

Clay chuckled.

"it's a good attitude. I don't fault it. Anyway, i'm glad to see your interests are more level-headed this time. I was a bit concerned about you a few years ago."

Caught off guard, Aynsley blushed. He recalled his infatuation with a girl at a cigar store and the surprising realization that his father had known all about it. Though Clay had never mentioned it, Aynsley had no doubt he would have intervened if necessary.

"well," he said, somewhat flustered, "i was at an age of sentimental foolishness, maybe, but not as naive as you seem to think. Miss neston was fine by me, and i'd appreciate you respecting that since you brought it up."

"fine, we'll drop it," Clay responded dryly. "i assume you have a better understanding of your worth now. But you don't seem to be making much headway with ruth Osborne. Do you really want her?"

They had passed the steepest part of the hill, but Aynsley downshifted to the lowest gear and quietly turned to his father.

"you have a rather blunt way of phrasing things; but yes, you can take it that i want her more than anything in the world."

"very well."

"i can get her for you."

Aynsley shifted abruptly, then spoke with deliberate calm, "i think not. This is something i need to handle myself. I need you to understand that."

Clay was taken aback by Aynsley's firmness, a rare display from the usually easy-going man.

"care to explain?"

"i'll try. You've been incredibly generous to me, and i'm thankful for everything, including the sawmill. You've guided my career choices, but i believe choosing my life partner is something i should decide."

Clay chuckled, "you're young. You'll learn that it's seldom a man with real passion who gets to choose his wife. Often, the decision is mutual. If you could go around with a checklist for the perfect girl, you wouldn't really be my son. I'm not objecting to your choice, though."

"that's enough. But if i did agree, how would you get miss Osborne for me?"

Clay smiled despite the awkwardness. The boy was sharper than he gave him credit for.

"well, i have some influence over Osborne. He owes me a few favors."

"a man wouldn't trade his daughter for a favor. What's your leverage?"

"not sure why you need to know that."

"you might be right," Aynsley conceded, but his tone remained resolute. "let's be clear. If miss Osborne marries me because she genuinely wants to, i'd be very fortunate. But the idea of forcing her, or pressuring her father, is out of the question."

"when i want something, i go after it any way i can."

"i believe that," Aynsley responded with a smile. "but this time, the method matters. I must ask you to stay out of it."

"very well," Clay agreed. "but remember, i'll be here if you need me."

"i suppose i haven't let you down yet."

"not at all, dad," Aynsley responded warmly. "hang tight; i'm going to fire up the machine."

CHAPTER TWELVE.

The train was delayed en route to the canadian border by a washout further up the tracks. Devereux Clay stood in the midday sun chatting with Osborne at a quaint wayside station, while clusters of frustrated passengers meandered along the tracks. Occasionally, they paused to peer through a gap in the dense fir trees where the sunlight glinted off the rails. The engineer, leaning out of his cab, also gazed in that direction. However, there was nothing to see but the ascending trees, their jagged tops rising one behind another up the steep hillside. The warm noon sun drew out a mix of pine fragrance and the sharp scent of creosote from the ties. Apart from the low murmur of conversations and the rhythmic panting of the locomotive pump, the small clearing was tranquil. From a deep hollow, the faint sound of cascading water reached them, where a lake sparkled amidst the firs. Clay leaned against the station agent's wooden shack, his watch in hand, knowing that every minute counted.

"another twenty minutes, according to that guy," he muttered. "got a cigar? i'm out, and there's no need for you to wait around."

"oh, i've got time," Osborne replied, glancing at his car parked outside the station. "i'm guessing the labor issues are what's taking you to Vancouver?"

"you've got it," Clay answered with a touch of secrecy. "i'm a bit concerned; spent the last two days debating whether to go or not."

He was rarely so indecisive, but Osborne thought he grasped the situation.

"it seems like the unions are serious," Osborne remarked. "with the current backlash against foreign labor, they seem to have the public on their side. Do you have any Japanese workers at the mill?"

"i think so. That's one reason i'm heading out. Until i read the papers this morning, i was inclined to stay put. I figured it might be better to let the kid handle it alone and see what he could achieve."

"let him earn his stripes?"

"exactly."

I told him to hang tight and i'd cover the costs as long as he delivered. But after the major blow-up in Vancouver yesterday, i figured i should tag along. Still, my plan is to stay in the shadows unless absolutely necessary.

His tone was half-apologetic, and Osborne smiled. Clay was not the type to hover in the background when things were happening, but Osborne understood the depth of his affection for his son.

"it might be smarter for you to be there; the crowd seems pretty riled up," he said. "how's Aynsley doing?"

"better than i thought. The kid has a good grip on things and he's tackling it head-on." Clay turned abruptly, locking eyes with Osborne. "i was a bit baffled by how quickly he decided to run the mill. Do you have any idea what might have convinced him?"

"well, since you ask, i have a hunch," Osborne replied.

"same here; probably the same as yours. Typical that a few words from a girl who knows less than he does would outweigh all my reasoning."

"it's not unexpected," Osborne grinned.

"then, let's assume we're right about what this implies? you know my boy."

"i like him. If i found out that ruth shared my opinion, i wouldn't object. But i can't read her feelings on this matter."

"i know Aynsley's," Clay said dryly. "we talked recently, and i offered to help him out."

Osborne scrutinized him, his expression shifting to one of caution.

"so far, you've managed to get your son everything he wanted, but you must understand, you can't make decisions for my daughter. Ruth will choose for herself."

Clay's eyes sparkled with a hard amusement.

"funny thing, my boy said the exact same thing. In fact, he warned me to back off."

"he knows how i've spoiled him and assumed i might sway your decision."

"in this case, it wouldn't matter much; but what you said has improved my opinion of Aynsley," Osborne replied.

"that's good to hear," said clay, placing a friendly hand on Osborne's arm. "we definitely can't afford to argue, and honestly, it's not so bad that our kids have higher standards than we do. Besides, we don't want them to figure us out. I'd feel terrible if my son disowned me."

Osborne flinched at the remark.

"Aynsley handles success well," he said.

"to me, it's much less harmful than failure. I'm glad i did all the dirty work for him, made things easier so he could stay clean. I've given him a solid foundation. My boy will have a better life than i had. I put him in business to teach him common sense—there's no better education than earning your own living. He'll learn the real value of people and things. Once he's shown he can stand on his own, he can do whatever makes him happy. I don't have any close family, and there was a time when my distant relatives weren't proud of me. Everything i have goes to my son. If your daughter accepts him, i'll rest easy knowing he's in good hands. If not, that's just something he'll have to deal with."

Osborne felt more at ease. Though clay's virtues weren't always apparent, his love for his son was genuine. Before Osborne could respond, Clay glanced at his watch, his demeanor shifting back to its usual tough exterior.

"if they get me into Vancouver after things start falling apart, i'll talk to the road bosses in seattle and have the superintendent of this division fired!" just then, the telegraph in the shack started its rapid-fire clicking, and moments later, the agent approached clay.

"they're through," the agent reported.

"we'll get you off in five minutes. I've been told to skip the next two stops," he said. As he informed the conductor, a sharp whistle echoed through the pine trees. A large engine, pulling flat cars loaded with a gravel plow and a group of dusty men, clattered down the tracks. Once it pulled onto the side track, Clay climbed onto the platform of his car and the train started almost immediately. Leaning back in a corner seat, his face grew hard and thoughtful. By the time he reached Vancouver, he had finished the cigar case given by his friend and rented the fastest car he could find.

While his father was being driven recklessly over the rough road cutting through dense bush, Aynsley sat on a lumber stack outside the mill with his manager. It was getting dark. The saws, which had filled the hot air with their screams all day, were finally still, and the riverbank was quiet except for the gurgling of the wide, green water swirling around the piles. A large boom of logs, moored in an eddy, strained at its chains with the current's push. A red glow lingered in the western sky, though trails of white mist were gathering in the thinning forest that bordered the clearing. Only trees too small for cutting remained, the gaps between them filled with massive stumps. Tall iron chimneys, scattered sheds, and piles of sawdust began to take on a rough, picturesque quality in the dimming light. The sharp scent of freshly cut cedar wafted on the faint breeze.

But Aynsley barely noticed his surroundings. Deep in thought, he realized that, somewhat to his surprise, his work was gripping him. The mechanical aspect, in particular, sparked his keen interest. There was a deep satisfaction in knowing that the power of the big engines was being harnessed to its fullest potential.

Managing the mill workers and running the business had always held a certain appeal for Aynsley. He prided himself on making few mistakes, thanks in part to the competent staff his father had put in place. But now, he faced an unforeseen crisis that tested the limits of his experience. There was a simple way out, but it wasn't an option he could accept. He had to navigate the tricky situation effectively, avoiding any form of injustice—a task that would inevitably compli-cate matters. The problem was old as time: he needed to protect his financial interests while maintaining his principles.

"you think the guys from Vancouver will cause trouble tonight, jevons?" he asked.

The young manager nodded. "that's what i'm expecting, and it's pretty likely the westminster crew will join them. They've been throw-ing around some nasty threats. I found this paper stuck to the door on my last round."

Aynsley read the notice: this is a white man's country. All aliens warned to leave. Those who stay, and those who keep them, will face the consequences.

"so, our only issue with them is that we're keeping the Japanese workers?"

"that's all they're saying."

"well," Aynsley said slowly, "if we give in on this, i bet they'll just find something else to complain about. Once you start making concessions, you usually have to keep making them."

"that's true," jevons agreed. "it seems like the workers are pushing their bosses, who can't rein them in. But the ones i've met are reasonable, and once the crowd cools down, they'll get back in control. They'd let us run the mill if you fired the Japanese workers."

Aynsley frowned. "i've received their delegations politely and put up with quite a bit these last few weeks. We pay standard wages, and i don't think there's a man here who's asked to do more than he can reasonably handle."

"but i can't let these guys tell me who i can hire!"

"you've got some big orders with tight deadlines," jevons reminded him. "you'd take a real hit if we have to shut down the mill."

"that's the problem," Aynsley admitted. "i don't want to lose the orders. But here's the thing: i hired these Japanese workers when i couldn't find any white men, and i promised their manager i'd keep them until we cleared the log boom."

"why don't you call him up and see what he'd take to step down? it might end up being cheaper in the long run."

Aynsley considered this. He hadn't realized it until recently, but he did have a bit of his father's mindset. Before taking over the mill, he didn't think much about money. But now, he found a peculiar joy in watching his profits grow and calculating the returns on the lumber he processed. The idea of sacrificing part of those earnings was frankly unacceptable. It wasn't greed so much as pride. He'd dived into this business seriously and wanted to prove his capability.

"no," he said firmly. "i don't see why i should let them punish me for being straightforward. I'd rather fight if it comes to that, and i guess you'll have to back me up."

Jevons chuckled.

"i'm not exactly eager to back down either. Just thought i'd suggest the easiest way out, out of duty. But there's merit in standing your ground. I don't think there are any more union agitators left in the mill, and i doubt the small-time ranchers want to quit."

Labor had been hard to find that year, so Aynsley had hired several local ranchers and loggers. In years when wages were high, they often came down from their remote homesteads to work at the mill.

The men were determined, reliable, and content with their pay.

"well," said Aynsley, "we should probably see what the Japanese workers plan to do; they're pretty set in their ways and seem to have their own organization. Anyway, they gave the mob in Vancouver a tough time a few days ago."

Their leader was called in and he explained, in excellent english, that their honorable employer had hired them to finish a specific job, and they intended to stay until it was done. When warned that this might be dangerous, he replied mysteriously that they had taken precautions, and the danger might not be limited to them. After some formalities, he left, and Aynsley laughed.

"well, that settles it! they won't leave, and i can't force them out. I sympathize with the argument that this is a white man's country, but since they couldn't provide the help i needed, i had to get it elsewhere. Now, let's talk to the white workers."

They found the men gathered in the large sleeping shed where the lamps had just been lit. They were robust and tough-looking, most of them owning small plots of land that couldn't support them in the wilderness. They listened seriously as Aynsley spoke. Then, one man stood up to speak for the group.

"we saw this trouble coming and discussed it. As long as you don't cut our wages, we don't have much to complain about and don't see any reason to leave our jobs. Now, it seems like the Vancouver boys are coming to force us out. We'll let them try if they can!"

A murmur of grim approval rippled through the group. Aynsley then divided them into teams and sent them off to guard the saws, booms, and engine house. Turning to the manager, there was a gleam in his eye.

"i think we're ready for whatever comes. You'll find me in the office if i'm needed."

Once in his office, Aynsley took a couple of books from the shelf and tried to focus on the business recorded within.

It was his first real crisis, and the thought of waiting around the mill for the impending trouble was more than he could bear. Surprisingly, he found himself absorbed in his work. An hour slipped by before he finally closed his books and walked over to the open window. The night was calm, dark, and warm. A couple of stars shimmered above the dark silhouettes of the pines, but the mist drifting along the riverside blurred the tall stacks and lumber piles. There was no sign of the men, and the deep silence was punctuated only by a faint hiss of steam and the river's gentle gurgle. Leaning on the sill, Aynsley inhaled the cool, soothing night air. Despite his anxiety, he was determined to keep his nerves in check.

As he stared into the darkness, a rhythmic sound began to emerge from the mist, growing louder, resembling the gallop of a horse. It approached the mill, but Aynsley stayed put. If anyone needed him, it would be better to be found calmly at work in his office. So he sat back at his desk, pen in hand, when a man was brought in. The newcomer was neatly dressed, except for his crumpled, damp white shirt. His face was flushed and resolute.

"i've come to prevent trouble," the man declared.

"i'm glad to hear that," Aynsley replied. "since we both want the same thing, that should simplify matters. As your group has the grievance, why don't you tell me what you want."

"we need a written promise that you won't keep a single jap here after tomorrow morning."

"i can't give you that," Aynsley said firmly. "i can promise not to hire any more and to let the ones here go once they've finished the work they were hired for, if that helps."

"it doesn't. I can't take that answer back to the boys."

"you have to get those japs out of here," the stranger insisted.

Aynsley leaned forward, a patient sigh escaping his lips.

"don't you realize that when two sides come to negotiate, they can't both get everything they want? compromise is the only way we might reach a settlement."

"you're wrong," the stranger said, his tone grim. "this can be settled quickly if one of them just gives in."

"is that what you're suggesting you'll do?" Aynsley asked.

"no way! i'm not bending! the boys wouldn't stand for it, even if i thought it was the right move."

"then, since i can't meet your demands, there's no point in continuing this discussion," Aynsley replied coolly. "it seems we've hit a dead end."

"i warn you, you're taking on a big responsibility and playing a dangerous game."

"that remains to be seen. But i won't keep you any longer. I'm sorry we couldn't come to an agreement."

Aynsley escorted the man across the yard, where the stranger's voice rose in anger.

"come out from your hiding spots, boys!" he yelled. "are you going to side with the foreigners and the bosses against your own friends?"

Aynsley grasped his shoulder firmly.

"i'm sorry, but we can't allow speeches like that. You have certain privileges as an envoy, but this crosses the line."

"and how do you plan to stop me?" the man demanded roughly.

"believe me, you don't want to find out," Aynsley replied calmly. "your horse is waiting over there. Goodnight."

The envoy mounted his horse and rode off into the darkness. Aynsley turned to find his manager.

"i think his allies are nearby," he said. "we should make another round and ensure everything is ready."

Chapter thirteen.

The night was pitch-black, and the road treacherous. Clay leaned forward in the swaying car, eyes fixed intently ahead. The headlights sliced through the darkness, illuminating wagon ruts and tall ferns that lined the rough track. Occasionally, the base of a massive fir would emerge from the darkness, only to disappear just as quickly. In the thinnest sections of the forest, Clay could see tiny wineberries sparkling red in the beam, but above, everything was swallowed by impenetrable gloom. They sped through the dense woods, the road straight but uneven, allowing conversation despite the bumps.

"there's been trouble in the city lately. How did it all start?" Clay asked the driver. "i'm new here, only know what i've read in the papers."

"the boys thought too many Japanese were coming in," the driver answered. "they took over most of the salmon netting, and when talk started about cutting prices, the white men warned them to quit."

The car jolted violently as it hit a pothole, and after a moment, Clay spoke again.

"the Japanese didn't back down?"

"that's right; they intended to keep their jobs. When the boys tried to drive them away, they didn't make much headway. As the Japanese started taking on more work, the conflict escalated. The city's practically overrun with foreigners."

"you had a major clash a couple of days ago."

"we did," the driver confirmed, steering around a deep rut. "the boys had planned to kick every last asian out of town."

"but they couldn't pull it off?"

"exactly. I don't care much for the Japanese, but i'll admit they fought back hard. Whenever the boys made a move, there was a group of them ready to counter. You couldn't catch them off guard. They shifted positions quickly and brought in reinforcements just where they were needed most."

The boys had fought like soldiers, and the police had easily dispersed both groups. Clay noted, "looks well-organized. It's smart to plan ahead before jumping in. Have the boys tried to chase off those working at the outer mills?"

"not yet, but we're bracing for it. They'd scatter them quickly if they went that route," came the reply.

This was exactly what Clay feared; it was the tactic he would have employed if he were leading the strike. Direct confrontation was risky, but smaller, isolated forces could be defeated more easily. Aynsley's mill was particularly vulnerable, sitting far enough from both Vancouver and new westminster that any help from the authorities would likely arrive too late. However, there was reason to think the foreign workers recognized the risk and had taken precautions. Clay respected the strategic thinking of the Japanese and chinese laborers. He asked no more questions, his silence blending with the driver's focus on maneuvering the rough road, the only sound the hum of the car speeding through the night.

Sometimes they flew across open fields where split-rail fences seemed to rush by in the headlamps' glow, with a few stars dimly visible overhead. At other times, they raced beside towering bluffs, dark fir branches reaching out over the road, the sweet, resinous scent mixing with the smell of dew on dust. Though the car was moving at a reckless speed, clay's impatience grew when he tried to check his watch. True to his nature, despite his anxiety, he didn't offer the driver any extra incentive to go faster. He rarely allowed his judgment to falter, knowing the risk of not arriving at all outweighed the benefit of shaving a few minutes off their journey.

Soon, they plunged into another dense forest, the engine's hum resonating among the thick trees. Outside the path illuminated by the headlights, everything was swallowed by darkness.

Clay was jostled roughly back and forth as the car swerved, but after a moment, he heard a sharp click, and the speed noticeably eased up.

"why are we stopping?" he demanded, impatience clear in his voice.

"men up ahead," the driver said, his eyes scanning the darkness. "just slowing down a bit."

Clay strained to see anything ahead, but the only thing piercing the gloom was a rhythmic noise—almost like the synchronized steps of an organized group.

"hold off on the horn," he warned as the driver's hand moved toward it. "let's see who they are first. Is there any way around?"

"no detours until we hit the mill."

"looks like we're going through them, then. Don't blow the horn or stop unless you absolutely have to."

The car rolled forward quietly, and soon enough, the rear of four men appeared in the beams of the headlights. More figures emerged as they moved along, their shapes silhouetted against the darkness. Many were armed with makeshift weapons, moving with a deliberate step. This wasn't a disorganized mob; it was a disciplined group on a mission. As the car drew nearer, one man spun around with a cry, and the rearmost quartet halted and faced them. Murmurs filtered from the front ranks, and with no clear path ahead, the driver stopped, leaving the engine idling nervously.

"move aside, fellas. We just need a bit of the road," the driver called out amiably. None of them budged.

"where are you headed?" someone in the front demanded.

"to clanch mill," the driver replied before Clay could cut him off. The men conferred briefly, then one stepped forward.

"you can't go there tonight. Turn around and get out of here!"

Clay was certain of their intentions, and he knew when a hefty bribe was necessary.

"floor it, they'll get out of the way," he whispered urgently. "i'll give you a hundred bucks if you get me through."

The car surged forward, accelerating rapidly. As it barreled toward the men, the nearest scrambled to clear the path.

They dove into the ferns as the horn blared a savage warning, and the driver floored the gas pedal, aiming the massive car into the gap. For a fleeting moment, it seemed like they might make it. Shouts rang out, blurred figures darted in and out of the beam of light as the car rushed forward. Some tried to strike the vehicle as it sped past; others turned to look, but those in front were either braver or simply couldn't move out of the way in time.

"straight ahead!" Clay shouted. A man lunged into the light, brandishing a thick stake. The next instant, there was a crash. The car veered wildly, ran up an embankment, and flipped over. Clay was hurled violently forward, landing unconscious in a patch of ferns. When he finally came to, he found himself lying on his back, surrounded by a group of men. His head throbbed, and he felt his face smarting—probably cut, he thought. As he weakly raised his hand to touch it, his fingers came away wet. One of the men struck a match and leaned over him.

"break any bones?" the man asked.

"no," Clay struggled to speak. "i don't think so, but i don't feel like i can stand."

"well," the man remarked, "you were warned to stop. Better stay still for now. If you're still here when we come back, we'll see what can be done."

Glancing around quickly, Clay saw the driver sitting by the over-turned car; then the match flicked out. In the darkness, the men whispered among themselves.

"what was your business at the mill?" one of them asked.

"i had some business there," Clay replied smoothly. "i deal in lumber from time to time."

The men appeared convinced.

"leave them," one suggested. "they won't cause trouble, and we need to move."

The others seemed to agree. There were shouts to those ahead, and the men moved on.

Clay listened as the sound of their footsteps faded into the night, feeling rather pleased that he had appeared more injured than he actually was. Now that the initial shock was wearing off, he realized he wasn't as hurt as he had first thought. Still, he took a few moments to gather himself before addressing the driver.

"how are you holding up?" he asked.

"i twisted my leg when i got thrown out; it hurts when i move, but i don't think it's anything serious," the driver replied.

"i need to get moving as soon as i can. How far do you think it is to the mill?"

"about two miles," came the response.

Clay rested for a few minutes more before unsteadily rising to his feet.

"if i don't catch you before, you can find me at the c.p.r. Hotel tomorrow," he said, summoning his strength and starting to limp down the road. The first half- mile was a struggle; his movements were unsteady and his head was still foggy. But as he continued, his mind cleared and his legs found their rhythm, allowing him to pick up his pace. There was no sign of the strikers; it seemed they had left him far behind. But he pressed on, knowing he had to get there soon—they were going to need him.

The landscape around him was open country, with nothing in sight but scattered clusters of trees and rough, wooden fences lining the road. The night was eerily silent, and darkness enveloped everything. Eventually, he saw the dark outline of a forest against the night sky, and when a couple of lights began to flicker amongst the trees, Clay knew he was approaching the mill. He quickened his stride, and upon hearing hoarse shouts in the distance, he broke into a run. It had been a long time since he had done any serious physical exertion, and he was still shaky from his earlier fall. Nevertheless, he pushed himself forward, breathing heavily. The lights became brighter, and though the noise had diminished, he knew that the trouble had already started.

He hadn't made any plans yet; he figured he'd make them on the fly, depending on how things panned out. If Aynsley could handle the situation, all the better. Clay's role was to be there if needed, as usual when it came to his son. As he sprinted through an open gate, dark buildings and stacks of lumber loomed ominously ahead. Reaching one of the massive lumber piles, he stopped in its shadow, panting heavily and surveying the scene.

The office was illuminated, and the glow from its windows revealed a crowd of men filling the space between the small building and the long saw sheds. They were shouting and seemed to be threatening someone inside the office. Another group of men gathered behind it, as far as Clay could discern. Then the door opened, and he felt a surge of pride as Aynsley emerged alone, stepping into the light. He looked calm and even good-natured as he faced the hostile crowd; nothing in his relaxed posture betrayed the tension Clay knew he must be feeling. Staring at his son's straight, confident figure and serene face, Clay felt a deep sense of validation.

"i'd hate to see you guys get into trouble for nothing," Aynsley said clearly. "if you think it through, you'll realize you don't have any grievances with the management of this mill. We pay standard wages and only hired foreigners when we couldn't find anyone else. They'll be replaced by local workers when their jobs are done."

"we're here to see you fire them tonight!" one of the strikers yelled.

"i'm afraid that's not possible," Aynsley replied firmly.

"listen up!" another shouted. "we're not here to mess around, and this isn't a bluff! the men mean business, and if you've got any sense, you'll do what they ask."

"tell me straight: is this your final word on the matter?"

"yes," said Aynsley. "that's my last word."

"that's clear," the spokesman affirmed. "now we know where we stand." he raised his voice. "guys, we need to drive those blasted japs out!"

A moment of hesitation followed, filled with a low murmuring for nearly a minute. From the shadow of the lumber pile, Clay wondered if he should have gone back to Vancouver for help; but given that the police were swamped in the city, it might not have made a difference. Plus, he was accustomed to the rough-and- ready conflict resolution from the mexican frontier and arizona twenty years prior. Shaken, bruised, and bleeding as he was, his adrenaline spiked at the thought of a showdown. As the strikers closed in on the office, Clay circled the lumber stack and found jevons, the manager.

"Mr. Clay!" jevons exclaimed, noting his battered face.

"yes," said clay. "don't mention i'm here. My son's in charge as long as he can handle things."

"it's looking bad," jevons admitted. "are you armed?"

"i have a pistol, but using it might not be wise. What's the plan?"

Before jevons could respond, a surge of dark figures swept toward the office, followed by a deep shout.

"get rid of the japs first! throw them in the river!"

"hold steady, boys!" Aynsley's voice cut through the chaos. "keep them back, crew a!"

A chaotic fight erupted amidst the shadows of the lumber stacks. Clusters of figures grappled, merged into a frenzied mass, split apart, advanced, and were forcibly repelled. There wasn't much shouting, and no shots had been fired yet, but Clay moved sharply, observing where the resistance was weakest, motivating defenders who didn't recognize him.

Clay showed surprising skill, shifting his men from the less threat-ened areas to where they were needed the most. Even though the garrison was outnumbered and was slowly being pushed back, they put up a relentless fight. The conflict grew more intense by the minute. Shouts of rage and pain pierced the air, mixing with the sounds of scuffling feet, labored breathing, and the clash of weapons. Orders and threats were yelled out, and clay's face hardened when pistols began to flash.

He had grabbed a heavy iron bar and felt confident wielding it. If he had to shoot, he wouldn't miss like he thought the rioters did. A red glow flared up from the end of a shed, spreading quickly into a blaze. The sharp crackling was louder than the chaos, and a thick cloud of acrid smoke hung over the struggling men. Clay could now see their faces clearly: Japanese and white men mixed together, all steadily losing ground. His son was in the center of the surging, swaying mass, taking the full force of the attack.

As Clay paused for a moment, it struck him that the small, sallow-faced foreigners remained remarkably composed, even though it was clear they were being overwhelmed. He wondered if they had a backup plan. There was no time to ponder; a pistol flashed amid the rioters. Aynsley's group reeled but then charged forward with renewed ferocity, their shouts hoarse and desperate.

"hold them off while we get him out! take down the guy with the pistol; he's hit the boss!"

Rage surged through clay, transforming him into a vengeful force. He had lived a hard, adventurous life, full of raw, primal instincts. His son had been shot, and the ones who did it would pay dearly.

"i'm his father, boys!" he roared. "charge and drive these morons into the river!"

The bravest of his men closed in around him, a tight-knit group of small ranchers and prospectors who had battled harsh elements and isolation in the rugged hills.

The factory workers were tougher than the city laborers, and with a leader who wouldn't quit until he dropped, they cut through the mob like a knife. One of the rioters fired a shot right in the leader's face but missed. Clay, however, didn't miss with the metal bar, and he trampled the man's body as he pressed on with fierce determination. It was a desperate gamble. For a while, they couldn't be stopped, but the rioters quickly formed up behind them, cutting off any chance of retreat. The advance slowed, and soon they gained only inches through sheer force.

Clay realized they were in serious trouble. The strikers were beyond reason and wouldn't show any mercy, but that didn't matter to him as long as he could take down a few opponents before they overpowered him. He fought with a cold, calculated rage, landing his blows with precision. The steel bar wreaked havoc, scattering the strikers, but soon he found himself backed against a pile of lumber. He felt the end was near. Bruised, disoriented, and bleeding, he stood his ground, swinging his weapon with deadly intent, eyes locked on his attackers.

Then, unexpectedly, the crowd recoiled, and he heard the frenzied sound of running feet and panicked cries. There was a wild shout, unmistakably foreign. Agile, fierce figures, moving with catlike grace, assaulted the rioters with relentless fury. The retreat turned into chaos; the strikers bolted for their lives, pursued by a swarm of furious Japanese workers. Clay noticed they far outnumbered the mill's Japanese workforce, but their origin didn't concern him now. He had to snap out of his daze, join the chase, and exact his revenge on the fleeing mob.

The rioters fled along the riverbank, scrambled over the log booms, and leapt into the water. Clay laughed bitterly as he drove the stragglers into the river. Whether they could swim or not was no longer his concern.

He returned to the office, his heart pounding with anxiety. Moments later, he stood beside the makeshift bed in his son's quarters. His hat was missing, his city coat torn to shreds, and his once white shirt smeared with blood from a gash on his cheek. Yet, he seemed oblivious to his own condition. Aynsley lay there, his breaths shallow, face pale with a small blue bruise on his chest, and a disturbing red froth forming at his lips. Clay placed a hand on his son's clammy forehead, and Aynsley's eyes fluttered open.

"do you know who i am?" his father asked softly.

"of course," Aynsley whispered with a faint smile. "you promised you wouldn't let me down. I guess you beat them?"

He turned his head and coughed, prompting Clay to signal jevons.

"help me lift his shoulders a bit; we should get some wet compresses on him. They've cut the phone lines, so send someone to the nearest ranch to fetch a horse and bring a doctor from Vancouver."

"i've already sent a man," jevons replied.

"good. Then send another one to westminster. We'll take the first doctor who arrives or keep them both if need be."

They adjusted Aynsley so he could breathe more comfortably, and Clay carefully wrapped him in damp cloths.

"i'm not sure if this is the right move, but it's all i can think of doing," he said. "we need to minimize any internal bleeding."

They waited tensely for the doctor. Jevons slipped out to restore order and ensure the fires were out, leaving Clay alone with his son. The room was silent, save for the strained breaths from the bed. After what felt like an eternity, jevons reentered, opening the door quietly.

"is the doctor here?" Clay asked, hope tinging his voice.

"not yet. Any changes?"

"none," Clay replied. "he can't hear me; i wish he could. Do we know who those men were that helped us?"

"from what i gather, they were city japs," jevons said.

It appeared that the group was well-organized. Anticipating a raid on their associates here, their leaders had dispatched some reinforcements. I'd been through the ringer, and it looked like it would cost about a thousand bucks to cover the damage.

"get out of here!" Clay barked. "i can't deal with the repairs now. Keep an eye out for those doctors and bring them in immediately!"

Jevons was relieved to leave, but it was nearly dawn by the time he returned with a surgeon from Vancouver. Moments later, the surgeon from westminster arrived, and the two of them ushered Clay out of the room. He paced back and forth in the hallway, filled with tension and worry. His own exhaustion and the painful gash on his face were forgotten in the face of his son's peril. When the spinning in his head became too much, he leaned against the rough banister, oblivious to the dizziness that threatened to overwhelm him. As the first light of dawn began to seep through the windows, Clay was finally allowed to enter the room. Aynsley was lying unconscious, but the doctors seemed cautiously optimistic.

"we got the bullet out," one of them informed him, "but there's still reason to be concerned. We'll do everything we can to ensure he pulls through. Now, let me tend to that cut on your face; it needs to be treated."

Clay allowed the doctor to patch him up and then sank wearily into a chair in a room downstairs, waiting for any news.

CHAPTER FOURTEEN.

Aynsley was in grave condition for an extended period, and Clay remained at the mill the entire time. Eventually, though, the boy began to slowly recuperate. Yet, as he regained enough awareness to observe his surroundings, the constant scream of the saws and the rhythmic throb of the engines began to unsettle him. The light wooden structure vibrated with the machinery's roar, and even when the machines were silent, the river's gurgle around the log booms disrupted his rest. He grumbled incessantly.

"how long does the doctor plan to keep me here?" he asked his father one day.

"i'm not sure, but it seems you can't be moved just yet," Clay replied. "are you uncomfortable?"

"can you expect me not to be, with this whole place clattering and shaking? if i'm going to get better, it has to be away from the mill."

"i'll talk to the doctor about it, but the problem is i don't know where to take you. You wouldn't be much quieter in seattle. It's strange, now that i consider it, that i haven't had a proper home in ages, though i didn't seem to notice until this happened."

Aynsley gave a faint nod of agreement. He had no memory of his mother, and his father had never really kept a home in his recollection. In recent years, they'd rented luxurious suites in a grand hotel that Aynsley shared with his father when he wasn't away on visits or sporting trips. But now, Aynsley recoiled at the thought of returning to the lack of privacy and constant commotion there. The hotel was a massive, ornate structure filled with the echo of footsteps and voices, the clang of streetcars, and the grinding of electric elevators.

"i want to go somewhere quiet," he insisted.

"then i'll have to rent a bushman's shack or take you out to sea in the yacht. Funny, it never occurred to me before, but finding quiet in this country is really tough."

"we're definitely not a calm bunch."

"i can't bear the thought of a sea voyage," Aynsley grumbled. "that boat takes on water at the slightest breeze, and i don't want to spend the trip dodging puddles. Besides, the genius who designed it put the only cozy rooms right where the propeller shakes you to pieces when the engines run."

In general, Clay felt relieved, particularly since Aynsley's picky discomfort suggested he was recovering. Clay had been busy at the mill with several projects on the go. If they were left unattended, his business could suffer—either overheating from neglect or cooling off before he could capitalize on them.

"how about we see if Osborne would take us in?" Clay proposed.

Aynsley's eyes lit up. Osborne's house was the closest thing he had to a home. Unlike other places filled with noisy guests and relentless activities, Osborne's was serene and beautifully arranged with artistic flair. The idea of resting there, soaking in the pine-scented air and ruth's gentle kindness, was incredibly appealing.

"that would be perfect! i feel like i could really recover there. Can you write to him?"

"first thing," Clay promised with a knowing grin, "but i'm not sure ruth is home. Either way, i've got a stack of letters to get through now."

"i've probably been pretty selfish taking up all your time, but if Osborne agrees to have me, it will give you a chance to head to town and manage your affairs."

"absolutely," Clay agreed. "in fact, some of them need attention."

The doctor hesitated but eventually agreed to move his patient. Clay spared no effort to make the journey comfortable. Concerned that the jostling train ride might be too much, he booked a private cabin on a large sound steamer. It was only Aynsley's stubborn refusal to use it that prevented Clay from arranging an ambulance to take him to the dock.

He reached the vessel safely by car, and as it cruised up the sound, he insisted on shedding his coat and trying to walk around. The effort drained him, and soon he found himself leaning on the rail at the top of a stairway from the lower deck, just as the steamer neared a pine-covered island. The tide swirled past the point, its sparkling white and green hues gleaming in the sun, and Aynsley let go of the rail to watch the shore glide by.

With his back turned, he didn't notice the jagged rock jutting out of the turbulent water ahead. When the helm was suddenly yanked hard to starboard, the vessel listed sharply. Taken by surprise, Aynsley lost his footing and tumbled down several stairs, crashing against a stanchion. Clutching it, his face went pale as he gasped for breath, a smear of blood staining his lips.

Clay rushed over and found him in distress. "i think it's started bleeding again," Aynsley managed to say. They helped him into the saloon, and Clay promptly called for the captain, who arrived quickly.

Unfortunately, there was no doctor on board, and the steamer still had multiple stops before reaching seattle. Cutting any of them was not an option. The captain proposed landing Aynsley at their intended stop and seeking medical help via a fast car. Aynsley weakly nodded in agreement.

"just get me ashore," he murmured. "i'll be fine there."

An hour later, the whistle echoed through the pines that lined the beach, and as the side-wheels slowed, a launch approached over the clear, green water.

Aynsley, stifling a cough, struggled to sit up.

"if ruth's aboard, she can't see me freak out," he muttered. "i'll go down like everything's fine."

"you're going down with the two strongest crewmen i can find," Clay countered. "if that's not okay, you're going in a sling chair."

Realizing he couldn't stand, Aynsley reluctantly agreed. Ruth, seated beside her father at the back of the launch, gasped when she saw him being carried down. His face, ashen and weary, triggered her compassion when they placed him on a cushioned bench. But it also clarified a long-held uncertainty within her. Yes, she was startled and sorry for Aynsley, but that was it; she didn't experience the fear or anxiety she thought she might. Aynsley noticed her somber expression and managed a faint smile.

"i feel utterly embarrassed," he said hoarsely. "had i known i'd end up looking like a fool—"

"quiet," ruth interrupted, gently placing a hand on his. She saw the effort it took him to talk. "you need to rest. We'll get you better."

"yeah," he replied unevenly. "i—i've been dreaming of this moment, imagined i'd feel better right away... Never thought i'd arrive like this..."

A coughing fit stilled him, and he hastily wiped his lips with a bloodstained handkerchief.

"it seems quite serious," Clay murmured to Osborne. "is it a few miles to the nearest phone?"

Osborne nodded silently, then waved at a man onshore as they approached the beach.

"get the car ready!" he shouted. "i'll secure the boat."

With considerable effort, Aynsley was carried into the house. The doctor, arriving hours later, wore a grave expression. By the following morning, he had brought in two nurses, as Aynsley teetered between life and death for several days.

He was delirious most of the time, but occasionally his fevered mind would clear enough for him to ask for ruth. Though he rarely spoke coherently when she arrived, her presence undeniably calmed him. His eyes would follow her with a dull sense of peace, and a few quiet words from her could sometimes lull him into much-needed sleep. Ruth recognized the power she held over him and wielded it effortlessly, driven by a curious mixture of pity and a protective tenderness. She found satisfaction in knowing he needed her, and it became both her duty and pleasure to aid in his recovery.

Clay observed her with growing admiration, but his persistent gaze occasionally made ruth uneasy. She felt he was beginning to question her motives, something she herself was still trying to fully understand. However, the pressing need was to focus on Aynsley's survival. The time to unravel personal motives would come later.

One night, after a long vigil with the nurse—who seemed powerless to calm Aynsley without ruth's help—she left his room with an aching head and heavy eyes. On the stairs, she encountered clay. His face looked drawn and exhausted, and his eyes searched hers with concern.

"he's finally asleep," she said. "i think he'll rest for a few hours."

Clay looked at her with a mix of gratitude and a rare hint of embarrassment.

"and you?" he asked. "how long can you keep this up?"

She sensed it wasn't kindness that drove his question. Ruth knew he could be relentless in his demands, yet she forgave him this because it was for his son's sake.

Besides, there was a subtle flattery in how he acknowledged her influence.

"i suppose i can manage as long as i'm needed," she replied with a smile. "after all, it's the nurses and the doctor who bear the real burden."

"rubbish!" he interrupted impatiently. "you know you're more valuable than all three combined. Why that is, doesn't matter right now; it's just a fact."

Ruth blushed, annoyed at herself for reacting visibly, as she didn't want him to provoke any display of emotion. But thankfully, he wasn't staring at her anymore.

"my dear," he said, "i need your promise that you'll help him pull through. You can do it if you're determined enough; he's all i have. He's been slipping fast these past few days, and you shouldn't hesitate to ask for anything you need from me."

"i'll do what i can, though it might not be much," ruth replied a bit more coolly. "but one doesn't expect—"

"payment for kindness?" Clay interjected. "sure, the best things are often given freely and can't be bought, but that's never been my luck. What i couldn't seize, i've had to pay for. The love of a deal runs in my veins. Help my son get better, and whatever i can do for you won't be enough to repay the debt."

Ruth fell silent for a moment. Lately, she had been feeling a vague unease about her father, and with a sudden insight, she realized it might be wise to have this man's gratitude.

"after all, i might ask you for a favor someday," she said, smiling.

"you won't find me breaking my word," he promised. As he strolled over to a seat by the water, he lit a cigar and tried to sort through his feelings, which were rather perplexing.

Aynsley yearned for the girl, and Clay gave his nod of approval; he'd always given the boy whatever he desired, but this time felt different. Though Clay had a marauder's code and wouldn't hesitate to snatch what pleased his son, ruth Osborne seemed untouchable, immune to his ruthless grasp. It wasn't just Aynsley's request for inaction; Clay felt an unseen barrier restraining him, a mystery he couldn't fathom. Yet Aynsley was young, wealthy, and strikingly handsome; surely, he could win the girl on his own merits. Just as Clay allowed himself a moment's hope, a gnawing anxiety returned. What if the boy didn't survive to see his love flourish?

A few nights later, Clay encountered the doctor descending the staircase. He pulled him into the hall.

"the boy's not improving," Clay snapped. "what's the prognosis? spare me the jargon."

The doctor sighed, shifting. "i'm baffled. He hasn't gotten worse, but there's little improvement. We've addressed the immediate physical damage, but his feverish agitation is depleting his strength. Oddly enough, miss Osborne is the only one who can soothe him. His reaction to her is quite extraordinary."

"that's irrelevant!" Clay cut in. "i want to know his chances."

"i expect tonight will be critical. If he can make it through the early hours, he might turn a corner; a lot hinges on his ability to sleep, and i've pushed the sedatives to the limit. Miss Osborne has volunteered to stay with the nurse, but she's visibly exhausted."

Clay turned away, and the hours that followed left deep imprints on him. Known for his hard-heartedness, he loved his son deeply; Aynsley was the epicenter of all his dreams and ambitions.

Social prestige and political clout meant nothing to clay; his sights were set on commercial dominance and wealth. He knew he had a knack for accumulating assets but lacked the know-how on spending them. When his son eventually made it in the business world, Clay wanted him to have the finest that society and culture offered. But at this moment, a few hours would decide if all clay's dreams would disintegrate. He trusted the doctor; still, with a strong man's skepticism of medicine, he trusted ruth Osborne even more. And, as it turned out, he was right to do so; ruth came through that night.

The air was hot and stagnant, seeping through the open door and window of the sick room. A small, carefully shaded lamp cast a dim glow, and every so often, a gentle breeze would stir the curtains, bringing with it a faint coolness and the scent of pine trees. Ruth, weary as she was, found the occasional draft a balm as she sat in a straight-backed chair near the bed. She dared not sit in a more comfortable one for fear that sleep might overcome her. Aynsley was restless, though perhaps a bit less than usual, and he occasionally mumbled weak but coherent words.

"don't leave," he pleaded in a feeble voice. Ruth responded with a warm smile, placing a cool hand on his hot, frail arm. For a while, he lay with his eyes closed, though clearly not asleep, then suddenly opened them, searching for her with a spark of eagerness.

"that guy's coming for me; he won't miss next time!" he muttered, presumably reliving the attack at the mill in his mind. Then, with great effort, he added, "you'll hold him off, won't you? you can do it, if you try."

"of course," ruth replied with a mix of compassion and a touch of admiring sympathy. She was young enough to still hold physical courage and manly strength in high regard, and her patient, though now pathetically helpless, had once stood bravely at his post. It was deeply unsettling to see such a formidable man brought so low.

When the doctor entered a little while later, he glanced at Aynsley before turning to ruth.

"still awake?" he asked softly. Aynsley, hearing him, looked up.

"no," he muttered. "i'm exhausted, but i can't sleep. How could i with those bastards burning down the gang-saw shed?"

The doctor shot ruth a warning look, whispered to the nurse, and left, passing clay, who had sneaked upstairs without his shoes and was now lurking in the shadows on the landing.

"no change," he said, steering the anxious man away. It was past midnight and getting colder. The house was quiet, with only the occasional faint whispering from the tops of the pines outside. A breeze had picked up, and ruth, worn out from the heat and fatigue, welcomed it. She checked her watch, then wrapped it in a handkerchief to muffle its loud ticking in the heavy silence. She knew the ominous hour, when human strength wanes the most, was approaching, and felt a strange awe as if death was hovering over Aynsley's bed.

"i can't see," Aynsley murmured weakly, reaching out a thin hand, searching for her. She grasped it protectively, and he sighed, settling down. After a while, the doctor returned, noiselessly, and looked down at Aynsley's still form with a nod of satisfaction, while ruth settled into the most comfortable position she could manage. She felt his burning fingers in her hand and it dawned on her with startling clarity that she was holding Aynsley's life; no matter what, she couldn't let go. Soon, she grew stiff and ached to move, but it was impossible: Aynsley was finally sleeping, and it might be fatal to wake him. Despite trying to relax her muscles, the fixed position became unbearable, but she summoned all her willpower to endure it. After all, the pain was welcome, because it kept her awake, and she was getting very drowsy.

Clay crept up again, stopping silently just outside the door. He couldn't see his son, but his gaze fell upon the girl, stirring something deep within him. The dim light illuminated her face, revealing a mix of weariness and empathy. Clay, neither a sentimental nor an imaginative man, found himself filled with a profound respect. It wasn't a lover's tenderness he saw in her eyes—there was no hint of passion there. Instead, what he witnessed was a deep, almost impersonal pity, protective and entirely selfless. For a moment, he wondered, somewhat embarrassed, how she would gaze upon his son if she loved him. Encouraged by her demeanor and the nurse's quiet presence, he retreated softly.

As dawn broke, the doctor descended into the hallway, with ruth trailing behind him. Clay beckoned, and the doctor paused.

"i have good news," the doctor announced. "he's sound asleep, and i believe the worst is behind us."

As the doctor continued, Clay turned to ruth, feeling an odd sense of relief wash over him. Her face was pale and drawn, yet serene, and Clay was struck by the absence of triumphant exhilaration.

"thank you," he said, his voice rough with emotion. "remember, my promise still stands."

"yes," ruth replied, smiling faintly. "but that doesn't seem important now. I'm very tired."

Clay stepped aside to let her pass, watching with heartfelt gratitude as she slowly made her way down the corridor.

CHAPTER FIFTEEN.

The scent of pine hung thick in the warm air. Sunlight poured over the grass, and the calm was barely disrupted by gentle waves lapping at the shoreline. Aynsley, in the throes of recovery, reclined in a cushioned hammock where shadows dappled the pristine lawn of Osborne's estate. His face was gaunt, his eyes half-lidded—not from slumber, but from an overbearing glare that tired him. His mind raced, haunted by uncertainties. Ruth sat nearby, engrossed in a book she'd been reading aloud. Her light summer dress draped elegantly over her graceful figure, her wide-brimmed hat casting a soft shade over her delicate features.

There was a serene, almost ethereal quality to her complexion, and her eyes shimmered with an unusual luminosity. Though not an artist, Aynsley felt captivated by the harmonious beauty she embodied. Usually, her calming presence had a soothing effect on him, but now, as he observed her, his heart pounded intensely. From the moment they met, he had been profoundly drawn to her, his admiration blossoming into love long ago.

Yet, Aynsley was perceptive enough to sense her lack of romantic interest. Her friendliness was too genuine, her warmth too open; he would have preferred a hint of awkwardness, a trace of hidden affection. He had waited patiently, hoping her attentive care during his illness hinted at deeper feelings. The fear that this hope might be in vain gnawed at him, but he could no longer keep his secret. Summoning his courage, he decided to find out where he stood.

"ruth," he began, "i'll need to head back to the mill next week. It's been wonderful here, but i've loafed around long enough."

She glanced up suddenly, her thoughts clearly miles away, showing no trace of his presence there.

"i suppose you must go when you're well enough," she replied, her tone distant. "still, you haven't fully recovered. Maybe they can manage without you for a while longer."

This was far from encouraging.

Her tone was kind, though she showed no urgency to keep him. If she wanted him to stay, a subtle hint would have done it. Nonetheless, he needed to know his fate.

"maybe," he started, "in fact, i have a feeling they actually do better when i'm not around. But that's not the point. I've been here for a while and have asked a lot from you. Now that i'm cured, i have no reason to impose on your kindness anymore."

"you're not imposing," she replied warmly. "honestly, i enjoyed taking care of you. Though it was the nurses who did most of the work, it's nice to feel useful."

Her smile did little to lift his spirits. Her care seemed impersonal, a kindness she would extend to anyone, even a stranger.

"i get it," he said. "you're naturally kind, and it seems like you need to share that kindness. It's a relief to you. Lucky for me, because i wouldn't be here, nearly healthy now, if you hadn't stepped in."

"that's an exaggeration," she said with a slight blush, which he eagerly took as a good sign.

"not at all," he said firmly. "you saved my life; i realized it the morning the fever broke. Even the doctor almost admitted it when i asked." he paused, holding her gaze though his heart raced. "since you saved my life, it belongs to you. That's a responsibility you've taken on. The life you gave back to me isn't much unless i can convince you to share it. Perhaps, in good hands, it could improve."

Ruth felt moved. She saw the depth of his trust and the longing in his eyes. He spoke with a touch of humor, a bravery she admired because she knew it masked his despair.

She couldn't doubt his love; she knew how much it meant. The realization brought color to her cheeks and made her uneasy.

"Aynsley," she began, "i'm sorry, but—"

He interrupted with a quick gesture.

"hold on a second. You didn't know i loved you. I could tell by your honest friendliness. I always felt i was aiming too high, but i couldn't let go of the hope that maybe someday i'd win you over. I intended to be patient. Now, it seems like i've thrown a wrench into things, but i'm leaving next week and i just... I couldn't keep it inside any longer."

"it's not a shock," she replied, smiling to mask her inner turmoil. "you're too humble, Aynsley. Any sensible girl would be proud of your affection. But still, i'm afraid—"

"please, think it over," he pleaded. "i know i'm probably not what you expected, but if there's one thing i can offer, it's that you can shape me into whatever you need. I'm starting a new chapter in my life, and no one could help me more than you."

Ruth was silent, caught in a whirlwind of thoughts. She knew his strengths and weaknesses and trusted him completely. Now, she felt a sting of guilt, realizing she hadn't been entirely innocent. She had sensed his feelings, and while she hadn't encouraged them, she hadn't discouraged him either—not entirely. She cared deeply for him, was even willing to love him, but somehow, she just... Couldn't.

"Aynsley," she said softly, "i'm more sorry than i can express, but you really must put me out of your mind."

"it's not going to be easy," he replied, his voice strained. "but you do like me, don't you?"

"the problem," she began, "is that i like you too much, just not in the way you want."

"i get it," he sighed. "i've always been more of a buddy than a suitor."

"but if i really gave it time, do you think you might come to love me?" Aynsley asked quietly.

"it's too much of a gamble," ruth replied, almost reluctantly.

"i'm willing to risk it, and i'd never hold it against you if it was too much," he said, his enthusiasm waning. He paused, his voice heavy with a tender seriousness. "ruth, is there any hope at all?"

"i'm afraid not," she whispered, though there was a resolute undercurrent to her words that Aynsley couldn't misread.

"alright," he sighed, showing remarkable composure. "this is something i need to come to terms with, but i don't want to burden you. The light out here is a bit too intense; if you don't mind, i think i'll head inside."

He rose, his movements betraying his frailty, and started for the house. Ruth stayed seated, understanding that his retreat was an act of kindness. She wondered why she had turned him down. He was everything she admired: modest, brave, generous, and positive. Yet, she couldn't picture him as her husband. She pondered this, wrestling with reluctant honesty, until suddenly, the embarrassing truth hit her, bringing a flush of shame and anger. The love she couldn't give

Aynsley had already been given, unbidden, to someone else who had left her behind and likely forgotten her.

She knew so little about Jimmy, while she knew Aynsley deeply. Aynsley was wealthy; Jimmy was clearly not—he might even have other issues. But these things seemed insignificant. Jimmy somehow felt like her own, and despite her efforts to deny it, she felt deeply connected to him. Coming to rationalize her feelings, she began to see she had judged herself too harshly. After all, though Jimmy never openly expressed his feelings, his actions had revealed them. There was no evidence to suggest he had forgotten her.

Poverty might have kept him quiet. Besides, it seemed he was out in some isolated place, completely cut off from the world. Maybe he thought of her often; but those were pointless thoughts, and forcing them aside, she stepped into the house. The next day, Clay found ruth sitting on the porch.

"so you turned down my boy," he blurted out.

"did he tell you?" she asked, feeling a bit uneasy.

"no, but i'm not an idiot. The look on his face said enough. I don't know if you're happy knowing he's taking it hard. Maybe it's flattering."

"i feel terrible," ruth retorted, annoyance creeping into her voice. "you're being unfair."

"and showing bad manners? well, i'm no gentleman, and i get nasty when i'm hurt. I assume you know the boy was dead set on being with you? i think you'd have realized that by now."

"i don't see what you expect to gain by trying to intimidate me!" ruth snapped back, her conscience gnawing at her. Clay chuckled harshly. He had outmaneuvered many tough and smart men in his time, and this young girl's defiance amused him.

"my dear," he said, "i'm not trying to intimidate you. If i were, i'd be using a completely different approach. Aynsley is a good son, an honest man without a hint of cruelty, and you could trust him with your life."

"yes," she said softly, "i know. I just can't say anything different."

Clay mulled over her words for a moment. Her honesty disarmed him, yet he couldn't fathom his restraint. He had won Aynsley's mother against fierce family opposition, and he had a primal side to him.

If all this had happened when he was younger, he might have pushed his son to take ruth by force. But now, even though times had changed, there were still ways to get her to yield. Despite his lack of scruples and the possibility of doing it behind Aynsley's back, he wouldn't consider it. She had saved Aynsley's life, and he had developed a strange respect for her.

"alright," he conceded, "you seem to know what you want, and i guess Aynsley will have to accept it."

Ruth felt a wave of relief as he left, accompanied by an odd sense that he no longer intimidated her. Despite his earlier gratitude, she had feared his anger; now, that fear had vanished. He hadn't said anything specific to reassure her, but she sensed that, while he regretted her refusal, he now saw her as a friend rather than a possible adversary. Later that evening, she shared the news with her father, who had been away for a few days.

"i'm not surprised," he said. "i even hoped you might choose him. But now it's too late, and if you didn't care much for Aynsley, i wouldn't have pressured you."

"i knew that," ruth replied warmly.

"and how did Clay handle your refusal of his son?"

"i think he handled it well. He even complimented me as he left."

She noticed a look of relief on her father's face, which struck her as significant.

"you should feel flattered," he said. "Clay tends to cause trouble when things don't go his way. It's a shame your feelings didn't align with his hopes."

"why?" ruth asked sharply. Osborne couldn't help but smile at her directness.

"well, Aynsley's got a lot to offer: money, status, good manners, and a solid character."

"you seem pretty hard to please," Osborne remarked with a wry smile.

"it's not that. I have no complaints about him," ruth replied, blushing. "but you don't exactly write a shopping list of what your ideal husband should be like."

"maybe that wouldn't be such a bad idea," Osborne laughed. "if only you could find someone who ticks all the boxes." his expression then turned serious. "i'm sorry you let Aynsley go, but if you're convinced it was the right move, then so be it."

He turned and walked away, leaving ruth deep in thought. Her father's reluctance to cross Clay was evident and only added to the vague, unsettling doubts she harbored about their business affairs. There was a nagging feeling that she hadn't yet uncovered the full extent of her father's dealings with him.

The evening was calm and suffused with a golden twilight as Aynsley, clay, and the Osbornes lounged on the veranda. Not a single breeze stirred, and the inlet lay before them, smooth as glass, reflecting the fading light. The tall cedars stood perfectly still, their silhouettes unmarred by even a whisper of wind. The beach was undisturbed, and the only sound punctuating the silence was the gentle lapping of water somewhere among the trees. The day's heat had been oppressive, and

Aynsley lazily admired the distant snow-capped peaks standing stark white against the azure sky.

"up there, it's bound to be cooler," he mused, yearningly. "that snow makes me crave the invigorating chill of the north. Times like this, i don't relish my role as a mill owner. Tomorrow, i'll be back in a hot, stuffy office filled with the din of machinery and piles of dusty ledgers."

"work is good for a man," miss dexter said pragmatically.

"true, but it has its downsides," Aynsley countered, glancing at her. "you'd understand if you'd ever been chased around your workplace by a pack of angry strikers. If i didn't have such tight business commitments, i'd tell the captain to fire up the yacht and take us all to a land of glaciers and mist, where the air is crisp and clean."

"wouldn't you miss the comforts—though i suppose you see them as necessities—that surround you here? they say life in alaska is quite spare," miss dexter replied, gesturing to the beautifully set table within arm's reach, laden with fine glasses and a large silver tankard brimming with iced drinks. Beside it, an array of exquisite californian fruits was presented on artistically designed plates.

"we could bring some of those comforts along. We're not as pampered as you think," Aynsley said with a chuckle. "honestly, right now, i'd rather live on canned food and swim in icy waters like those fishermen we met than sit in my sweltering office fretting about accounts and labor issues."

"those fishermen really left an impression on you, didn't they?" ruth interjected.

"can you blame me?"

"you have to admit, they even piqued your curiosity, and you didn't have my reason since you hadn't seen them," Aynsley said, a hint of a challenge in his voice.

"what fishermen are you talking about?" Clay asked. Ruth immediately regretted bringing it up.

"some men he met on an island up north," she replied with a forced laugh. "Aynsley seemed to envy their simple life. I guess it would be nice in this heat, but seriously? i can't picture him handling wet nets and slimy fish, for instance."

"it wasn't their lifestyle that got to me," Aynsley clarified. "it was the men themselves. Except for one, they didn't fit the typical fisherman profile. And as far as i could see, they didn't have many nets. Then one of them said something that made it clear he didn't care much about catching fish."

"maybe they were just like you, amateur explorers. They just didn't have the luck to own a big yacht. You probably wouldn't have been interested if you knew their whole story."

"where was this island?" Clay interrupted. Aynsley guessed that ruth was eager to change the subject, and he was fine with that.

"i remember the latitude," he said nonchalantly, "but there are a lot of islands up there, and i can't recall the longitude."

Clay gave Osborne a sharp look, and ruth noticed her father seemed uneasy.

"could you locate it on a chart?" Clay pressed Aynsley.

"maybe. But i don't carry charts around. They're bulky and only useful when you're at sea."

"i have one," Osborne said, and ruth felt a wave of anxiety as he rang a bell. She regretted her lack of discretion in bringing up the topic. She wanted to drop it but hesitated to give Aynsley a warning look—his father might notice, leading to an awkward explanation later. Standing up, she quickly made an excuse to go inside. She knew where the chart was kept and thought she could hide it.

CHAPTER SIXTEEN.

S he was too late. Just as she was retrieving it from the bookcase, a servant entered the room.

"Mr. Osborne sent me to get a large roll of thick paper from the top shelf," the maid instructed. Begrudgingly, ruth handed over the chart and returned to the veranda, where Aynsley pointed toward the island. Ruth noticed her father's lips tighten.

"what kind of boat did they have?" Clay inquired.

"quite a smart sloop, but rather small," Aynsley responded, trying to steer his father away from the subject. "at least, that was the rig she was designed for, based on the position of the mast. They had split the single headsail for easier handling. We're conservative out west; you'll still find people sticking to the big old jib, even though it's a hassle in a strong breeze. They've done away with it on the Atlantic coast, and sometimes i think we're not as advanced as we believe compared to those folks down east."

"what was her name?" Clay cut in. Aynsley saw no reason to avoid answering, especially since he knew the question would resurface sooner or later.

"she was called Resolute."

Ruth quietly observed the group. Miss dexter seemed genuinely disinterested, and Aynsley appeared unsure whether revealing the name had been the right move. Osborne's face was firmly set, and Clay had a dangerously focused and determined look. Ruth began to regret bringing up the topic, sensing she might have stirred trouble, though she wasn't sure how. Nonetheless, she felt compelled to gather more information.

"was it the island where you were wrecked?" she asked clay.

He shot her a sharp look, then chuckled.

"i think so, but the experience wasn't pleasant, and i'm not eager to revisit it."

Afterward, he effortlessly shifted the conversation to lighter topics. About thirty minutes later, he stood up.

"it's probably cooler on the beach," he said. "anyone want to join me?"

Everyone stayed put except for Osborne, who got up and followed him. Once they were out of sight, concealed by the trees, Clay stopped.

"i guess what you heard was quite a shock," he said.

"it was surprising. I don't think you showed much tact by making such a big deal out of it."

"sometimes you have to take a gamble. If i'd waited to get Aynsley alone and then grilled him, it might've looked suspicious. Generally, if you're willing to discuss something in public, it's less likely to be taken seriously."

"that's true," Osborne agreed.

"i don't want the boy to overthink things," Clay continued. "i assume we're both keen on our children seeing the best in us."

He looked at Osborne intently, and Osborne nodded in agreement.

"so, what's your plan?"

"i'm going to track down the sloop. We can't have mysterious strangers poking around that reef. Once i gather enough information, those guys will either need to be bought off or driven away."

"fine, i'll leave it in your hands."

"not really your field anymore, is it?" Clay said with a mocking smile. "but i admit, you do deserve some sympathy."

"in that case, we both do. You're not any better off than i am."

"i beg to differ," Clay replied. "my reputation is well-known and has been hit so many times that no one takes a new scandal seriously; in fact, people tend to find my antics amusing. You're in a tougher spot. Even though you slipped up once, you've led a safe and steady life since then."

Osborne lit a cigar to mask his emotions; clay's jab had struck a nerve.

When he was struggling with poverty and the temptation was high, he had gotten involved in an illegal scheme with clay. The money he made from it had allowed him to start what he now considered a respectable business career. Occasionally, especially when he collaborated with clay, his actions might not have passed a stringent ethical test. However, on the whole, he could justify them, and he had earned a solid reputation in the market. Now, a misdeed from the near-forgotten past—a deed he sincerely regretted and would undo if he could—was threatening to resurface and haunt him. Even worse, he might be forced to take crooked measures again to cover up his error.

"we won't gain anything by debating who might suffer the most," he said as calmly as he could manage.

"no, that's pretty pointless," Clay agreed. "well, i need to track those guys down and see what i can do."

They walked along the beach for a while before heading back to the others. While Clay traced her movements as far as they could, the Resolute was slowly making its way north. She encountered light, un-predictable winds, and calms, and was eventually driven into a desolate inlet by a fresh gale. They were stuck there for a while, and even when they set out to sea again, adverse winds continued to hound them. These were no longer gentle breezes but carried a biting chill from the polar ice. The crew grew anxious and moody as they stubbornly fought the wind with reduced sails, mindful that every additional day at sea strained their finances further, and the open-water season was short. On a sharply cold, blustery morning, Jimmy dragged himself off the locker where he had managed to catch a few hours of heavy sleep. His limbs were stiff, his clothes damp, and as he moved, he bumped his head against a deck beam. Sitting down with a muttered curse, he pulled on his soaked knee-high boots and glared around moodily. Daylight was filtering through the cracked skylight above, revealing the underside of the deck dripping with moisture.

Large drops raced each other down the slanted beams, splashing into the lee bilge below. Water oozed in through the seams on the weather side, pooling several inches deep on the inclined floor as the boat plunged wildly through the waves, the wind roaring around it. Jimmy muttered complaints at his crewmates for not pumping out the water and shivered as he pressed himself against the centerboard trunk, trying to light the rusty stove. The wet stove wouldn't draw, and smoke billowed out, nearly choking and blinding him as he placed the kettle on it. Frustrated, he climbed back on deck with a sour temper.

Moran sat stolidly at the helm, wrapped in a soaked slicker with spray whipping around him. Bethune crouched under the coaming, while white-capped waves with gray sides tumbled around the boat. A furious red glow was spreading high in the eastern sky.

"you're making a lot of smoke," Bethune observed.

"yeah, i am," Jimmy replied. "if you could get forward and swivel the funnel- cowl, which you could've done earlier, it might help. It's your turn to cook, but you should probably pump a bit before you start."

Bethune stretched and laughed apologetically as he rose. "well, i was so cold i didn't want to do anything."

"that's a common feeling," Jimmy said. "the best way to get rid of it is to work. If you adjust that cowl, i'll prime the pump."

Bethune shuffled forward, adjusted the cowl, then returned and pumped a few strokes before stopping to lean on the handle. "do you really think we'll reach the island today?" he asked.

"yes. But it's tough to shoot the sun when you can barely see it and the horizon's all over the place," Jimmy answered.

After setting our course for the past two days, i don't have much faith in the log we're trailing."

He pointed towards the wet line extending over the stern, leading back to a glint of brass visible amidst the waves.

"what did you expect?" Bethune asked. "we got it for half the regular price, and to be fair, it works pretty well after a good soak in oil. But when it stops, it stops completely. You know how to handle a distance recorder that decides to stick and then miraculously start again—it's a real hassle."

"talking's easier than fixing it," Jimmy insinuated.

"true, but i need to vent a bit. These thoughts came to me last night while i was sitting behind the coaming, chilled to the bone. Have you ever noticed how the ambitious underdog is always at a disadvantage? no one cheers him on when he chooses the tough, moral route. It takes guts to start, and instead of things getting easier, all sorts of unexpected challenges crop up. Even the weather seems to work against you; it's always an uphill battle."

"are you saying you regret coming here?"

"not exactly, but i'm starting to question the point of all this. I haven't slept in dry clothes for two weeks. It's been a full seven days since any of us had a decent meal, and my slicker's given me a nasty sore on my wrist. Meanwhile, i could have been enjoying three square meals a day, spending my free time reading a lousy newspaper, and watching them sweep up dead flies in the hotel lounge."

"what i want to know is whether any ambition is worth the price you have to pay for achieving it?"

"i suppose that depends on your temperament."

"moran's been known to say some outlandish things," moran commented from his post at the helm. "when you make your living at sea, you have to brace yourself for whatever comes your way. If you don't fight hard enough, the ocean will defeat you. That's why you should finish your pumping before a big wave hits."

Acknowledging this with a subtle nod, Bethune returned to his work, soon heading below deck while Jimmy took over the helm. The breeze picked up steadily throughout the morning, causing the sea to grow rougher, but it calmed down again by the afternoon, when they encountered a dense fog bank. Jimmy speculated that it meant land was near. With daylight hours shortening, they hoisted the topsail and scanned the horizon eagerly until a faint gray silhouette emerged through the mist, roughly a mile away. As they closed in, they could discern the shoreline, which Jimmy examined through binoculars after referencing his notebook.

"luff!" he called out to Bethune. "keep it steady; i've got my first two marks." then he signaled to moran. "get the anchor ready!"

Moments later, having completed his precise four-point positioning, the Resolute came to a stop, head into the wind, the sound of the anchor chain rattling in the still air. The sea lay relatively calm in the shelter of the land, undulating with a long swell that occasionally crested into a rolling wave of foam.

Bethune picked up the binoculars and focused on the shoreline.

"it's been a while since high tide; she should be appearing soon," he said, scanning the horizon. "i'm trying to locate that large boulder at the point." he paused and lowered the binoculars. "see anything?"

"no," moran replied curtly. "she should be visible by now."

"agreed," Bethune nodded. "the tallest mast used to stick out above the water when the top of the boulder was just submerged, and now the bottom of it is a foot above the tide."

Jimmy remained silent, but with a burst of energy, he grabbed the dory, heaved it over the railing, and leaped in with a coil of rope. Moran followed, letting out a length of the rope as Jimmy rowed. Minutes passed with no sign of contact, and Bethune watched from the sloop, his expression tense. It seemed like the wreck might have disintegrated and vanished. But then, as the dory shifted course, the rope tightened and moran looked up.

"got it now! it's shifted, and there might not be much of it left intact."

Jimmy stopped rowing, and there was a moment of silence. It would take a while to set up the diving gear, and sunset was approaching, but they couldn't stand the suspense until morning.

"it might get rough by morning," Jimmy remarked.

"true," moran agreed, pulling off his heavy coat. "i'm going down."

The wind was biting, the tide strong, and the water chilled by arctic ice; yet moran stripped off his damp clothes with urgency. For a moment, his figure, stark and white against the gray rocks and dark water, was perfectly poised. Then he dived, and the others watched the surface ripple as he disappeared. Moments passed before his head emerged farther out than expected. Jimmy rowed toward him, and after a clumsy scramble that nearly tipped the boat, moran was aboard, struggling back into his clothes.

Then he spoke.

"she's there, but from what i can see, she's heeled over with her keel buried deep in the sand."

Jimmy and Bethune felt a wave of relief. Getting to the strong-room might still be tricky, but knowing the wreck hadn't broken apart in their absence was reassuring. Jimmy grabbed the end of the rope and secured a buoy to it. He then rowed back to the sloop, where Bethune was busy preparing a surprisingly lavish supper.

CHAPTER SEVENTEEN.

When Jimmy stepped onto the deck the following morning, a heavy fog cloaked the land, and the slate-green sea heaved sluggishly through bands of mist. The air was unusually crisp, and the furled mainsail sparkled with a thin layer of frost. This was worrisome; they had to complete their task or give it up before winter arrived in full force. But Jimmy reminded himself that they should have a few more weeks before the real cold hit. As he watched the smoke from the stove pipe rise in a faint blue column, he heard the splash of oars. Bethune was approaching in the dory.

"i took the water breaker off before you got up," he announced as he came alongside. "there was ice on the pool. Looks like a sign that we can't waste any time."

"that's clear enough," Jimmy replied. "pass me the breaker. Let's get the pumps set up immediately."

Breakfast was rushed. The weather was perfect for their work, and they couldn't expect it to stay that way. Within an hour, they had maneuvered the sloop close to the wreck, and Jimmy donned the diving suit. Despite thinking he'd overcome his initial reluctance to descend, he found himself feeling an instinctive dread. But he couldn't let that stop him, and he forced himself down the ladder resolutely.

After a few minutes, he reached the wreck. One side was deeply embedded, but the other was lifted, exposing a broad strip of torn planking. With his lamp, Jimmy could see into the interior, where the tide had washed away some of the sand that had previously blocked their path to the bulkhead sealing off the strong-room. The bulkhead had been strained by the wreck's movements, making it possible to loosen the beams. Jimmy attacked the nearest one with his shovel, using all his strength as he found leverage, but the timber was firmly mortised in. He lost track of time as he strained to pry it free, not stopping until the pressure began to take its toll on him.

His heart pounded and his breath came in harsh gasps, but the beam remained undisturbed. Staggering out of the hold, he made his way toward the ladder. When his teammates finally removed his helmet aboard the sloop, he sat still for a few minutes to catch his breath. The crisp, natural air was indescribably refreshing. Eventually, he recounted what he'd found below and suggested:

"we could carve out an opening for the saw and then cut through the stanchion to pry off the cross-timbers."

"the issue is we don't have a large drill," Bethune pointed out. "when you need a specific tool, you often find it's the one you're missing."

"a mortise chisel might work," moran proposed. "how thick's the wood?"

"about three or four inches. Given how tough it is, i reckon it's oak or hackmatack."

"well, that's a big job," Bethune grumbled. "in my experience, as soon as you drive a chisel into old timber, you hit a spike. And we don't have a grindstone."

"stop whining and get the chisel!" moran snapped. "i'm going back down."

They watched the line of bubbles marking his descent rise to the surface and then halt in a stationary cluster. Sooner than expected, the bubbles began to move back, and moran looked dejected as they removed his diving suit.

"did you manage to cut much?" Bethune asked.

"no," moran replied, showing the chisel. "hit a massive spike on the second cut."

Bethune chuckled. Even Jimmy cracked a smile. A deep notch marred the tool's edge.

"your so-called philosophy isn't much help," moran grumbled. "it lets you predict problems but not avoid them."

"we'll need to work on that nick for a while," said moran.

"i'll try the engineer's cold-chisel," replied Bethune. "with some luck, i might be able to cut the spike."

He grabbed the tool and a carpenter's chisel and headed back down. When he returned, the edge of the chisel was broken.

"i've cut the spike and managed to dig out about an inch of the wood," he reported. "why the frown, Jimmy?"

"it's looking like we might spend a week just on that timber. Those endless preliminaries are driving me nuts!"

"it's all part of the process," Bethune started philosophizing. "anytime you take on something a bit out of the ordinary, most of your effort goes into preparation. Once you get to the actual task, it often feels like less work."

"save it!" moran cut him off. "Jimmy, it's your turn."

Jimmy stayed below deck as long as he could bear it, furiously hacking at the hardwood with broken chisels, scraping out the debris with his bruised fingers. When he couldn't take anymore, moran took over. The job was grueling and only got worse as they slowly made an opening for the saw. The tool had to be driven horizontally at an awkward height above the sand, straining their wrists and arms.

Fortunately, the weather was on their side for once. They worked tirelessly until exhaustion overtook them at dusk. Moran sent Bethune ashore to find stones with a cutting grit, and they sat in the cabin, patiently sharpening their tools as frost began to blanket the deck above them. Two days passed before the beam finally gave way, and by the time they succeeded, the temperature had plummeted. Jimmy was cooking dinner when moran called him up on deck, pointing towards the sea.

"look at that," moran said. "i think we've got a signal to leave."

Scanning the western horizon where the sea cut a dark blue line against a dull red sky, Jimmy saw a faint patch of white shimmering in the distance.

Grasping the binoculars, he noted that the mass was low and jagged, with waves crashing along its windward edge. This indicated it was a floe of thick northern ice, submerged enough to pose a threat.

"yes," he responded solemnly, "we need to hurry."

They dedicated the next week to breaching the bulkhead. Jimmy thought it would have held them off longer if it hadn't been constructed in such haste. Here and there, the reinforcing irons had torn away due to the hull's movement. They worked ceaselessly, but the labor was grueling and tested their endurance. By late afternoon, a brisk wind made diving treacherous. Jimmy prepared for what he hoped would be the final dive, pausing briefly to survey the scene. Wisps of gray fog drifted in from the sea, and the long swells had broken into choppy, white-capped waves. The sloop plunged through the spray, straining at its cables as the tidal current surged past.

"we might hold out for another hour," Bethune said optimistically, but then pointed out to sea. "that settles it. If we can manage it at all, we need to cut through the bulkhead tonight."

A tall, glimmering form materialized from the fog about a mile away, irregular and bright, as if a ghostly crag glowing against the grey mist. It advanced smoothly with the tide, towing a smaller mass in its wake, and then a third shape emerged behind it. The men watched with anxious faces. Jimmy reached for his helmet.

"they'll run aground before they get to us, but we need to get to work now," he said.

A bent iron plate dangled from a shaky beam as he crawled to the aft end of the hold. With a fierce determination, he set to prying it free with a bar.

The effort was draining, but just as Jimmy felt he could push no longer, the timber gave way, and he tumbled forward into the gap. It took a moment to regain his balance, crouched on hands and knees as the disturbed water surged ominously into the dark void. Raising his lamp, he saw the floor carpeted in deep sand, from which two wooden boxes jutted out. He tried to extract them but soon realized it was futile without proper tools. While fumbling around, he stumbled upon a bag. It was a plain canvas bag, heavily sealed, though some of the wax had chipped off. Lifting it, Jimmy noted it was still robust enough to withhold its contents. He sat there for a few moments, heart pounding with exhilaration. The sand was significantly deeper on the far side of the small, tilted room. He couldn't guess what might be buried there; however, he could clearly see two boxes and now clutched a weighty bag. Gold was fetching around twenty dollars an ounce, and a considerable fortune could fit in a small space. It seemed like wealth was within his reach.

The strain of the pressure began to take its toll, and Jimmy quickly maneuvered out of the hold. He struggled up the swaying ladder, and upon reaching the deck, he found moran occupied at the front, adjusting the cable. Bethune helped remove his canvas suit and took the bag from him.

"you got in?" Bethune exclaimed.

"yes. Here's a bag of gold. I saw two boxes and believe there are more buried in the sand," Jimmy replied.

Bethune clenched his fist tightly.

"and we can't hold on! it's maddening! she's dragged the kedge up to the anchor and is pushing her bow in. Still, i'm going to give it a shot."

Jimmy glanced at the sea, shaking his head.

The waves swelled as the tide rose, and the sloop crashed into them fiercely, water cascading over the foredeck, shaking the anchor line.

"no," he insisted. "i struggled to reach the ladder earlier, and she might drift to leeward before you could get back. It's too risky."

Moran, moving aft, felt the weight of the bag and glanced longingly at the diving suit but nodded in agreement with Jimmy's decision.

"i really don't want to bail, but we need to get the sails up."

Crouching in the spray that swept over the bow, they painstakingly hauled in the anchor chain with numb, battered hands. Leaving Bethune to hoist the reefed mainsail, they coiled the soaked kedge line in the cockpit. Then they set the small storm-jib, and the Resolute shot forward, cutting through the waves toward the sheltered cove.

"another hour, and we'd have known for sure," Bethune grumbled, shifting his grip on the wheel to ease his sore wrist. They were too tightly wound to chat after supper; the weight of the bag suggested its contents were valuable, and it seemed wiser not to break the seals.

Jimmy grew drowsy and had just lain down on a locker when moran opened the hatch.

"now that it's too late to dive, the wind's dropped and is coming off the land," he said. Jimmy fell asleep, only to be awakened at daybreak by an unusual sound. It reminded him of breaking glass, though sometimes it sounded like tearing paper. He leaped to his feet, curiosity growing. The noise was loudest at the bow but seemed to come from the entire length of the boat's waterline. Moran was sound asleep, but when Jimmy shook him, he came awake instantly.

"what is it?" Jimmy demanded.

"ice; splitting on her stem."

"so it's too thin to worry about."

"that's the most dangerous kind," moran replied, slipping into his pilot coat. "get your slicker on; i'm heading out."

There wasn't much to see when they reached the deck.

The clammy fog wrapped around the boat, but Jimmy noticed a glassy film covering the water's surface. Unlike opaque, white ice, this was clear, with frosty streaks weaving in erratic patterns. As the rising tide pushed it up the channel, the ice splintered at the bow, sending sharp shards scraping along the waterline. It didn't seem strong enough to cause severe damage, which made moran's anxious expression even more puzzling to Jimmy.

"shift the boom to the other side!" moran ordered, his voice cutting through the damp air. Jimmy moved the heavy spar, causing the boat to tilt slightly. Moran, lying on the deck, leaned close to the water. Jimmy joined him, and they both saw a rough, white line etched along the planks where the ice had grazed the hull, resembling the mark of a dull saw.

"she can't take much more of this," Jimmy said seriously, tracing the shallow groove the ice had carved.

"that's right. I've seen boats ripped apart by this stuff. The real issue is, the current runs strong through here, except at low tide."

Jimmy nodded. This was his first encounter with thin sheet-ice, but he grasped the danger it posed. Driven by a swift current, the ice broke on the hull, its edge constantly renewed with sharp shards. He could envision it scoring even a boulder in its path. Unlike most tidal currents, this one ran in the same direction regardless of the tide, as often happens around islands. Bethune joined them and peered over the side, his face instantly registering their peril.

"what do we do now?" he asked.

"i'm not sure," moran admitted, looking bewildered. "the ice piles up along the beach and freezes together as the tide pulls it out."

She'd be safe in the still part of the stream, but this bight was the only spot where we could find any protection from the wind and sea.

"we can't stay here; we need to leave as soon as we can," Jimmy said firmly. "we can stick to the wreck unless it starts drifting, but i need the water containers filled before we go."

"that's going to take some time," Bethune argued. "i'd prefer we retrieve those crates from the hold first."

"i agree," Jimmy replied. "but we can't take any risks with the chance of getting blown out to sea."

"the captain's right," moran chimed in. "we'll load the dory, and he can let her drift with the tide."

They worked together to shorten the cable. After raising the anchor, they maneuvered the dory toward the shore through the slushy ice, while the sloop drifted gradually seaward. Jimmy felt a wave of relief as the unsettling crackling of the ice ceased. He moved deliberately to set the sail, given the light breeze. He needed enough canvas to keep the sloop maneuverable until the others returned.

The wait in open water was tedious, filled with an anxious desire to get moving. The gold was right there in the wreck's hold, and it would take only an hour or two to transfer it to the sloop. But doing this immediately was crucial—the drift ice was closing in, and an onshore breeze could spring up unexpectedly. They had no other safe haven now; the only one available was no longer an option. Still, Jimmy felt he had been prudent to insist on fetching the water.

The air was almost calm and biting cold. The sky and water blended into a uniform drab gray, and while the mist had thinned near the land, it still obscured the view toward the horizon. At one moment, Jimmy thought he saw an eerie pale glow amid a stretch of haze, but as a fickle breeze swept it away, the vision disappeared, leaving him in a void of uncertainty.

For two hours, he navigated back and forth in half-mile stretches, just managing to counter the tide with the light wind. As his patience wore thin, a wave of relief washed over him at the rhythmic splash of oars approaching. Minutes later, the dory pulled up beside him, and Bethune hoisted the casks aboard.

"we had to break the ice with a rock, and i doubted we'd make it through," Bethune said. "it froze over again as we carried the first load down."

"doesn't matter much now," Jimmy replied. "if things go our way, we'll be out at sea by dawn tomorrow."

As they secured the breakers, the wind died down, and Jimmy, watching the slack sails, made a gesture of irritation.

"luck's against us! feels like we'll never get that gold! there's a two-knot current against her bow, and she'll drift leeward quickly."

"then we'll tow her," moran said resolutely. "get in the dory; you didn't carry those casks, and i'm not worn out yet."

Despite resting since the previous evening, Jimmy found the work grueling. The past week's underwater exertions had taken their toll, and the tide working against them meant the line bore a heavy strain as the sloop rose and fell. The smaller craft was often yanked back nearly under the bowsprit, demanding arduous rowing to straighten the slackened line. Still, they progressed and finally anchored beside the wreck by early afternoon.

"now," moran said, "shall we dive, or do you need some food first? we haven't had breakfast yet."

Bethune chuckled and turned to Jimmy.

"think you can eat?" he asked.

"not a chance. I won't feel hungry until those boxes are up. Secure the ladder while i hook up the pump line!"

Bethune was the first to descend into the depths.

Upon his return from an unexpectedly long dive, he reported an inability to extract the nearest box. Although he had cleared the sand from it, he was forced to surface. Jimmy then took over, working furiously to drag the box towards the bulkhead. The tight space, further restricted by broken timbers, made it impossible to lift the box through the opening. As he exerted every muscle, a timber shifted beneath his feet, causing him to lose his balance and extinguish his lamp.

Rising again, Jimmy felt a change; he was less buoyant and panting heavily. Heat built up uncomfortably. Suddenly, a chilling realization hit him—his air-pipe was compromised. Panic was close, but he fought it down fiercely. There was no time to lose, and he needed to stay calm. He ran his hand over the now slack canvas suit, fumbling for the lamp. As he did, a wavering beam of light flickered through the water. He deduced that falling had jarred the switch.

Raising the lamp, he saw the air tube bent sharply around a jagged timber. His heartbeat pounded painfully, his breathing growing harder. He retreated to reach for the tube, but found his hands weak and his legs unsteady. Stooping to free the line, his dizziness overcame him, and he pitched forward across the timber, clutching the air line as he fell.

CHAPTER EIGHTEEN.

D espite the cold, Jimmy lay sprawled on the sloop's deck after being stripped of his diving gear. The memory of how he had crawled out of the abyss and climbed the ladder was hazy. He figured he must have untangled the line during his fall, driven by an overwhelming desire to breathe the open air. Struggling to explain what had happened to moran, he still felt weak and shaky, shuddering at the mere thought of plunging back into the deep.

"once we get that box out of the hold," he said, "hauling it on board should be smooth."

Moran took his time, leisurely smoking a pipe before taking his turn. When the copper helmet vanished beneath the surface, Jimmy gripped the signal line tightly, eyes scanning their surroundings. The days were noticeably shorter, and dim light cast a murky pall over the horizon, encroaching on them through wisps of smoky fog stirred by a rising wind. Ripples splashed around the sloop, and the swell grew steeper.

"i hope Hank manages to sling that box," Jimmy remarked to Bethune, who nodded while methodically turning the pump.

"we might get another turn or two, but that's it. There's a breeze pushing in with the swells."

With no more words exchanged, they waited as patiently as they could until moran surfaced.

"i got the box out of the hold before i had to quit; the next guy shouldn't have much trouble getting a sling around it," he said, casting a glance toward the sea, adding with a sense of urgency, "he better hurry."

A gust of wind tore through the fog, revealing a long, low mass, shining with a dead, cold glow. As the haze swept back, another pale streak appeared off the opposite bow.

"they're all around us!" Jimmy's voice cracked with tension.

The crew were seasoned veterans, forged by their trials in the north, but the sight before them was unnerving, causing their steadfast courage to wane. Only moran had faced such a threat before, and he knew better than to underestimate it. The pack ice was closing in around the island, trapping their sloop in a deadly embrace that could shatter it like glass. To make matters worse, a biting wind lashed at their anxious faces, and the sea churned with menacing, sharp waves.

"we've got no choice but to leave," moran said with a heavy heart. "but i still want that box."

"you'll get it, if i can rig the sling," Bethune replied. "help me get into the suit—fast."

He cast a nervous glance around. A jagged raft of ice was drifting closer, and the fog, stirred by the rising wind, streamed across the sea in thick tendrils.

"looks like it's up to me to finish the job this time," he said with a grim chuckle. "no more easy escape to a cheap hotel for me."

After he had been submerged for some time, Jimmy, working the pump in response to the tug of the signal line, began to wonder when he would resurface. Bethune seemed particularly cautious about his air supply, and Jimmy guessed he was trying to maneuver the case along the ocean floor to get a clear path for the lift line, since the Resolute had shifted position. Moran took over the crank when necessary, but otherwise he stood still, his imperturbable brown face fixed on the encroaching ice. As a distraction from the tension, Jimmy found himself wondering about moran—what he was thinking, what drove him. Despite their hard work and shared dangers, Jimmy realized he knew little about the man. Moran's stoic reserve and calm demeanor were a mystery.

When a demanding task came up, he was always dependable. He rarely moved hurriedly, though, and his actions often conveyed an impression of an unthinking, automatic strength. But Jimmy knew better; he had witnessed the cool judgment and unyielding courage that guided his friend's formidable strength when under pressure. This wasn't particularly important right now, though.

Jimmy kept his eyes fixed on the patch of bubbles breaking the surface of the swells. The bubbles remained in place, and Bethune had been down longer than usual. He wasn't in trouble; Jimmy's tug on the line had met with a reassuring signal. It seemed Bethune was confident he'd bring up the case. Meanwhile, ice was drifting closer, driven by the wind and tide, and its low profile hinted that it had formed in shallow waters. If that were true, it might not ground before reaching their sloop. Still, its progress was slow, and Jimmy felt there was no urgent need to recall Bethune, especially since he needed to finish his task or abandon it altogether.

Finally, the bubbles started to move towards the surface. Following them was tricky; the swell was streaked with foam, and the bubbles would vanish momentarily before reappearing. Soon, the top of the ladder banged against the rail, and the copper helmet emerged from the sea. Bethune threw an arm over the deck and grabbed a cleat, struggling to rise further, so they pulled him onboard. When released, his face was pale, and he lay back against the skylight, catching his breath. After a few moments, he gasped out painfully:

"the case is slung; i had to clear it from her. Heave it up!"

The crew lunged for the line he brought up, hauling it in with Jimmy battling his fierce impatience. Care was essential to prevent the sling from loosening while dragging through the sand.

The line finally dropped straight down, and they were heartened by the weight they felt as they pulled it back up. Even moran couldn't hide his excitement as the corner of the box broke the surface. With a powerful heave, he hauled it on board, then he and Jimmy collapsed onto the deck, their eyes locked on the treasure before them. The box was thick, reinforced with heavy iron, and the wood was thoroughly waterlogged. Despite that, it was clear it contained a substantial amount of gold. Jimmy felt a surge of triumph, but that was soon interrupted by Bethune.

"look at the ice!" he cried out. The floe was closing in on them, and through the fog, they could see a taller mass seemingly stuck on the reef. Spray leapt around it, and heavy chunks of ice fell off with loud splashes. Moran glanced at the floe and sprinted forward. Jimmy joined him, and together they hastily pulled up the chain cable. With Bethune's assistance, they reefed the mainsail and stored the folding ladder and pumps below deck. They struggled to lift the kedge anchor, which seemed to be tangled in some waterlogged timber. Yet, knowing it might be a long time before they could return, they refused to abandon it. When they finally freed it, Bethune had already hoisted the mainsail. There was no time to waste; the fog thickened even as the wind picked up, and a foreboding mass of ice approached dangerously close. The light was fading, and the sea grew rougher. Quickly setting a small jib, they headed for the open sea.

"get as far away from here as you can," Jimmy instructed, leaving moran at the helm. "i'll get the stove going, and after dinner, we'll open the box."

It had been almost twenty-four hours since he'd last eaten, and Jimmy was beginning to feel weak from hunger. He struggled to get the fire started, his movements hampered by a frustratingly sluggish clumsiness.

When the meal was ready, he called down to Bethune and handed over moran's portion.

"i've been a bit indulgent today, but after what we've done, we deserve a feast," he said, exuding triumph. They ate voraciously as the water splashed beneath the deckboards and the lamp swung erratically with the rolling of the cetacea. Bethune didn't object when Jimmy lit his pipe afterward. The box lay undisturbed against the centerboard trunk. They felt no rush to open it. This was a thrill that could wait; for now, they reveled in their triumph within the cozy cabin.

"technically, we're probably not supposed to break into this thing," Bethune remarked. "it might even make us look suspicious. But i don't think i can resist until we get back. Grab the tools, Jimmy."

Jimmy complied, then, opening the hatch, called out to moran.

"we're about to open the box. Can you come down safely?"

Moran seemed to shake his head in refusal, though Jimmy could barely make him out. Darkness had fallen, and a dense fog was sweeping past the boat, with spray beating through the rigging, hinting that they were sailing hard. Dropping back below deck, Jimmy closed the hatch and picked up a hammer.

His fingers trembled, nerves buzzing, as he wedged the tool beneath the first band.

"i wish we'd cleaned out the strong-room, but we can come back," he said, his voice laced with optimism. "we've got enough to clear our debt and live in comfort through winter. Imagine staying in a nice hotel, maybe even take a trip to california. And if Jaques can find someone to manage the store, we'll bring him and his wife to the city."

"that's not exactly aiming high," Bethune laughed. "but it sounds doable. Though, we still don't know what our share will be."

"i'm insisting on half," Jimmy declared with resolve. "in fact, we'll negotiate before handing over the goods."

Working with eager determination, he loosened the band and slipped a chisel under a board. Within moments, he pried it free, revealing thick layers of decayed canvas.

"looks like there's a lot of packing," Bethune observed. "there's a seal here we need to break—but we've already broken one. Don't waste time. Rip it open!"

Jimmy slashed at the canvas with his knife, plunging his hand into the box. The feel of the contents startled him.

"it feels like small ingots," he remarked.

"that's odd; there's no smelter around here. Cut through the wrapping, let's see what it is!"

Jimmy did as instructed and then yelped as he dropped the object he pulled out. Dark-colored, it landed with a heavy thud.

"it's lead!" he exclaimed. In a fit of anger, he tilted the box, shaking out several small gray lumps. They scattered across the floor, and when he sliced one open with his knife, the metal inside was soft and revealed a silvery sheen. Letting the knife fall, Jimmy's face became stark with disappointment. A heavy silence hung in the air until Jimmy, snapping out of his stupor, flung the lid back.

"hank!" he called, his voice rough and strained.

It seemed moran recognized the urgency in their voices. The changing rhythm of the boat told them he was altering its course, yet he maintained his cool, not skipping a single sailor's task. Jimmy listened to the jib being hauled aback and the mainsail tightened. The boat leaned into an easy lurch as it was brought to a halt. Moran reappeared from below deck, a heavy frown darkening his face.

"someone's played us for fools!" he exclaimed.

"first the underwriters, but still," Bethune responded, fighting to keep calm. "open one of those bags, Jimmy, and let's see if it's all the same."

Jimmy grabbed the bag he'd salvaged from the wreck. Slicing it open, a few coarse, yellow grains trickled out.

"it looks fine, but there's not much here; and the bag Hank brought isn't any bigger," he muttered gloomily.

"sew it back up before you lose any more," moran suggested, sitting down on the box. "if there's any fixing to be done, we should do it quick. The boat's carrying all the sail it can handle, and i can't afford to leave it unattended for long."

"are we heading back?" Bethune asked. "we haven't emptied the strong-room. What we left behind might still be the real deal."

"that's off the table," moran said grimly. "with the wind like this, the drift ice will lock up the shoreline solid by tomorrow."

They sat in silence, each weighing their options. There was only one clear choice, but none wanted to voice it, admitting their defeat. Finally, Jimmy let out a sigh of resignation.

"set course southward," he said. Moran gave a silent nod and headed back up through the hatch. Jimmy slumped down on the locker, while Bethune lit his pipe, the glow of the flame briefly illuminating the tension on his face.

Neither of them spoke until they heard the clatter of blocks and the rush of water along the lee side, signaling that the Resolute had swung around.

"our winter plans are shot," Bethune said. "we'll be lucky if we can get jobs at a mill and crash at some cheap motel. But let's save this talk for tomorrow; i'm not up for it right now."

Jimmy gave a brief nod and pulled a damp sail over him. To his surprise, he soon fell asleep. When moran woke him for his turn at the helm, the wind was howling and the cold seared his skin. Nestling into the coaming as best he could, Jimmy faced his bleak watch. Long, white-topped waves chased the sloop, pummeling her weather quarter, while the spray hammered down on Jimmy's slicker. Visibility was near zero; he could barely see the boat from end to end. He knew he was taking a risk with potential ice, but he figured stopping would make them no safer. Fixing his eyes on the compass, he let the sloop ride the storm.

Their exhaustive efforts had come to nothing, and Jimmy, worn out and disheartened, couldn't muster the energy to ponder future attempts. They were returning bankrupt. He couldn't see how they could even keep the sloop. At best, they'd be stuck until spring. The outlook was grim, and what made it worse was the sliver of hope Jimmy had clung to. Since Bethune had first proposed the scheme, a faint, alluring prospect had kept him going. He hadn't dwelled on it, but it had lingered in the background, urging him forward. There was always that slim chance their project might succeed, in which case, his share of the salvage would have been enough to turn things around for him.

Opportunities were plentiful in western canada for someone with energy and a bit of capital, and Jimmy saw no reason why he couldn't succeed. He dreamed of the day he could reconnect with ruth Osborne. Over time, he had thought of her often, and reminiscing about their shared voyage, he dared to think he had made some impression on her. He recalled small moments, stray words, and fleeting glances that carried meaning. If he could elevate himself to her social standing, perhaps he could win her love. This hope had driven him forward relentlessly. But now, he had failed miserably. He was returning home, defeated. His only hope was that through relentless hard work on the docks or in the sawmills, he could earn enough to pay back the storekeeper who had extended him credit. Beyond that, the future seemed bleak. He knew he had to forget ruth. As he shivered at the helm, bitter spray stinging his face, and the sloop lurched through the darkness pursued by surging waves, Jimmy's heart sank.

CHAPTER NINETEEN.

A sudden cold snap had gripped the northern half of Vancouver island, blanketing the towering pines and unpaved streets with a layer of frozen snow. An icy wind swirled around Jaques' store, making the loose windows rattle and tiny icicles dangle from the eaves. But inside the cozy back room, warmed by a polished lamp and a glowing stove, Jimmy and his friends found a comforting refuge. They had just cleared away supper and now gathered around the table, pondering their next move after the second failed attempt to recover the gold.

Jaques leaned his head on his hand, his elbow resting on the table. Across from him, mrs. Jaques sat with eyes fixed intently on Bethune, who had taken the lead in the conversation. Jimmy, with a gloomy expression, stared toward the single window where a frozen pine bough occasionally scraped against the pane, its rasping sound cutting through the rattling sashes. Moran sat in the lamplight, his face downcast. For a few moments, the only sound was the cheerful crackle of the stove. Then Jaques broke the silence.

"we might as well go over everything from the start," he said. "the first thing to decide is what we should do with your boat."

"that brings up another issue," Bethune replied. "what we do with her now depends on our future plans, and we haven't made those yet."

"then let's consider the possibility of you trying again in the spring?"

Jimmy glanced at mrs. Jaques and thought he saw an encouraging look in her eyes.

"you're assuming we can get out of debt," Jimmy said.

"if it were possible, we'd pull her up and strip her down for winter with the first big tides."

"not here," Jaques interjected sharply. "for one thing, she'd get spotted. And trust me, that's something you want to avoid."

"i can see why," Bethune replied with a resigned grin. "you're not our only creditor, and the other guy won't be any more forgiving."

"let's put that aside for now. Do you know any secluded creek where she'd be safe and hidden away?"

"i think we could find one," Jimmy answered.

"then i'll fill you in. Shortly after you left, a man from Victoria paid me a visit. Said he was an accountant specializing in helping small businesses. He talked about collecting overdue accounts, teaching clients how to keep their books in order, negotiating the best buying terms, or even helping sell their business. He mentioned that some of his city friends were thinking about merging the grocery stores across the small island ports."

"sounds like he offered you a good deal for your own store," Bethune observed.

"i wasn't too eager. Business had picked up since you were last here, and things were looking better. Still, i showed him my books, and he took a particular interest in your account. He asked if i knew you were a remittance man who lost his allowance and that your partner was a steamboat mate who'd been kicked off his ship. I told him i knew, and then he said your chances of success were pretty slim. He gave me some useful advice and left."

"intriguing," Bethune mused. "did you hear from him again?"

"i did. Not long ago, he sent me an offer to buy my business as it stands, with all unsettled claims and liabilities included."

When i asked a Vancouver contact to look into it, he assured me it was a safe bet and the money was good."

"so, someone has definitely noticed our worth. Did you accept the offer?"

"no, sir. I declined for two reasons. First, i sensed that the buyers either anticipated a boom in the island trade, making it wise for me to hold on, or they had some compelling reason to want to get their hands on you. After giving it some thought, i decided not to help them."

"appreciate that. I wonder if mrs. Jaques had any input?"

"she certainly did," Jaques admitted, clearly moved. "she believed it wouldn't be right to betray you, and thought that standing by you might ultimately be for the best."

"we're grateful, but i'm not sure if her decision was the wisest. It's apparent that there was something shady about the wreck, and what you've told us suggests that some well-financed individuals are eager to cover their tracks. I suspect they've become wealthier since the fake gold shipment and might be willing to shell out a good sum to keep things quiet. The guy who approached you probably knew nothing about this; he was just working on commission for them."

Silence fell over the group as they contemplated their situation. They were ordinary people, and they didn't doubt that wealthier individuals were scheming against them.

"it seems you've stumbled onto a dangerous secret," mrs. Jaques said, breaking the silence.

"at the very least, an important one," Bethune agreed. "it could potentially land us in hot water, but our position's fairly solid. Still, i must admit, i'm not sure what the best course of action is."

Mrs. Jaques observed him intently.

"have you considered striking a deal with the people who insured the gold?"

"they'd probably pay you well if you put the screws to them."

Jimmy jerked slightly, a frown creasing his forehead, but Bethune motioned for silence.

"did you really think we'd go that route?" he questioned the woman.

Her lips curled into a knowing smile. "no, i didn't. So, what's the alternative?"

"we could approach the underwriters and see what they'd offer us. It's the logical move, but i'd rather hold off. If we can clear out the strong-room, we'd have all the leverage we need."

"in your hands, you mean," she retorted.

"no, i meant what i said. My idea is that your husband should drop his claim against us and take a small share in the venture. If he agrees, we could return next spring. It's not a suggestion i would've made earlier, but circumstances have changed, and we need another man on board."

Jaques leaned forward, his expression thoughtful. "i half-expected this and have been crunching some numbers. The mills are swamped with orders for dressed lumber, a pulp factory is under construction, and business is picking up now that trade is flowing into town. Still, there's a risk involved."

"of course," Bethune replied. "we're three freewheeling adventurers without a penny to our names, up against serious men of business and influence. They might crush us. But i think we've got a fighting chance." he turned his gaze to mrs. Jaques. "what's your take on this?"

"oh, i love a good adventure! and i have this gut feeling that you'll pull it off."

"thank you! it's clear that our rivals can't do much at the wreck site while we're there, and the ice will protect our claim during the winter. But we must return before they can dispatch a steamer come spring. Meanwhile, we need to handle those bags of gold."

"that's a challenge," Jaques admitted. "we really should hand them over to the underwriters."

"true, but as soon as we do that, we lose our edge. We've got to hold on to them and keep everything under wraps until we've wrapped up the whole operation."

"isn't that risky?" mrs. Jaques asked, a hint of worry in her voice.

"you've cut one bag and broken into the box. If the folks working against you found that out, they'd claim you'd stolen the gold. You'd be in a tight spot."

"not the first time," Bethune replied with a chuckle. "we have to take risks, and we'll lock the gold in your safe. What gives me hope is that several different consignments of gold were sent by the steamer and insured. I can't believe all the shippers were in on the conspiracy. There's no reason to distrust the remaining cases."

"you hadn't deciphered the marks when i last inquired," Jimmy interjected.

"no, they were nearly illegible; but i think i have a lead now. I'm inclined to believe one of the cases was shipped by a man named Osborne. His name's on the vessel's manifest, and he's been connected with the owner for a long time. I found that out while looking into the salvage plan."

Jimmy looked startled. "his first name?"

"henry. I heard he has a house on the shores of puget sound. Looks like you recognize him!"

Jimmy stayed silent for a few moments, aware that others were watching him keenly. Bethune's suggestion hit him hard because it seemed preposterous that henry Osborne, the amiable and refined gentleman he'd met aboard the empress, could be involved in a common fraud. Moreover, it was unthinkable that ruth Osborne could be the daughter of a criminal.

"i do know him; we met on our last voyage. But you're mistaken," he said firmly.

"it's possible," Bethune conceded. "time will tell. I only have a suspicion to go on."

"and how do you plan to act on it? what are you going to do?"

Bethune gave him a penetrating look. "nothing, until we've emptied the strong-room. Then we'll decide on the best course of action."

"the opposition will likely make their move soon; there could be developments over the winter," he declared, turning to Jaques with purposeful intent. "we'll hide the sloop with the next high tide, then head south to find work. Come spring, we'll ask you to support us and return to the wreck as soon as the weather allows. It's our best plan."

The others nodded in agreement, and shortly after, the gathering dispersed. As they walked back to the boat, Bethune addressed Jimmy.

"feel like telling me what you know about Osborne?" he inquired.

"i just know you're barking up the wrong tree. He's not the type to be involved in the conspiracy you're implying."

Bethune remained silent, and they continued down the snowy street. Jimmy struggled to believe that Osborne had any part in the deceit, though a sliver of doubt began to edge into his mind. He toyed with the idea of abandoning the hunt for the gold, but he was committed to his comrades and couldn't convince them to forget the matter. Besides, if Bethune's suspicions were somehow right, he might be able to help miss Osborne. Regardless of what they uncovered, Jimmy was determined that she should not suffer.

The next day, they set sail and found a safe spot to dock the sloop. After pulling her onto the beach, they walked to a nearby siwash village, arranging for an indian to take them back by canoe. Upon reaching Vancouver by steamboat, they struggled to find work due to the influx of laborers and railroad crews descending from the mountain ranges to the coast as winter approached. Despite the mild temperatures in the coastal valleys, it was tough, but eventually, Jimmy and his friends secured positions with a contractor clearing land.

Their pockets were empty, and it wasn't a job they would have chosen otherwise. The trees they felled were monstrous in size, and since moran was the only one skilled with an ax, the rest had to handle the heavy crosscut saws. Pulling those double-handled saws through the sticky wood day in and day out was grueling, made worse by constant rain that turned the clearing into a swamp. Whenever a log fell just outside the clearing, they had to wade waist-deep into soaked brush and rotting ferns to retrieve it.

Bethune and Jimmy soon realized that sawing was the easy part. They were soon tasked with piling the timber for burning. These logs were massive, and rolling them into place through knee-deep muck was back-breaking work. Building the logs into pyramids, several tiers high, was a herculean task, fraught with danger. Each row was a gamble, any misstep risking the logs crashing down on them.

Jimmy and Bethune kept at it because they had no other option. They labored, drenched and exhausted, from dawn till dusk, returning to their sorry excuse for a sleeping shack at night. The shack was a slapdash construction, hardly waterproof. Its dirt floor was a muddy mess, the stove barely provided warmth, and the place reeked of cooking odors, stale tobacco, and soaked clothes.

Bunks were stacked along the walls, damp and dirty from the men's perpetually wet garments. More often than not, Jimmy would be jolted awake by water dripping from the leaky roof onto his face. His nights were restless, his body aching, and the constant discomfort wearing down his spirit.

He was convinced that the moment he set them down, he'd never want to see a cant-pole or a crosscut-saw again. However, the liberation he craved arrived in an unexpected manner.

CHAPTER TWENTY.

A heavy mist clung to the edges of the clearing, shrouding the somber pines in a ghostly veil, but sparing the rows of trunks below, which stood straight and uncovered. It was a gloomy morning. Jimmy, drenched and tired, paused for a breath beside Bethune and a few others near the growing log-pile. His muscles ached from the previous day's grueling work. Two sturdy skids, arranged to form an inclined bridge, led to the top of the log-pile, and the soil between them had been churned into a slick, muddy mess, making it hard to keep their footing.

They were trying to haul a massive log onto the top tier, already cluttered with timber. Using their poles, they inched it upward bit by bit. Halfway up, one of the poles slipped, and for a few nerve-wracking moments, the men strained with all their might, preventing the log from rolling back while another found a fresh grip. The log had to be held. There wasn't time to jump clear if it slipped.

Sweat poured off them as they lifted it a few more inches, until it seemed just possible to hoist it onto the lower logs with one final effort. They made the attempt. Then one of the skids broke.

With one support gone, it seemed impossible they could manage it, yet they pressed their shoulders beneath the heavy log, fighting to keep it from crashing down and crushing them. For a moment, they held it—but no more. Jimmy felt the veins throbbing on his forehead, a strange buzzing filled his ears, and his heart pounded painfully. He knew he couldn't endure the strain much longer, yet they had no choice but to overcome it or be maimed.

"lift! you've got to land her, boys!" someone shouted, their voice half-choked with desperation.

They gave it their last push. The mass hovered for a moment, then lifted an inch. With another heave, it edged forward before their muscles could fail. Its weight gradually shifted onto the lower logs, and another shove sent it rolling, eliminating the risk. That was it, but Jimmy collapsed onto the wet fern, breathless, and was still catching his breath when the foreman approached and signaled him.

"we won't need you and your partner after tonight," he said curtly. Jimmy stared at him, puzzled.

"we haven't messed up, so what's the reason?"

"you can ask, but i can't tell you. Orders are orders. You're fired."

Canadians are often blunt, and Jimmy nodded.

"fine," he said, "we'll leave now. It wasn't the cushiest job anyway."

"your call," the foreman replied. "the boss's clerk is in the shack; i'll get him to settle your accounts."

Jimmy followed him to the office and collected his pay, but the clerk couldn't clarify the termination.

"probably because this rain's killing productivity," the clerk hedged.

"but why pick us?" Jimmy pressed. "not that i'm dying to stay, but i'm curious. We've stacked as many logs as the rest."

"i've got work to do!" the clerk snapped. "take your money and go!"

Bethune diverts Jimmy and they cross the clearing to where moran is working. He seems unsurprised by their news.

"alright," he said, "i'll finish out the week and then join you in the city. We'll need the cash."

"sure," Bethune nodded, "if you get to stay that long; but i doubt it. You know where to find us."

They head to the sleeping shack to gather their belongings.

"what did you mean by saying he might not get the chance?" Jimmy asked.

"i have a hunch Hank will get his notice in a day or two."

The boss wouldn't want to make it too obvious, and Hank is a skilled chopper. He's cutting some tricky trees where he's working."

"but why would they want to get rid of him, or us, for that matter?"

Bethune offered a grim smile.

"i think we've been marked. We'll know soon enough if i'm right."

Bethune's intuition was spot-on. Within a few days, moran joined him and Jimmy in Vancouver. After a week of fruitless job hunting, they finally landed work with a lumber-rafting crew. It lasted only two weeks before they were let go without a plausible explanation. That evening, they found themselves in the drab lobby of their hotel. It was quiet, with most of the other guests lounging by the windows, their hats on, feet propped against the radiator pipes, idly watching people pass by.

"i ran into the guy we got the pumps from earlier," Jimmy said. "last time i saw him, he was fairly polite, but today he was downright hostile. He demanded to know when we'd pay the rest of what we owe and threw some nasty comments our way."

"that won't bother us," Bethune laughed. "we have nothing left to give him, and the sloop is well-hidden. He can't make much trouble. I heard something more interesting today. A friend mentioned that the clanch mill needs to cut a huge lot of lumber and is looking for more men. If we can get jobs there, we might actually hold onto them."

"it feels like we can't hold onto anything," Jimmy muttered. "why is that?"

Bethune chuckled, a knowing glint in his eyes.

"sometimes, boldness pays off. I bet our mysterious enemies won't think to look for us at the clanch mill. We'll head out there tomorrow."

The trek to the mill proved long and grueling. Not long after they left the city, the rain started pouring down, making the road even more challenging.

When they arrived at the mill gate, they were directed to the office. Jimmy, soaked and sullen, waited by the counter for the indifferent clerk's attention. Just then, an inner door swung open, and a young man emerged. Jimmy recognized him instantly as the yachtsman they'd met on the island. Aynsley stepped forward, smiling.

"well, this is a surprise! glad you decided to look me up."

"actually, we're here for work," Bethune said flatly. Aynsley laughed and gestured to the door behind him.

"come in and sit down. I'll be with you in a minute, and we'll see what we can do."

They entered his private office, well-appointed with sleek furnishings. Reluctant to use the polished hardwood chairs while drenched, they hesitated. The hum of engines and the shrill buzz of saws made it unlikely their conversation could be overheard. Jimmy turned to Bethune with a frown.

"you made a cryptic comment about boldness paying off when you suggested coming here. Did you know he was in charge?"

"no, that's a twist i didn't see coming. But i did know this mill belongs to his father."

"clay? the guy who owned the wreck?"

"used to own it. It's with the underwriters now. There's a sort of irony here. We might end up working for the man who's been after us."

"you suspected Osborne recently," Jimmy said curtly.

"they're partners. But from what i've picked up, clay's more likely the one on our trail. Registering with an employment agent probably helped them track us. Should we consider changing our names?"

"i'm sticking with mine!" Jimmy declared, and moran agreed.

"yeah, it's a weak move anyway and wouldn't fool someone like him," Bethune conceded. "he's clearly got a pretty detailed description of us."

"but why would someone like him waste time hunting us?"

"wouldn't that lead to rumors?"

Bethune chuckled. "he'll work through intermediaries. Plenty of down-and-out adventurers in Vancouver would jump at the chance to do his dirty work. This city's full of desperate souls; i should know, i was one of them."

"maybe we should clear out," suggested Jimmy. "i don't like the idea of taking his money."

"don't worry about it. If it makes you feel any better, the mill fore-man will get every penny's worth of work out of you. But," Bethune paused as Aynsley walked in.

"didn't have much luck fishing, did you?" Aynsley said, setting a box on the table. "have a cigar."

"not worth the net we cast," Bethune replied, declining the offer. "actually, we probably shouldn't muddle things right from the start. Look, we didn't know you were the manager, but we came here hoping you'd have room for three hard-working men."

"if i didn't, i'd make room," Aynsley said. "as it happens, we do need extra hands, but i can only offer rough work."

"it can't be rougher than what we've been through. We can handle ourselves, and Hank here can probably move more lumber in a day than any man in your mill. But there's no obligation to take us."

"let's not worry about obligations; i need the help. You can start with the stacking crew, and something better might come up. Now, tell me about your trip up north."

Bethune shared only what he deemed necessary. Even with tactful omissions, Aynsley occasionally gave him sharp glances, as if sensing there was more to the story. Before Aynsley could comment, Bethune stood up.

"i'm sure you're a busy man, and we shouldn't waste your time. Shall we start in the morning?"

"you can start now."

Aynsley rang a bell, summoning his foreman. For the next few weeks, the men found themselves contentedly integrated into the mill's operations.

The work was tough, but the pay was fair, and the accommodations were decent. Aynsley always made it a point to pass by with a friendly word. Jimmy had grown to like him a lot, though it was really Bethune who kept their roles as employer and workers clear-cut. One day, after Aynsley had been gone for over a week, the foreman approached them with a grim look.

"i hate to do this, but you guys have to pack up," he said. "we're letting a few of you go."

"packing up?" Jimmy burst out, indignation flaring in his voice. But he saw Bethune's stern glance and quickly added, "oh, well, i guess this has to be Mr. Clay's decision?"

"no, no," the foreman admitted unwittingly. "Mr. Aynsley had nothing to do with it. He didn't even know..." he cut himself off abruptly. "anyway, you're done here."

Without another word, he walked away. Bethune casually sat down on a pile of lumber, lighting his pipe with an air of nonchalance.

"since i'm out of a job with no explanation," he drawled, "i'm not about to break my back lugging planks around. Did you catch that slip about Mr. Aynsley not being responsible? the foreman regretted it right after he said it. And the fact he used Aynsley's first name is telling, especially considering that big car parked at the gate all day yesterday. I wouldn't be shocked if old man Clay himself had a look at the payroll."

"what do you reckon that greedy old hog's got against us?" moran muttered angrily.

Bethune paused, looking reflective.

"he might want to push us out, but i think his plan is to wear us down and then propose a deal once he thinks we're vulnerable."

"he'll be sorely mistaken if he thinks we'll cave in." Jimmy paced back and forth, his face flushed with anger. "and i'm certain Aynsley is clueless about all this."

"you're right," Bethune responded with a grim smile. "i've seen firsthand how a wayward son tries to hide his antics from his up-right family. But, it's often the unscrupulous parent who's better at keeping secrets from their kids. None of this matters much right now, though. We have a bigger problem if we don't clear the lumber from the saws—they'll be on us in no time."

The next morning, they left the mill and trudged back to Vancouver, their spirits noticeably dampened.

"so, what's our next move?" Jimmy asked as they neared the city's edge.

"why not head down to the states and test our luck?" Bethune suggested. "clay's reach won't extend much beyond seattle."

"run? are you serious?" Jimmy snapped, eyes blazing. "i'm not going anywhere."

"same here," grunted moran. Bethune let out a chuckle.

"well then, how about we take the fight to them? i'd certainly relish a good, no-holds-barred clash, whether it's a fistfight or a war of words."

"that's not gonna work," moran objected. "we need to know exactly what's in those other boxes in the strong-room before we're ready for any confrontation. But i have a feeling our adversary will make his move before we get the chance."

And he did.

CHAPTER TWENTY-ONE.

J immy's resolve was at rock bottom, dragging with it any hope and ambition he once possessed. Every avenue for escaping poverty seemed firmly shut. He had spent days wandering the streets of Vancouver, combing the wharves and mills for work, finding nothing but rejection. The wet streets were a dismal patrol; his dingy room in a run-down hotel offered no comfort. The curt refusals that greeted his job applications were utterly dispiriting. Worst of all, he felt an ever-widening distance from the girl who was never far from his thoughts. His faith in the salvage scheme was nearly extinguished, yet he was bound by his promise to his friends—they would attempt another venture if they could secure finance through Jaques. They had to find a way to scrape by, save a few dollars before it was time to make another start.

One bleak afternoon, Jimmy stood outside an employment agency among a gathering of similarly downcast, shabbily dressed men, some of whom had distinctly disreputable looks. One man had rudely shoved him aside from the window, yet Jimmy didn't muster energy to retaliate. He felt listless and low; waiting a little more would simply pass the endless time. Besides, he believed he had read all the available job notices and had already tried for several positions, all in vain. When his turn at the window finally came, he left it despondently, but as he reached the sidewalk, he stopped abruptly, feeling a sudden rush of blood to his face. Ruth Osborne was crossing the street toward him.

Jimmy glanced around desperately, but it was too late to hide; he could only hope miss Osborne would pass without recognizing him. He dreaded the idea of her seeing him among such a bedraggled crowd. His own clothes were threadbare, and he knew he looked utterly defeated. The employment bureau's sign blatantly hinted at his purpose there, and he couldn't bear the thought of her witnessing how far he had fallen.

Jimmy had turned his back to her and pulled his worn-out hat low over his eyes when her voice reached him.

"Mr. Farquhar!"

He spun around, caught off guard yet pleased, as ruth gave him a warm smile.

"you don't seem to remember me," she teased. Jimmy noticed the curious gazes of the passersby. Ruth carried herself with grace, her upscale outfit reflecting her status, contrary to his disheveled appearance. He found their speculations unbearable and stepped forward reluctantly.

"oh, i remember you well enough," he said, meeting her gaze with confidence.

"that makes it worse. It seems like you were trying to avoid me."

"i'll admit, i was. But can you blame me? you saw what i was doing."

Ruth's eyes sparkled, and her face flushed with a hint of annoyance.

"i do blame you. That's a poor excuse. Did you think i would let something like that stop me from talking to you?"

"honestly, i can't imagine you being mean," Jimmy replied boldly. "maybe i was being sentimental, but everyone has their weak moments."

"true. Mine's a quick temper, and you nearly made me lose it. I don't like being ignored by people i know."

"that can't happen often. Anyway, i've admitted my mistake."

"then, as your punishment, you must come to our hotel and tell us about your trip to the north. My father will be back late, but i think you'll like my aunt."

Jimmy's surprise was evident.

"you knew i was up north?"

"yes," she said with a sly smile. "is that so shocking? maybe you think it's easy to forget a pleasant acquaintance."

"it was quite difficult," Jimmy said earnestly, then paused, realizing he might be going too far. "anyway," he continued more cautiously, "friendships made during a voyage don't always last once you're back on land."

A steamboat officer's privileges end when he reaches land," Jimmy remarked.

"is that where you lose your confidence? you're either unusually modest or unfairly bitter," ruth replied, her brow slightly furrowed.

"it's not that," Jimmy sighed. "i hope i'm not a fool."

Ruth felt a mix of impatience and sympathy. She understood why he hadn't tried to strengthen their acquaintance, but she thought he was putting too much emphasis on their social differences.

"i assume your father found out where i went?"

"no, it was Aynsley Clay who told me. My father did ask one of the empress's mates about you, but all he learned was that you had left the ship. You remember Aynsley, the yachtsman you met on the island?"

"yes," said Jimmy cautiously. "my partners and i worked in his mill until a couple of weeks ago. Then we were let go."

"let go? why? i can't imagine Aynsley being a tough boss."

"he isn't. We got along well. I don't believe he was behind our dismissal."

Ruth started, her mind racing with possibilities. Jimmy's words confirmed her suspicions, and she remembered pressuring Aynsley to speak about Jimmy in clay's presence. Guilt gnawed at her conscience.

"so whatever you were doing up north didn't pan out?" she ventured.

"it didn't," Jimmy replied with a grim look. Ruth studied him quietly. It was obvious he wasn't doing well, and he looked weary. Her heart went out to him, though she knew she couldn't help. His pride was a wall between them.

"i'm sorry," she said softly. "you might have better luck next time. Do you have any plans for the future?"

She seemed genuinely interested, and Jimmy could see it. Though it was impossible she knew about the plot between her father and clay, he still couldn't bring himself to be fully open with her.

Loyalty to his friends kept him from taking a different approach, wary that she might accidentally mention what she knew. Asking her to conceal it from her family was out of the question.

"they're uncertain," he replied. "i think we'll find something that suits us soon enough."

Sensing his guardedness, she felt a pang of hurt, especially since she'd made several attempts to break the ice. Then, she glanced down a road leading to the wharf and spotted a ship's towering funnel and a mast, with a white and red flag fluttering in the breeze.

"that's your old ship; she docked this morning," she said. "do you think we could go aboard? after that delightful trip, i'd love to see her again."

"as you wish," Jimmy replied, though his hesitation was clear. Ruth regretted the misstep, thinking she understood his reluctance. He looked like a man who had fallen on hard times, and she imagined revisiting the ship where he had once been an officer might be a painful experience for him.

"maybe we don't have time after all," she said quickly. "i told my aunt when i'd be back at the hotel, and we're almost there. She'll be glad to see you."

Jimmy glanced at the building and paused. Several luxurious cars were parked out front, and a group of well-dressed people stood on the steps. He felt conspicuously out of place.

"i'm afraid i must excuse myself from coming in," he said.

"but why? do you have something pressing to attend to right now?"

"no," Jimmy admitted with a smile. "sadly, i can't use that as an excuse. I wish i could."

"you're not being very flattering."

"i'm truly sorry."

"i meant that i've kept you long enough already, and i shouldn't intrude," Jimmy said.

She held his gaze steady, offering no relief from his awkwardness.

"you're very kind," he asserted with determined conviction. "but i won't take advantage of that by coming in."

"very well," she replied, extending her hand. She let him go with a calmness that baffled Jimmy as he walked away. Had he offended her? undoubtedly, he had behaved clumsily, but there seemed no other option. It was fortunate he had maintained his composure, and perhaps she'd come to understand that he was thinking of her well-being. Then a bitter realization struck him: she might not dwell on it at all. It would be more productive to focus on finding a job.

However, ruth did dwell on it. That evening, she and her father sat in the grand rotunda of the luxurious hotel with Aynsley and clay. The spacious hall was richly adorned, filled with well-dressed men and women mingling between the columns or chatting comfortably on the lounges. Some were passengers from the *empress*, while others were prominent locals who dined at the hotel, as was common in the west.

A fall of sleet was clear from the way men entering the vestibule stomped their feet and shook wet flakes from their fur coats, handing them to the porter. Maybe it was the opulence, the affluent company, or the glittering surroundings that made ruth think of Jimmy out in the wet streets. The stark contrast between his reality and her own comfort struck her, stirring a sense of concern and pity.

Yet, this could not help Jimmy; and despite him pointedly avoiding any presumption on their friendship or seeking her sympathy, ruth longed to offer him some tangible support.

She needed to learn more about his business without being too obvious; she was generally straightforward but wasn't opposed to a little subtlety if it served a good purpose. It was clear she was up against a clever opponent in clay, but that only made the challenge more exciting. She trusted in her abilities.

"ran into Jimmy Farquhar this afternoon," she mentioned casually to her father.

"the empress's first mate? what's he doing in Vancouver, and why didn't you invite him in?"

"he wouldn't come. Seemed like he's been going through a rough patch lately."

Her comment, made on a whim, had hit the mark. Her father's relaxed manner was genuine, reassuring her that he had nothing to do with Jimmy's troubles. This was a relief, but she also made another crucial observation. Watching Clay closely, she noticed his slight frown. It was barely perceptible, but she had expected him to control his reactions. His displeasure at the mention of Farquhar suggested he had a good reason to keep his dealings with Jimmy hidden.

"then i'll have to try convincing him if i run into him again," said Osborne. "i always liked the guy."

"the c.p.r. Sure knows how to pick their officers," Clay remarked, flashing ruth a nonchalant smile. "still, he didn't show much sense in turning down your invite."

"it didn't bother me," ruth said lightly, gauging if he was fishing for any slip in her response.

"i suppose he isn't worth much of our attention," Clay concluded.

You wouldn't have had to ask me twice when i was young," Clay said, his voice edged with the nostalgia of years past. "but it seems like the younger generation now doesn't have the same fire."

"isn't that what every old-timer says?" ruth laughed, her eyes sparkling with mischief. "your father probably thought the same about you."

Clay seized the moment to shift the conversation away from the criticism. "actually, that's where you're wrong," he chuckled. "my folks were the backbone of a little church back east. They did their best to tame my wild side. It wasn't their fault they couldn't; i just had a rebellious streak inherited from the old puritan bloodline. The more they tried to rein me in, the wilder i got. That's why i give Aynsley some freedom—he stays steady without trying to break loose."

Ruth listened half-heartedly, her mind racing with thoughts of clay's involvement in Jimmy's affairs. She sensed an underlying reason for his attitude and was relieved when Clay and Osborne stood up to head to the smoking-room. She seized the moment to interrogate Aynsley.

"why did you fire Jimmy Farquhar from the mill?" she asked as soon as they were alone. Aynsley looked taken aback.

"actually, i didn't fire him," he replied, somewhat defensively.

"then did he and his friends leave voluntarily?"

"no," Aynsley admitted awkwardly. "i can't say they did."

"so someone must have dismissed them," ruth persisted. "who was it?"

Aynsley squirmed under her direct questioning. Lacking his father's artful dodging, he felt a pang of jealousy. Ruth's insistence suggested she had a vested interest in one of the men. He assumed it had to be Jimmy, with his charming looks and demeanor. But ruth's curiosity was broader; she sensed deeper layers and was fishing for clues.

"the old man came by when i was away and slashed the yard crew," Aynsley explained. "he's clever with cost-cutting, thought i was spending too much on wages."

"but why did he target those three specifically?" ruth pressed.

"did they perform well?" ruth asked, her eyes searching Aynsley's face for any sign of deceit.

Aynsley hesitated, feeling a mixture of confusion and frustration, but he chose honesty over evasion. "from what i could tell, they were pretty competent. But honestly, i'm not the best judge of that. Besides, he didn't really explain much."

"you brought it up with him, though?" ruth persisted.

"yes," Aynsley admitted, somewhat awkwardly. "but i couldn't push too hard. I didn't want him to think i was upset about his involvement. After all, he did buy me the mill."

Ruth understood Aynsley's doubts about clay's intentions, echoing her own suspicions. Realizing there was nothing more to learn from him, she mercifully steered the conversation elsewhere, much to his relief.

CHAPTER TWENTY-TWO.

In the sleek and polished confines of the hotel's elegant smoking room, Clay leaned forward, settling into the deep leather arm-chair, and fixed Osborne with a sharp gaze.

"what exactly is your interest in this guy Farquhar?" he demanded curtly.

"i'm not particularly invested," Osborne responded casually. "he was helpful to us on the trip back from Japan and seemed like a capable young man. I just thought i might return the favor for a few small assistance he provided."

"forget about him! has it not crossed your mind that your daughter might have developed her own opinions about him? the guy is quite charming."

Osborne's head snapped up, eyes narrowing.

"i won't discuss—"

"we must discuss it," Clay interrupted firmly. "you can't have that man around your place; he's one of the guys from that wreck."

"is that so? well, that changes things. I assume you've been investigating them, but you haven't shared anything with me yet."

"i had a feeling you preferred not to know the details. You're a refined sort of guy, and i suspected you'd rather leave the dirty work to me."

"you're right," Osborne conceded. "i trust you'd manage it better. But now, i'm curious about what you've uncovered."

"i've done as much as is prudent. Had the men sacked from several jobs and made it tough for them to find new ones; but it wouldn't do for my agents to suspect my true intent." Clay chuckled. "Farquhar and his crew are either braver or craftier than i thought; they were even taking my money from the clanch mill."

"so you aimed to ruin them?"

"absolutely! a man without money doesn't pose much of a threat; but wages are decent around here, and if left to their own devices, they might save enough to get back on their feet. Now, i doubt those poor devils have ten bucks among them."

"so, what's the next move?"

"i don't know yet."

I pondered letting them discover their vulnerability and then negotiating a payoff. But if i'm not careful, that could backfire and give them power over me.

Osborne looked pensive.

"i wonder if the insurance company would consider an offer for the wreck? i wouldn't mind chipping in."

"it wouldn't work," Clay said resolutely. "they'd get suspicious. I guess you felt guilty and wanted to return their money."

"i did, yes."

"then why did you take the money in the first place?"

"you should know. I had about two hundred dollars from you back then, and i wanted to give my girl a good start in life."

"and now she'd be the first to feel ashamed if she knew."

Osborne winced.

"what's the point of digging up skeletons best left buried!" he said impatiently. "the important thing is the wreck. If we could buy it, we could destroy it."

"we can destroy it anyway. That is, if we get there before the Farquhar crew. We have steam while they rely on sail, and i've complicated their boat fittings. Unless i can strike a deal with those guys, i'll set off in the yacht once the ice melts."

"your crew might talk."

"they won't have much to say; i'll make sure of that. Now, i don't know what claims insurers have on a ship they've paid for and abandoned for years, but i don't see anything stopping us from recovering its cargo as long as we account for what we find. The yacht's been known to cruise in the north, and it wouldn't be too surprising if we discovered that a storm or change in currents had washed the wreck into shallow waters after the salvage mission abandoned it. If there was anything shady, we'd have acted sooner."

"alright then, since we know more about the ship and its cargo than anyone else, let's see what we can do. If we fail like the salvage teams, no one can blame us."

"you'd be taking quite a risk," Osborne pointed out thoughtfully.

"true enough. If Farquhar and his associates were savvy businesspeople, i'd be worried. He's holding all the aces, but he doesn't realize it. If he did, we would have heard from him or the insurers by now."

"that sounds likely," Osborne agreed. "still, i'll feel better once winter is over and you can get out there. It'll be a relief to know the ship is gone."

"you'll have to wait, but there won't be much left of her once we start with the dynamite," Clay assured cheerfully. They continued discussing the plan late into the evening. The next morning, the group dispersed; the Osbornes returned home while Aynsley headed back to his mill. Clay, however, remained in Vancouver to visit a doctor who was gaining a good reputation. There were plenty of doctors in seattle who would have gladly seen him, but he preferred the anonymity of the canadian city.

Lately, Clay had been troubled by strange symptoms that baffled him. He decided it was best to keep any potential weaknesses to himself. Known for his formidable mental and physical strength, as well as his reputation as a daring, unscrupulous fighter, it would be dangerous if rumors of his frailty started spreading. His work was far from finished and his ambitions only half-achieved. Aynsley possessed his mother's sophistication; a woman of refinement who had once succumbed to the charm of the dashing adventurer. Clay was determined that his son would have the wealth necessary to be a prominent figure on the pacific coast. Clay knew his own limitations and was content that his son should reach social heights he never could.

This was one reason why he was more concerned about Farquhar's salvage operations than he'd ever admitted. He was well aware that his personal reputation wasn't stellar, but his business ventures, as far as the public was concerned, were tolerated and would eventually be forgotten. The shipwreck, however, posed a much more serious problem and could potentially damage his son's career if the truth ever came out. This had to be prevented at all costs. With his business expanding, he would need all his mental faculties sharp in the coming years, and the mysterious bouts of weakness he experienced were clouding his focus. Reluctantly, yet pragmatically, he decided to see a doctor.

The doctor examined him with a meticulous interest that Clay found troubling. After questioning him about his symptoms, the doctor stood quietly for a few moments.

"you've lived pretty hard," the doctor remarked.

"i have," Clay admitted, "but perhaps not in the usual sense."

The doctor nodded, studying him intently. Clay's face bore the traces of indulgence, but they were not pronounced. He didn't strike the observer as someone who habitually exercised strict self-control, but neither did he seem a complete hedonist. Still, a practiced eye could detect signs of wear.

"you haven't exactly been careful with yourself."

"i didn't have much of a chance," Clay responded with a grim smile. "in my younger days, i endured scorching heat and parching thirst in the southwest. Later, i trudged through the alaskan snow on half-rations, carrying a heavy pack. Perhaps i got into the habit of prioritizing my goals over basic necessities."

"over food, rest, and sleep?"

"something like that."

"and you work hard now?"

"i start as soon as i wake up. Usually, it's eleven at night before i finish. That's one of the perks of living in a city hotel."

"you can meet the people you work with after office hours."

"not much of a perk," the doctor said. "you need to change that. Don't you have any hobbies or ways to unwind?"

"i don't have time. My business demands too much attention. That's why i'm here—to find out what's wrong."

The doctor explained that Clay had a serious heart condition, likely inherited but worsened by the excessive strain he had put on himself. Clay's expression grew stern.

"so, what's the treatment?" he asked.

"there isn't a cure," the doctor said calmly. "easing the pressure will help. You need to take it easier, reduce your working hours, avoid stress and intense focus. And you should take a vacation whenever possible. I'm recommending three months of complete rest, but be aware that there will always be some risk of an episode. Your goal should be to minimize that risk."

"and if i keep going as i am?"

The doctor studied him with a sharp eye. He recognized clay's determination and lack of fear.

"you might live another three or four years, although i have my doubts. But the first severe attack you provoke could be fatal."

Clay showed no alarm. Instead, he appeared thoughtful, as if an idea had just occurred to him.

"would you advise a trip to a cold, invigorating climate, say, in the spring?"

"i'd advise going now. The sooner, the better."

"i can't leave yet. Maybe in a month or two. In the meantime, i assume you'll give me a prescription?"

The doctor went to his desk, wrote on two slips of paper, and handed them to clay. He had laid out the situation plainly and felt he could do no more.

"the first medicine is for consistent use as directed. But you must be cautious with the other," he warned. "when you feel the faintness you mentioned, take the prescribed number of drops, but do not exceed that amount under any circumstances."

The dispenser would label the bottle.

Clay thanked him, lighting a robust cigar as he stepped outside. He hesitated, recalling the warning against excessive smoking. Momentarily, he considered discarding it, but he quickly put the cigar back between his lips. If the doctor's predictions held true, this minor indulgence wouldn't do much harm. With a bit of luck, he'd see all his plans come to fruition within the next year or two. He had no intention of abandoning his ambitions now. Over the years, risks had become second nature to him, and he had too much on his plate to start acting cautiously.

Still, it wouldn't hurt to follow through with the prescriptions. Clay scanned the area for a discreet pharmacy. No one could suspect that his illustrious career teetered on the brink of an abrupt end.

CHAPTER TWENTY-THREE.

C lay didn't change his lifestyle much after seeing the doctor. Not long afterward, he found himself locked in a battle with a group of savvy speculators who were challenging one of his business ventures. They had the brains and the bucks to be serious threats, and Clay knew he had to throw everything he had into the fight if he wanted to come out on top. Despite the fierce resistance, he managed to defeat them and set terms for a hefty compensation. The battle took a toll and lasted a grueling month, with Clay getting little rest day or night. Even after the office doors had closed, he would host his allies in his hotel suite. He'd be up at the crack of dawn, tweaking and perfecting his strategies before the business day began.

To his surprise and relief, he felt no ill effects; yes, he was worn out, but it seemed only a natural reaction to the relentless stress. With victory in hand, he decided to take a well-deserved break. He sent a telegram to Aynsley, confirming he'd be spending the weekend at Osborne's house, a place always open to them both. Buoyed by the sweet taste of early triumph, evidenced by some enticing offers that reached him just before he left the office, Clay headed down the sound with a content heart. His satisfaction peaked further when he learned that Aynsley had landed a series of lucrative lumber orders.

Saturday evening saw dinner served earlier than usual, and clay, his appetite unusually keen, indulged more than he typically did. He assured himself he was in good health, though the recent stress had left him needing a bit of fortification. Miss dexter, meanwhile, watched him with a critical eye. After dinner, he was standing in the hall with a large glass in hand. Although he had a high color, his eyes seemed strained and his lips took on an odd bluish tint. He appeared sober, which surprised her, but his talk was getting freer and his laughter harsh. In that moment, she thought he looked crude and domineering, a stark contrast to his usual self.

The large hall had a stylish cedar paneling, with pine logs crackling in the open hearth, casting a warm glow across the room. Small lamps hung from the wooden pillars, adding to the cozy atmosphere. Adjacent to the hall were a drawing-room and a billiard-room, both inviting with warmth and light. Osborne, the host, let his guests choose their own pastimes, and no one seemed eager to move. Near the hearth, ruth and Aynsley were deep in conversation, while miss dexter busied herself with some embroidery. Osborne lounged comfortably in a deep chair by the table, and clay, with an empty glass in hand, leaned against it, feeling quite pleased with himself. He wasn't one for polished manners, and he knew it, never pretending otherwise. He grinned when he noticed miss dexter's disapproving glance.

"i often find myself in trouble, ma'am, and fighting on coffee and ice water just doesn't cut it," he joked.

"maybe that's one of their benefits," miss dexter replied dryly. "but since we're not a quarrelsome bunch, you should enjoy a few days of peace."

"that's right. I guess i got a bit worked up telling your brother-in-law about my latest scrap." he turned to Osborne. "frame and nesbitt showed up this morning, ready to take whatever crumbs i'd toss them. Fletcher tried to bluff his way through, but he crumbled when i turned up the heat. I've got the whole gang cornered, and they'll go under before they can escape."

Clay's flaws included a taste for coarse bragging, though he usually had the sense to reign it in when necessary. Tonight, however, he felt expansive, eager to savor his victory.

"the funny thing is, they were dead sure they'd bled me dry," he continued. "they latched onto a tip about the land development plan, never realizing i'd set the whole thing up to bait them. Morgan cost me a pretty penny, and he's skittish, but he's a clever little rat and does his best work in the shadows."

"didn't the opposition buy him off?" Osborne asked.

"they did," Clay chuckled. "now they want his head, and i think denby's angry enough to have him taken out."

That works in my favor, because the guy will stick with me for protection. If he tries to ask for more money, i just need to threaten to leave him to the wolves. Judging by the way they're howling, he's already pretty scared."

"have you started the clean-up yet?"

"i washed out the first pan before i left," Clay responded in miners' talk. "ten thousand dollars for two small back lots. It's all good pay-dirt, loaded with heavy metal."

"in a way, i feel sorry for fletcher. He's had a rough time lately, and now that he's hit rock bottom, this might just finish him off."

"he chose to join the gang. Now he has to live with the consequences."

Clay noticed miss dexter listening with a look of disapproval. He didn't mind having an audience and had been speaking rather loudly.

"if you saw the people who tried to rob you get ruined by their own greed, what would you do, miss dexter?" he questioned.

"i would try not to gloat over their downfall," she replied sharply.

"that does sound better," Clay admitted. "but when i have someone down, it seems smart to make sure they don't get back up too soon."

Miss dexter observed him. While she thought a bit more humility would suit him, she didn't believe he was just bragging. There was strength in the man, though she suspected he often used it poorly. She disliked his principles and he often repelled her, but sometimes she felt drawn to him. She thought he had a better side that he rarely showed.

"doesn't it ever pay to be merciful?" she asked.

"rarely. In my line of work, it's usually a matter of break or be broken. It's a tough fight out there. I stick to the rules of the game. Sometimes those rules are pretty loosely interpreted, but if you go too far, you get kicked out. In this business, the stakes are high, but i've been through the toughest training since i was a kid, and i have to win." he paused, glancing toward Aynsley. "sounds pretty egotistical, doesn't it?"

"but i know my powers, and i can't be stopped."

His assertive tone lent him an air of dignity, mitigating the audacity of his boast. Osborne eyed him with curiosity, while miss dexter was partly intimidated. She deemed his stance arrogantly defiant, foreshadowing inevitable repercussions for such pride.

"that sounds recklessly bold," she remarked. "you don't know what you might be up against."

Clay let out a harsh laugh.

"i have an idea; but there comes a moment, usually after years of battling, when one realizes they just need to persist and they'll win.

Strange, isn't it? but you just know, and you grit your teeth as you gear up for the final push that will secure the victory."

He spoke with fervor, his face flushing. Miss dexter wondered if the last glass of whiskey and soda had addled him; yet the color abruptly drained from his face, his lips turning a disturbing shade of blue. Osborne was the first to notice. He leaped up, grabbing Clay by the arms and steering him towards the nearest chair. Clay collapsed into it, fidgeting with his vest pocket, but soon his hand fell weakly. Within moments, Aynsley was at his side. Although the hall was spacious and Aynsley had been seated at a distance, he moved swiftly and silently. He had inherited his father's quick reflexes, a fact ruth noted with concern as she followed, alarmed by the turn of events. Her perceptions were somewhat muddled, and it wasn't until later that the scene crystallized in her memory.

"maybe we should get the car ready," Aynsley suggested urgently. "we might need it if this keeps up."

Osborne rang a bell, and for a few moments, they stood in anxious silence. Clay's face was ashen, his eyes half-closed. He seemed oblivious to their presence, appearing to wrestle against the weakness overtaking him.

His lips were set tight, his brows furrowed, and his hand clenched into a fist. Osborne gave a quick order to a servant, who promptly vanished, allowing clay's tense demeanor to soften. He collapsed into the chair, his body suddenly loose and limp, as if all his strength had been drained. To the onlookers, this abrupt transformation was even more unnerving than the initial tension. They were accustomed to his vigor and determination; now he lay slumped, his head drooping forward, a bulky, lifeless figure, stripped of the very traits that had made him formidable. His helplessness was almost grotesque, and ruth couldn't shake the odd feeling that it was inappropriate, even indecent, for them to watch him like this.

Yet, it seemed he was still conscious. When Osborne brought a glass to his lips, Clay weakly shook his head in refusal, and his slack fingers fumbled for his pocket.

"there's something he wants there!" ruth exclaimed with urgency. "maybe it's something he needs to take!"

Aynsley reached into the pocket and pulled out a small bottle.

"six drops," he read, preparing to lift his father's head when miss dexter intervened.

"no," she insisted. "you'll spill it. Wait for a spoon."

She fetched one, and with some difficulty, they managed to administer the dose. For a moment, there was no noticeable effect, but then Clay sighed and shifted slightly. A little later, his eyes fluttered open and he beckoned weakly.

"the medicine!" Aynsley demanded, his voice hoarse.

"no," miss dexter stated firmly. "he's had his six drops already."

Aynsley relented, recognizing that his father was indeed starting to recover. A moment later, Clay sat up in the chair and gave miss dexter a feeble, apologetic smile.

"sorry i made this fuss."

"are you feeling better?" Aynsley asked.

"i'll be fine in a minute," Clay responded, then turned to Osborne. "it wouldn't be right to blame your cook; guess it was my mistake."

He grabbed breakfast early, leaving no time for lunch.

Despite having a substantial dinner, his quick explanation didn't sit well with the others, and ruth found his promptness suspicious. They didn't bombard him with questions, though, and after a while, he stood up and moved to another chair.

"the car won't be necessary," Aynsley said to Osborne.

"the car?" Clay interrupted. "why did you need it?"

"we were thinking of calling a doctor," Aynsley admitted reluctantly. Clay scowled.

"nonsense! you scare too easily; i wouldn't have seen him. Where's
that bottle?" he quickly pocketed it and turned to ruth. "i'm really
sorry about all this; i'm ashamed of myself. Now, i wonder if you'd
play us some music."

They moved into the drawing-room, and Clay settled into an easy
chair a bit away from the others. He wasn't one for music, but he
felt unsteady and welcomed the chance to sit quietly. Plus, he needed
time to think. It seemed like the doctor, whom he'd started to doubt,
was right after all. He'd had a warning he couldn't ignore; and as he
observed the girl at the piano, it dawned on him she might have saved
his life. The others thought he was out of it, but she had realized he
was searching for the remedy that had revived him. It was unfortunate
she had turned down Aynsley, but he held no grudge—even though
he usually showed no mercy to those who crossed him. He wanted
to thank her, but he couldn't admit he'd had a serious attack. Then
it hit him: if the threat was real, he needed to take precautions. He
had a good offer for a property he wanted to sell, which he'd delayed
answering because not all terms were settled, and he didn't want to
appear too eager. Maybe it was time to close the deal now.

After expressing his gratitude to ruth for the music, he quietly
retreated to Osborne's study. There were several letters that urgently
needed writing, but his hands were unsteady, and his thoughts seemed
elusive. Determined not to let physical frailty defeat him, he firmly
gripped the pen once more. No one could know how shaky his hand-
writing was becoming. He tore up the first attempt and resolutely
rewrote it with a steady hand, though sweat beaded on his forehead
from the effort. His plans needed conclusion, his affairs required order,

and he would see it done before conceding to weakness. Ruthless and unscrupulous as he was, his courage and will were unyielding. Meanwhile, in the billiard room, Osborne conversed with Aynsley.

"what do you think about your father?" Osborne inquired, leaning forward with a concerned look.

"i'm worried. He downplayed it, but i've never seen him like this before. Something about his demeanor just isn't right," Aynsley replied.

"the fact that he saw a doctor caught my attention," Osborne noted. "the medicine bottle, with its detailed dosage instructions, indicates it was prescribed. He's been pushing himself too hard lately. You should probably check on him. If he's working, get him to stop and bring him down here."

Aynsley went to the study but was brusquely dismissed within minutes. Frustrated, he sought out ruth in the hallway.

"i need a favor, ruth," he said earnestly.

"of course. It's about your father, isn't it?" she asked.

Aynsley nodded, worry creasing his brow.

"he's in there writing letters, and it's taking a toll on him. He doesn't look well at all. I suggested he stop, but he just ordered me out. Given what he's capable of, i didn't press further."

He tried to sound casual, but ruth could read the anxiety he was trying to mask.

"do you think i could persuade him?" she offered.

"i'd really appreciate it if you tried," Aynsley replied, his eyes pleading.

"don't worry, he won't be rude to you. Besides, i think you have some sort of influence over him. You should be flattered; nobody else does."

Ruth walked into the writing room and stood next to clay, wearing a reproachful smile. He looked unwell, and she felt a wave of sympathy.

"we can't let you leave us like this," she said softly. "it's too late for business anyway."

"i suppose Aynsley sent you," he replied curtly. "you should focus on him instead of me. The boy needs looking after; he's got no nerve."

"it's not fair to blame him for being concerned about you. Besides, as your hostess, i don't think it's polite to treat me this way. If i ask you to put those papers away, you'd better do it."

Clay fixed her with a steady gaze. "i'll do whatever you ask," he said. "just give me five more minutes."

"alright. But i'll wait here, just in case you take longer."

Before the time had elapsed, Clay sealed the last envelope with a firm hand. Moments later, they entered the drawing room, and Aynsley threw a grateful glance in ruth's direction. When Clay returned to Vancouver, he visited the doctor immediately. His face hardened as he left; the doctor had been clear—he was getting worse and needed to change his lifestyle now. But Clay couldn't agree to that.

He had money tied up in various ventures, none of which had yet to achieve the success he anticipated. They needed time to mature, and selling out now would mean sacrificing the handsome profit he was expecting. He'd be left with only a moderate fortune, but he intended to be rich. Clay was ambitious, not just for his son's future but also because he had a profound sense of finishing what he started. Clearly, he needed to hold on for another year or two.

Additionally, the doctor had cautioned him against increasing the dosage of the restorative, which Clay sheepishly admitted he'd been doing. The potent drug had bolstered him whenever he faced the aftermath of any severe strain, and he had come to see it as a dependable fallback. Now, he had to cut back, and the loss would be palpable. Given the risk he was taking, it was wise to take some preventative measures. First and foremost, the wreck had to be obliterated. If he were suddenly cut off, there couldn't be any evidence left that might ruin his son's future. Aynsley needed a spotless name.

The initial step was to get Jimmy Farquhar and his associates out of the picture—to bribe them if necessary; if not, well... A steely determination hardened clay's features as he sat down and swiftly penned a brief note to Jimmy.

CHAPTER TWENTY-FOUR.

The pacific province wasn't exactly thriving, and that left a lot of men from the interior swarming to the coast, hoping to find work. It was tough for Jimmy and his friends; employment was scarce. For the past month, they'd barely scraped by, taking on the odd job here and there. Their hotel bill was overdue, and their prospects weren't looking good.

One evening, after a meager supper, they sat gloomily in the lobby of their run- down hotel. Jimmy, having found some temporary work, had spent his day in the relentless rain, loading a ship with lumber. He was drenched, exhausted, and sore. His clothes hung off him more loosely these days, a testament to the weight he'd lost. He had the gaunt, determined look of a man hardened by tough times.

"what's this?" Jimmy muttered, eyeing an envelope that had just been handed to him. "i don't know anyone in Vancouver who uses fancy stationery." he opened the envelope, skimmed the note inside, then looked up with a puzzled frown. "it's from clay! he wants to meet me in the smoking-room of his hotel—the swanky new one."

"oho!" Bethune said. "i've been expecting this. So, you planning to go?"

"what do you think?"

"well, ignoring the invitation might be smarter; but, i don't know. I'd like to see the guy and hear what he's got to say. It's odd we haven't run into him yet, even though we've felt his influence."

"either way, i'm not going alone. I could mess things up; he's clearly a sly operator."

"if you think it's wise to see him, you'll have to come along."

"we'll all go," Bethune replied with a grin. "i think he already knows us, and he won't get much out of hank."

"i'm not much of a talker," moran admitted. "but if he tries something shady and you need me to handle it..."

"we're not at that point yet," Bethune laughed. "the guy's more subtle, but just as dangerous." he glanced at the note. "it's about time; let's head out."

Clay was seated at a small table, looking up in surprise as the trio walked in. He couldn't help but feel amused at moran's unwavering, defiant gaze. This, he thought, was a curious match for Bethune, who he immediately recognized as the leader. Jimmy, he concluded after a quick look, was less of a threat—likely the efficient seaman, but with Bethune's intelligence steering their course.

"take a seat," Clay said, pulling out his cigar case. "i wrote to Mr. Farquhar, but i'm glad to see all of you here. Drink?"

"no, thanks," Jimmy said quickly, adding, "i hope this isn't too much of an intrusion, but since we move as a team, i thought it best to bring my friends."

Clay registered Jimmy's refusal as a hostile stance but smiled nonetheless.

"suit yourself," he said, lighting a cigar and studying them closely. The room was spacious and elegant, with an inlaid floor and towering pillars, adorned with pictures of snow-capped mountains. It was almost empty, amplifying its grandiosity, though two very polished and somewhat haughty attendants lingered in the background. Farquhar and his friends were plainly dressed, and Clay had hoped this environment might make them feel out of place or uncomfortable in silence. But there was no sign of that. Bethune looked slightly bored, while moran glanced around with innocent curiosity.

Despite their best efforts, they looked exhausted, a tension hanging over them like a dark cloud. They had felt the pressure Clay had expertly applied, but whether they had buckled under it was still uncertain.

"alright," Clay started, breaking the silence. "we need to talk. You've been diving on that wreck in the north, right?"

"yes," Jimmy replied curtly.

"you don't seem to have had much success."

"our appearance probably gives that away," Bethune chuckled. "honestly, we haven't even covered our costs yet."

Clay was unsure what to make of such openness; typically, if someone was aiming for the best deal, they wouldn't be this straightforward. He realized he had to tread carefully. Bringing Farquhar into this meeting had been a gamble. He'd have preferred to handle the wreck before these guys got to it, but time wasn't on his side—his warnings had been clear, and he couldn't leave loose ends.

"it's clear the original salvage team abandoned the wreck for a reason, which means you've been handed a rare shot," Clay observed. "however, it's obvious you don't have the funds for the right equipment. You need a strong vessel and top- notch diving gear—and those don't come cheap."

"we could certainly do better if we had those," Bethune conceded.

"alright then, are you open to taking on a partner?"

Jimmy's face showed outright defiance, but he stayed silent. Clay guessed Bethune had given him a warning kick under the table. He was right; Bethune was buying time, deep in thought, trying to navigate this delicate negotiation.

Declining would suggest they were confident about their chances and that the salvage could be easily managed with the limited gear they could acquire. But this wasn't a wise move, as it would make Clay suspicious.

"maybe we could bring in a silent partner satisfied with a cut of the profits," he proposed.

"so, you're planning to handle the actual salvage yourself?"

"yes," Bethune replied. "you can assume that."

"then that's not going to work for me. I know more about the wreck than you do and have always taken charge. But i'll offer you five thousand dollars for your stake in the wreck."

"technically, we can't sell an interest we don't truly have."

"that's fair; but i'll pay for your insights on where she lies and the best method to access her cargo. Naturally, once you have the money, you'll leave the wreck alone."

"it's quite the offer," Bethune mused. "but let's be honest. From what i gather, you were one of the original owners and the insurers settled with you. So, what would you stand to gain?"

"not all the gold on board was insured."

Bethune scrutinized him, and Clay grinned. "it's true. So there's no reason i shouldn't try for the salvage myself. I'm game for anything that promises a reasonable profit."

"i suppose that's fair," Bethune agreed slowly. "would you consider ten thousand dollars?"

"no, sir!" Clay responded resolutely. "my offer stands."

"then i'm afraid we can't make a deal." Bethune turned to the others. "is that how we all feel?"

"definitely," Jimmy confirmed, and moran nodded. Clay remained silent for a few moments. He would have happily offered ten thousand dollars to settle the issue, but he doubted Bethune would accept it now, and raising his bid too much would only breed suspicion. It seemed like he'd gotten nowhere, but he had learned his adversaries were more competent than he'd thought. He decided it was wiser not to press them further.

He didn't want them to find out that he was the reason they'd had such a hard time finding work. It would suggest he had a significant motive for keeping them away from the wreck.

"well," he said, "it's unfortunate we can't reach an agreement, but i have no new offers to make. You're up against quite a challenge."

"indeed," Bethune replied amiably. "we'll have to manage as best we can. And now, since we shouldn't waste your time, i'll say good-night."

Clay let them leave, and as they walked down the street, Jimmy turned to Bethune.

"what do you think of the interview?" he asked.

"a stalemate. Neither side has gained the upper hand; but i've picked up two key insights. First, he has no idea we've discovered the fake case."

"how do you figure that?"

"because of his perception of us. Remember, we're broke adventurers, not people he'd think would be principled. He'd assume that if we had found anything suspicious, we'd have tried to leverage it against him. He was waiting for a clue from us, and i made sure not to provide one."

"and the second insight?"

"he plans to clean out the wreck before we can get there. That's the real reason he let us go. You might have noticed how careful he was not to seem eager to buy us off. Interestingly, i think he was honest when he said not all the gold was insured."

"if it had been a straightforward deal, with nothing shady about it, i think i'd have taken the five thousand dollars," Jimmy said. "he won't have much trouble getting ahead of us once the ice thaws. Outfitting the sloop will be costly, and we're flat broke."

"oh, there's still time," Bethune answered with a light-hearted laugh. "something might come up."

Luck was on their side the next week. Bethune landed a job as a hotel clerk, and moran went inland to help repair a railroad track that a snowslide had damaged.

In no time, Jimmy landed a job as a deckhand on a sound steamboat. He got lucky when one of the directors, who happened to be on board, noticed his quick thinking and cool-headedness in preventing an accident after a passenger gangway broke. Impressed, the director chatted with Jimmy and, learning he was a steamship officer, offered him a position in charge of a gasoline launch. Jimmy's new role involved ferrying passengers from minor landings to the main boats. The job was straightforward, paid decently, and Jimmy had settled into it with a sense of satisfaction over the past month.

One evening at dusk, Jimmy set off to meet a northbound steamer. He had no passengers, and the weather was rough, with gusts of wind and sleet showers. The fierce gusts turned the leaden waters into frothy turmoil, and as he steered away from the shore, the ripples chasing the launch grew into larger, more aggressive waves. When he navigated past a headland, these waves transformed into short, choppy seas, and the small craft bucked wildly over the strong tides. Islands occasionally loomed through the dim haze, but the shoreline had vanished into the mist.

Initially, the launch had an additional crew member, but he had left and wasn't replaced due to the sluggish winter trade. Jimmy anticipated some difficulty getting passengers on board that night, though he doubted there'd be many. He was late as his engine was acting up, and when he finally halted, there was no sign of the steamer. The boat languished, rolling on the waves with spray lashing over the rail, rattling on Jimmy's slickers and stinging his face. Yet, compared to what he had faced in the north, the cold was almost bearable. He sat sheltered behind the coaming, casting glances up the sound intermittently.

Suddenly, a fierce sleet storm engulfed him. When it cleared, a blinking white light and a colored one emerged from the swirling clouds.

Jimmy ignited a blue flare, revved the engine, and aimed for the island's edge. When he halted, the steamer loomed ahead, a towering, gray silhouette outlined by rows of lights. It swayed as it cut through the tide, foaming around the massive paddle wheels and trailing smoke from tilted stacks. It didn't seem like it was going to stop, and Jimmy was about to steer clear when the deep wail of its whistle pierced the tumultuous seas. Moments later, he was parallel to the gangway, and caught the rope tossed down while keeping the launch a few yards from the steamer. A ladder was lowered, clattering awkwardly against the vessel's side. Jimmy steadied the launch with one hand on the tiller as a deckhand descended to the lowest rung, tossing a valise into the boat before turning to assist a woman who followed. Although the dim light obscured her features, Jimmy noted her poised and fearless demeanor, which he found reassuring. Cautiously, he nudged the launch closer.

"grab my hand and jump!" he called out. She obeyed, and once she was safely aboard, he looked up at the gangway.

"that's it!" someone shouted. Jimmy released the rope, the side-wheels churned, and the steamer surged forward as the launch drifted clear, its propeller rattling. Jimmy pulled up a canvas hood over part of the cockpit and lit a lantern beneath it before turning to his passenger.

"if you sit here, you'll be out of the wind and spray. Where to?"

"pine landing." she jumped at the sight of Jimmy as he stooped near the engine, the light spilling over him. "you!" she exclaimed. "Mr. Farquhar!"

He stared at her in astonishment, his heart pounding.

Despite the dim light and her swift motion, he thought he caught a hint of color in her cheeks.

"i didn't recognize you until you spoke, miss Osborne," he remarked, striving for a composed tone. "i wasn't expecting to see you here."

"our house is just a mile from the landing."

"the charming place in the woods? i had no idea it was yours. I've seen it from afar, but never visited."

"you could have come by; you're the only one to blame for that," she said, half- teasing.

"i was staying on the canadian side until a few weeks ago," Jimmy chuckled. "besides, my opportunities for visits were pretty scarce."

Ruth's gaze softened with sympathy as she recalled how he had looked the last time they met. But now, he was busy tinkering with the engine, his face obscured.

"so, how did you end up in this boat?" she inquired.

"i'm the captain, though right now i wish i were the engineer," he replied with a humorous undertone. "the engine's not running smoothly, so this trip might take longer than expected. We should probably swing around behind the island where the waters are calmer. Will your family be worried if you're late?"

"they aren't expecting me until tomorrow. I joined some friends traveling on the boat, thinking i'd get home before dark."

Jimmy felt a rush being so close to her, but he knew he had to guard himself against her allure. Her friends were his adversaries, and involving her was out of the question. He needed to bide his time until fortune smiled upon him, if it ever would. But patience was proving difficult.

"you never mentioned how you ended up running this boat," she reminded him with a curious smile.

"well, the truth is, i didn't want to leave this area," Jimmy began, choosing his words with care. "my partners and i have a plan that's on hold for now, meaning we have to stay close to Vancouver. I'm not certain anything will come of it, but it's worth a shot."

"one lives in hope."

Ruth felt a wave of relief at his response. The thought of him grappling with a rough job, or worse, aimlessly wandering the city streets in search of work had been troubling. It made her angry to think of him being satisfied living among those destitute souls she'd seen loitering around budget hotels.

"Mr. Farquhar," she began, "even in this country, it's hard for anyone to go it alone, and sometimes it's perfectly fine to accept help from friends. You've been so kind since the empress, and i'm sure my father..."

He interrupted her with a sharp movement, and she paused. Just then, the launch dipped its bows into a wave, sending a spray of water under the hood.

"it's impossible," he said bluntly after a moment. "maybe i'm stubbornly independent, but i have my partners to think about. They count on me to see our plans through. Who knows, things might turn out as we hope."

"and if they do?" she asked.

"if they do," he responded nonchalantly, "then i won't be hauling lumber or steering boats like this anymore."

Ruth felt frustrated, even a bit angry. She'd had plenty of suitors who didn't mind her father's wealth. Jimmy's stance was certainly more admirable, but she thought he clung to it too rigidly. When she remembered his worn-out appearance and tattered clothes when they met in Vancouver, she felt a pang of pity. But offering him sympathy that he didn't seem to want would be pointless.

"i hope you succeed in your venture," she said.

"thank you," he replied. "we'll give it our all. Now i need to watch out, there's a rock in the channel."

There was tension in his voice, and she felt a bit of satisfaction seeing his reserve cost him something. But when a gray mass of stone loomed out of the darkness, with waves crashing around it, she understood the necessity for caution.

After that, she didn't try to break the silence again. They continued on, each acutely aware of the awkwardness but neither wanting the journey to end. As they rounded a rocky outcrop, Jimmy killed the engine, and the launch coasted toward a small wooden pier. Dark pines loomed down to the water, and the waves crashed fiercely against the shore and swirled around the pilings. The place was deserted, but Jimmy managed to catch a trailing rope beside a set of steps where the water lapped rhythmically, while the launch bumped against the mossy timbers.

"i'll help you out," he said. Ruth hesitated when she saw him standing knee-deep on the lowest step, holding out his hand. But there was no dry way ashore without his help. In the next moment, he had wrapped an arm around her, standing tense and concentrated, struggling to maintain his balance. She knew it would be silly to fall into the water, so she yielded to his grip, her head resting on his shoulder as he lifted her. He stumbled on the slippery step, and she clung to him, alarmed. As she thrilled at the contact, she felt his heartbeat quicken, his muscles tensing. He gasped, a sound not from exertion but something deeper. She lay motionless, not limp but compliant, until he gently set her down away from the water's edge. She was grateful that the darkness concealed her flushed face, and Jimmy stood silently, his fists clenched. No words were needed. Both felt that something profound had shifted between them in those last few moments—something that might be ignored but not forgotten. They were no longer merely acquaintances; the fragile thread of friendship had snapped, and anything growing in its place would have to be stronger and more resilient. Ruth was the first to break the spell.

"my valise is in the boat," she said with a nervous little laugh.

For a tense moment, Jimmy stayed silent. Then he said, "yeah, i forgot," and quickly jumped down to retrieve the bag. "i hate to say it, but you'll have to head back alone. If i leave the launch here, it might get damaged. Plus, i can't bring it near your landing tonight."

"it's not too far through the woods," ruth replied, hesitating slightly before extending her hand. "i'm glad we ran into each other, and i look forward to hearing about your success."

Jimmy swiftly let go of her hand and climbed back aboard, while ruth stood rooted to the spot, watching the launch disappear into the night. As she started her walk home, her nerves tingled, and her heart raced. She knew what Jimmy felt for her, and she wondered when the time would come for him to express it openly.

CHAPTER TWENTY-FIVE.

Aynsley sat by an open window in his office, momentarily pausing from his work to take in the scene outside. The sight of the lumber raft ready to embark down the river filled him with a sense of accomplishment. Workers moved briskly, unfastening the mooring chains. The pond was brimming with logs recently delivered by a freshet, and the rapid, green waters swirled noisily around them, signaling the swift melting of snow on the distant mountain ranges. The sharp, resinous aroma from the cedar stacks permeated the air as the hot sunlight beat down on them.

A plume of smoke drifted across the long sheds, leaving a grimy trace against the sky and streaking the pines behind the mill. The incessant screech of saws and the thudding crash of boards being tossed around filled the air, signifying bustling activity. Aynsley's satisfaction deepened as a clerk handed him a stack of letters. They were filled with orders, forecasting the need to expand the mill's capacity soon. As he mulled over the expansion plans, his father entered the room.

Clay, smiling at Aynsley's evident surprise, settled heavily into the nearest chair.

"why don't you set up on the ground floor? those stairs are a real pain," Clay said, breathing heavily.

"from up here, i can keep a better eye on everything," Aynsley replied. "saves me a bit of money here and there."

Clay's face lit up with pride.

"there was a time i never thought i'd hear you say something like that. But you've got a capable mill boss and secretary, don't you? do you think they could handle things for a while?"

"i guess they could," Aynsley responded, not entirely convinced. "they know more about the business than i do, but i still prefer being here. Things tend to go awry if you don't keep a close watch."

"they sure do. You're learning quickly, my son."

"looks like the mill is starting to get to you," Clay remarked, watching Aynsley's furrowed brow.

Aynsley reached into a drawer and pulled out a set of blueprints.

"what do you think of this?" he asked. "we could keep the new saws busy, but the job would cost about twenty thousand dollars. Can you lend me the money, or should i head to the bank?"

Clay studied the plans closely.

"it's a solid plan," he said. "if the market remains steady, you'll recoup the cost quickly. I could lend you the money, but maybe you should consider going to the bank. You need to stand on your own at some point. Besides, you're steadying out; not regretting i made you work, are you?"

Aynsley paused, contemplating. While he didn't love the business, it was becoming a major focus of his life. Directing and planning for the future, seeing tangible results—it all had a certain allure.

"no," he admitted. "in fact, i'm finding it a lot more satisfying than i expected."

"that's good. It'll help with something else too. You won't be as torn up about not getting Osborne's girl."

Aynsley sat quietly, his forehead creased with thought. Honesty with himself was a habit, and he could see that his father had a point. He thought of ruth with a deep, tender sadness, and he knew he always would. But the sharp sting of his initial loss had faded. His new responsibilities had somehow dulled the pain.

"that's true," he said softly.

"but your real challenge will come when you see her getting close to someone else. How will you handle that?"

Aynsley flinched.

"it's hard to even imagine, but if the guy is good enough for her, i'll try to accept it and wish them well."

"you'll do fine," Clay said with dry approval. "but i've wandered off topic."

"you've been working hard lately, and considering how things are, you can afford to take a break without much risk. I need you to take me north for a few weeks on the yacht. The doctor says i could use the trip."

Aynsley noticed that his father wasn't looking well. He'd lost his usual healthy complexion, his face gaunt and pale under the eyes, and he had a tense, anxious demeanor. Aynsley had pressing business matters that required his personal attention, but he also recognized his responsibility to his father. Besides, the north held its own allure, with its promise of battling fierce seas, dense fogs, and biting winds.

"alright," he agreed. "when do you want to leave?"

"as soon as possible. Next week, if we can manage it. You should inform the captain to assemble the crew and stock up on coal."

Aynsley called his secretary, and by the time Clay left, they had arranged to meet at Victoria in two weeks. However, their plans were delayed; when prepping the yacht for the voyage, necessary repairs to the rigging and engines were discovered, taking longer than anticipated. Eventually, Clay received word that everything would be ready in a few days, so he paid a visit to Osborne. Arriving in the evening, he found himself in the library after dinner, conversing quietly with his host. A shaded lamp stood on a table adorned with wine and cigars, the only light source, casting long shadows across the spacious room. The polished wood floor gleamed, interrupted only by a plush rug leading to the door, which was framed by heavy drapes.

"the Farquhar gang split up, and i've lost their trail. I'd be surprised if they've managed to scrape together even three or four hundred dollars," Clay said, in a hushed, confidential tone as they smoked. "they're going to struggle outfitting their boat; it's quite a small vessel, anyway."

Although the delay has got me worried, we should still reach there well ahead of them. We only need a few days of good weather to wrap this up."

"you're taking a risk by bringing both the diver and Aynsley," Osborne warned. "it might be tough to keep them both in the dark."

"it shouldn't be an issue. I'll take the owner's berth with the small attached sitting room. Everything we bring up will go straight in there and i'll keep the key. The diver's job ends once he places the stuff on deck, and then i'm the only one touching it."

"Aynsley might want to see it and ask questions."

"well, he's not going to get the chance. I've trained him well and he knows when to stop. Besides, he'll be useful. If we need to discuss anything, i can consult with him instead of hiring someone new. The skipper's basically just a sailing- master anyway. Aynsley has the actual command."

"still, you can't keep everything from him," Osborne persisted. "there are too many people you need to take into your confidence to some extent. That's where Farquhar has the upper hand. He only has two partners he can trust."

"don't worry so much! some of the gold will be there, and i can use that if needed. Still, i'd prefer a partner who knows as much as i do, and it bothers me that i don't have one. It's your job to back me up, but you've become so annoyingly picky lately."

"i'm not going," Osborne replied quietly, as Clay raised his voice. "i've had enough dealing with the wreck."

Clay gestured to the luxurious room and its opulent decor.

"you've had your share of the loot, and you didn't even have a place to stay when i first found you. Now, when i'm facing a tricky job, you decide to bail on me."

But before he could complete his thought, he was interrupted by a sudden draft of cooler air sweeping into the room. Osborne turned abruptly and saw ruth standing by the hearth. She was cloaked in shadow, just beyond the reach of the lamp's warm light, but her posture seemed relaxed and natural.

"walter just got back with the car and brought this telegram," she said, holding out an envelope. "i thought it might be important."

Osborne felt a slight sense of relief at the sound of her voice. It was steady and normal, though he wished he could see her face more clearly.

"thank you," he said, tearing open the envelope. "we'll be done with our conversation soon."

Ruth exited silently, and Clay scrutinized Osborne intently.

"do you think she overheard?"

"i doubt it. I hope not."

"if it had been a man, i'd have found out quickly enough," Clay said with a grimace. "in any case, whatever she might have heard wouldn't give her much to go on."

He was mistaken. Ruth's suspicions had already been kindled, and clay's careless words only fueled them. She knew he was heading north to where Jimmy, who had spoken about some scheme to boost his fortunes, was involved with the wreck. Clay's reference to sharing the loot confirmed her worst fears. Even more troubling, he seemed to be persuading her father to join him. It took all her effort to maintain her composure while handing him the telegram, and her face was pale as she descended to the empty hall below.

Ruth was deeply shaken. She had always offered her indulgent father unwavering love and respect, believing his hard years had finally paid off through sheer courage and integrity. Lately, though, his association with Clay began to sow seeds of doubt in her mind. Puzzling inconsistencies started to align within her imaginative thoughts, forming a theory that linked odd bits of knowledge she had inadvertently gathered.

She knew that sometimes shipowners orchestrated the loss of their vessels to perpetrate fraud against insurers. The thought was disheartening, but clay's words suggested something of that nature. As she shook off the initial shock, pity welled up inside her, and she sought to justify her father's actions. He must have been desperate to succumb to such temptation, likely spurred on by his partner's influence. The urge to shield him consumed her. He needed to be rescued from the malicious forces that had led him astray. Recalling clay's assertion that he owed her a debt of gratitude, she was filled with a peculiar confidence that he'd honor it if she pleaded her case. Steeling herself, she waited until he came downstairs, then gestured for him to join her in the vacant drawing room.

"i suppose my father's occupied?"

"yes, he's drafting a letter," Clay replied, casually leaning against a chair, his eyes scrutinizing her as she stood before him, intense and composed. Her demeanor spoke volumes. She was close to the truth, and he genuinely felt for her; if he could allay her doubts, he would gladly do so.

"then he won't be down for a bit," she noted. "i need to speak with you. You've been trying to persuade him to go north with you, haven't you?"

"not exactly. I'm not sure i could persuade him; he's quite resolute. Do you not want him to go?"

"no!" she exclaimed. "you mustn't take him! and from now on, you must leave him alone. I can't let you pressure him into things he despises!"

Clay's grin widened at her fervor.

"it seems you suspect me of leading him astray. That's unfair to both of us. Don't you think your father has a mind of his own?"

"i know you have some influence over him, and i implore you not to wield it."

Clay pulled out a chair and gestured for her to sit.

"i think it's best we sit and thoroughly discuss this."

First off, your father and i go way back; we've faced tough situations together and shared some pretty rough patches. I think that gives us some kind of bond."

"that's not what i mean," ruth said firmly. Clay wanted to protect her feelings as much as he could.

"if you think there's some other influence, let me tell you, you're too young and inexperienced to really get what's going on. You hear something shocking and, without really understanding it, you jump to conclusions. Your dad's known as one of the most honest business guys in the state." he paused and chuckled. "honestly, he's getting so picky that i'm almost scared i'll have to drop him."

"that's what i want," ruth replied. "i mean, i want you to stop being business partners."

"so, you wouldn't mind still seeing me as a friend?"

"no," ruth answered slowly. "somehow, i think you might turn out to be a good friend."

"thanks. Now, listen up. I'm not going to defend my business reputation. I've taken on some risky deals and pulled them off, fighting off anyone trying to bring me down; but not all my business moves have been about taking over someone else's turf. You can't play the pirate all the time. Sometimes, when i'm doing a clean deal, i need a respectable partner as a sort of guarantee, so i'd ask your dad to join in. He's known as an honest guy, and having him with me made people less suspicious; i used him for that. I hope i've explained enough to ease your mind?"

Despite his humorous tone, ruth felt somewhat reassured. His explanation made sense, and she was glad to hold on to it, but it didn't completely eliminate her doubts.

"i don't want him involved in your northern trip," she insisted.

"why?"

Ruth hesitated, and Clay felt a surge of sympathy.

Her face was a mix of distress and confusion, but what struck him most was the unmistakable trust in her demeanor, a silent plea for his help.

"i'm scared; i fear nothing good will come of this," she said, her eyes imploring him. "please, don't let him be involved."

"alright," Clay replied, leaning in, his voice steady and sincere. "rest assured. I promise your father will have no role in what i plan to do at the wreck. Besides, he isn't aware of all my intentions concerning her. There's nothing in them that could harm him; in fact, if things go as planned, it'll benefit him in ways he wouldn't expect—and you won't disapprove of."

Ruth sensed the honesty in his words; he was offering a guarantee more significant than she could fully comprehend. His tone had a calming effect, and she felt a rush of relief.

"thank you," she said, standing up. "please excuse my bluntness—it felt necessary."

"take it as a compliment; it shows you have some faith in me after all." he smiled softly. "you won't regret it."

Ruth departed with a newfound lightness. She wasn't sure if she had been too demanding of clay, but she felt confident in his trustworthiness.

CHAPTER TWENTY-SIX.

As soon as Aynsley joined her at Victoria, the sleek schooner-yacht, equipped with auxiliary engines, set sail. For the first couple of days, the wind was favorable, but even with plenty of canvas spread, Clay insisted on maintaining full steam.

"she'd glide along efficiently with the propeller disengaged and the gaff, topsails up," Aynsley argued. "keeping the fires stoked is just wasting coal."

"i'm fine covering the cost," Clay responded. "i'm just used to moving fast, and i like to feel like we're making progress."

"we might get there too quickly," Aynsley warned. "we could encounter ice near the island."

"if that's the case, we can wait until it clears. Keep her at top speed for me."

Aynsley agreed, though his father's urgency troubled him. Honestly, Clay was aching to start work on the wreck. He'd never ruined a project by rushing in the past, but he had a nagging sense that delaying could mean missing his chance. His life was under threat, and he needed to wrap up his current tasks while he still could. Once they lost sight of Vancouver island, the wind shifted against them, so they furled the sails and continued under steam power. She made good progress for two days, but as the wind picked up and the sea grew rougher, her speed dwindled. The heavy masts weighed her down, causing her to struggle through the churning waves.

By the third afternoon, the weather had only worsened. Clay stood impatiently on the drenched aft deck, scanning their surroundings. Gray mist shrouded the horizon, and row after row of frothy waves rolled in front of them. The yacht lurched over the towering swells, pitching violently, her bow plunging into the surf, which washed over her low bulwarks and cascaded through the gap amidships in streaky torrents.

The soot plumed out from her funnel, trailing far to leeward, and Clay could feel the steady pulse of the engines. Despite this, it was clear she was barely moving, and he motioned to Aynsley, who made his way to join him.

"i've been monitoring that log since lunch. She's struggling badly," he pointed out, tapping the brass dial on the taffrail. "there's hardly enough rough sea to explain it, and it looks like they're really pushing the engines."

"saltom's having issues with his condenser," Aynsley clarified. "he didn't want to stop since you're eager to get moving, but the vacuum's dropping."

"let's go have a word with him. But i'm no engineer, so you'd better come along."

Descending a slick iron ladder, they found saltom in the engine room, crouched by a large iron casting. Nearby, the piston-rods and connecting-rods flashed with a silvery glint between the rhythmic cylinders and the spinning cranks, spraying oil everywhere as the floor-plates and frames vibrated in sync with the engine's clamorous beat. The engineer, holding a flickering lamp, watched the vacuum gauge needle bob anxiously.

"you've lost another half inch since i last checked," Aynsley said, bending down beside him.

"she's giving me a hard time," saltom responded. "soon, i'll need to cut back on the hot-well feed, and our fresh water supply isn't abundant."

"are you sure it's not the air-pumps?"

"i can't find anything wrong with them. I suspect there's an obstruction in the main inlet valve, and the tubes might be clogged, although the last batch i pulled out were clean."

"why didn't you replace that faulty condenser if you had doubts?" Clay interjected sharply. "i haven't skimped on your budget, and this boat needs to move when i say so."

Saltom looked up, startled by clay's harsh tone.

"i don't squander company resources," he began, but Clay cut him off.

"forget that! she's not running. What's your plan to fix it?"

Aynsley watched the exchange with growing concern.

Clay had a fiery temper, but he usually managed to keep it under control. Now, however, his voice was rough with fury.

"i want to stop her right away and see what's wrong, but it's a big job to tear apart a surface-condenser, and these castings are heavy to move," he said.

"she'd drift into the trough of the sea when her propeller stopped, and the rolling would make it nearly impossible to work," Aynsley explained.

"well," Clay said curtly, "what do you suggest?"

"i'd like a day or two to overhaul her in calm waters, maybe in some inlet," the engineer replied.

"do you know a suitable spot?" Clay asked Aynsley.

"yes, but it's a bit off our course. It'll take a day to get there."

Clay frowned and turned to the engineer. "he'll sail her in, but if you're not done in forty-eight hours, i'll fire you and scrap this machine!" he then touched Aynsley's arm. "let him handle it, and give your orders to hartley."

They headed up to the deck, and Aynsley watched as his father lit a cigar, only to angrily toss it away. After speaking to the skipper, Aynsley returned to find Clay standing in the deckhouse with a small bottle and a wineglass. Recognizing the bottle, Aynsley quickly exited. A few minutes later, the yacht altered her course to the east and they set the foresail and two jibs. By midnight, with the wind blowing hard, the engines stopped and they hoisted the reefed mainsail.

Aynsley was surprised to see Clay back on deck but didn't speak to him, sensing his father's dangerous mood. At dawn, the schooner was slicing through the waves, close-hauled, with her lee channels submerged and white seas crashing over her bow. Aynsley found his father sitting at the foot of the mainmast, the only dry spot on the deck.

It seemed like he'd been up on deck since midnight.

"she's moving fast, but hartley thinks she's pushing her limits," Aynsley noted. "there's a lot of pressure on the rigging, and it might be safer to slow her down and reduce the sail."

"let her ride it out," Clay replied. "the designer insisted on the finest oregon timber for the masts, and i remember paying a premium for them. Now it's time for them to prove their worth."

"all right," Aynsley agreed; but as the wind continued to pick up, he remained on deck, observing the increasing tilt of the vessel. The ship, driven hard by the sails and submerged in the froth, fiercely cut through the churning waves. By mid-morning, the wind shifted to the east, knocking the schooner off its course and forcing them into long tacks. It was late in the day by the time a range of forest-covered hills emerged ahead. Rocky points and scattered islands broke the coastline, and as they drew nearer, Aynsley climbed the fore rigging with his binoculars. He spotted a gap in the surf some three or four miles away, identifying it as their target. Descending, he conferred with the captain before explaining the situation to clay.

"from the tidal charts, we estimate the ebb tide started about two hours ago," he said. "that means the current is flowing strong out of the inlet, and we'll be facing the wind as we go in. I know the area quite well since i once took shelter there, but hartley wasn't present then. After checking the chart, he's a bit uneasy about attempting it during the ebb tide."

"if we wait for the flood tide, how long would that take?"

"about nine hours. There's a rocky patch at the entrance and not much room to maneuver. Plus, saltom wants to beach her, which means we'd have to wait until near high tide unless we go in right away."

"it's still a risky spot."

"let's go for it. We'll take our chances!"

As they drew closer, Aynsley stood in the rigging, examining the shore through his binoculars. He noticed the wet band above the surf line, indicating the water level had dropped; the inlet looked ominous. On the starboard side, massive boulders peeked through the frothy waves; to port, a rocky shoal loomed. Beyond these hazards, a deep, narrow channel cut its way inland between the hills. The wind howled down the channel, whipping the water into a frothy frenzy.

"we'll need speed; better unfurl the mainsail all the way," he advised the skipper when he came down. For a few minutes, the crew bustled about, shaking out the reef, and then, as the yacht leaned hard into the wind, Aynsley took the wheel. The sea calmed a bit closer to shore, but the yacht strained under the full sail, with water splashing over her bow and flowing ankle-deep across the sharply tilted deck. The tall masts bent toward the leeward side, the rigging sang with tension, and the crew stood steady on the inclined, wet planks, ready to adjust the sails. Up front, a drenched sailor swung the lead line through the spray that whipped around the rigging, his voice barely audible through the roar of the water.

"seven fathoms!" he missed a beat and his next shout came sharper. "shoaling, sir! down to six and a quarter!"

There was a tense silence as he gathered the line, the yacht charging towards the beach.

"four fathoms deep!" he called.

"ready about!" Aynsley shouted, pulling the wheel hard. "helm's a-lee!"

The sails flapped furiously as the yacht leveled out, rocks and pine trees closing in as her bow swung around. Then she shifted to the opposite tack, aiming for the channel entrance, with boulders dangerously close to leeward and the tide pushing against her.

The boat veered back, hampered by the trailing screw. When a fierce gust leaned her over until the sea was level with her rail, clay, clinging to a shroud, shot a sharp glance at his son. Aynsley stared ahead, his expression firm but calm, even as the frothing waves roared around the boulders, seeming to rush towards them. Clay wasn't much of a seaman, but he could tell they were barely making headway. Still, he trusted his son. The leadsman had found bottom at three fathoms, yet Aynsley hadn't turned her around. There was a lull along the shore, and he was determined to exploit it, even though it looked like they might crash any second. Then, she suddenly straightened, swung, and surged off on the opposite tack toward a chaotic white turmoil where the stream and shore-running sea clashed over the shoal. They were almost upon it when she swung around again, and five minutes later she raced back with the ominous white patch off her lee bow—not quite far enough to clear it. On the other side, a narrow tongue of beach jutted out, closing in the entrance. It seemed impossible to squeeze through, and in those few moments as they hurtled toward the rocks, Clay felt a newfound respect for his son. Aynsley had proven himself shrewd in business, a popular figure socially, and now he was entirely admirable at the yacht's helm. His finely built frame was tense, his wet face resolute, and his eyes sparkled with intense focus. The boy exhibited impressive nerve and judgment. Clay's pride in him deepened his resolve to protect his son's future. Aynsley must carry an honored name, and it was unthinkable that any disgrace should shadow him because of his father's mistakes. Aynsley shouted to the skipper, who anxiously watched the shore.

"there's not much room! i'll let her shoot well ahead before i fill on her."

"look at those boys handling the fore-sheets!"

Hartley gripped the helm tightly as he issued the command. The schooner swung around, charging forward with its sails flapping in the wind. It was a daring but precise maneuver—Aynsley had to rely on the ship's momentum to navigate the treacherous waters against the tide. If the schooner lost speed before he could set her on a new tack, the rocks would be unforgiving. The skipper stood firm amidship, just clear of the jerking foresail-boom; the crew readied the fore-sheets, and clay, leaning on the aft rail, intently watched his son. Aynsley's stance was poised yet relaxed; his eyes sharp and confident, hands gripping the wheel with authority.

"lee sheets!" he commanded, yanking the wheel hard. The schooner's bow slowly turned, the flapping sails caught the wind, and she gained speed. As the deck tilted, boulders drifted past her side. With another careful turn, she left them behind, gliding swiftly into open, calmer waters. Ten minutes later, they lowered the headsails, and Aynsley gently steered her onto the beach. There she would sit, waiting until engineer saltom finished the necessary repairs.

CHAPTER TWENTY-SEVEN.

Late on a dreary evening, Jimmy and his friends sat down for a few minutes' rest on the beach of a desolate island along the northern coast. With Jaques' assistance, they had equipped the sloop, setting sail far earlier in the season than advisable, driven by the fear that Clay might beat them to their destination. The journey had been grueling; they spent days hove to in relentless gales that pushed the sloop off course, often seeking shelter from the punishing weather. Yet, they resolutely continued their voyage northward.

The strong winds battered their smaller boat, a violent contrast to the more stable schooner-yacht that Clay commanded. Pushing through the steep, attacking waves caused the shrouds to strain heavily, eventually starting a leak beneath the channel plates. After hours of relentless pumping, they reluctantly conceded to find a sheltered harbor for crucial repairs. Fortunately, the task required nothing more than some dedicated caulking, but accessing the leak meant they had to beach the sloop. Jimmy seized the opportunity to refill their water-breakers.

Taking the water containers ashore in the dory, they hauled the small craft up and, after filling the breakers, decided to explore the island. Their vessel wouldn't float again until near high tide, giving them ample time. The island was desolate, with only a few patches of stunted trees, but they enjoyed the walk despite their weariness, the unusual exercise, and gnawing hunger—they hadn't troubled themselves with lunch.

Bethune, finding a sheltered spot, lit his pipe and lazily gazed around. Dingy clouds raced across the sky, and the dark, leaden sea crashed restlessly against the stones. A light breeze from the sea had ushered them ashore initially, but it had since shifted, now blowing cold and brisk from the land. The raw chill cut through them, a reminder of the harsh, unforgiving nature of the place.

Bethune shivered.

"we really should get on board," he stated. "but i wish we had a crew to handle the heavy lifting and row us to the yacht. I'd enjoy my dinner more if i didn't have to cook it myself. Funny how we cling to the idea of luxury."

"if you were a lobster fisherman, you'd know better," moran replied.

"true enough," Bethune laughed. "guess it's how you're raised; but it's rare for you to drop these insights on us. Still, i can't stop thinking about our rival, sitting in his yacht's saloon with a sharp steward ready to serve him, while we hunch over tin plates in our cramped cabin, knees pressed against the centerboard trunk and heads brushing the beams. It's a tough comparison."

"the sooner you stop philosophizing and get moving, the sooner we'll have dinner," Jimmy reminded him.

"i wish it was hank's turn to cook, although eating his food isn't much fun. At least we don't have to fight the stove on a tilt anymore;

it'll be nice to cook upright for a change. That's why i was waiting for the tide to lift her."

"she's afloat now," moran pointed out. Bethune glanced up, confirming it as the sloop's mast began to shift against the rocky backdrop. Then a chain clattered, and the boat started drifting faster.

"she's taking up slack on her anchor," said Jimmy. "we should get on board. I didn't give her much anchor line because i wanted to keep her off the rocks."

"let me finish my pipe first," Bethune said lazily, and they remained seated for a moment longer. The sloop bobbed, swaying in the swirling gusts. When moran glanced back at her, he sprang up suddenly.

"she's moving away!"

They watched as a gap formed between the mast and a boulder.

It was clear she was drifting out to sea.

"the wind's shifted since we left!" Jimmy shouted. "when she swung around, her cable twisted around the anchor and yanked it free."

"we need to get to the dory!" Bethune cried, racing along the shore.

"no point!" Jimmy called after him. "there's no time." as he kicked off his heavy sea-boots, he added, "she's dragging the anchor along the bottom, but it won't hold her for long."

The others could see he was right. The water deepened sharply beyond the half- tide line, and once the boat lifted her anchor, she'd move quickly.

"it's too cold to swim, and you won't catch her!" Bethune argued, gasping for breath.

"i have to try," said Jimmy, flinging off his jacket and diving into the icy water. The others left him and sprinted along the beach, stumbling over the rocks. The dory was some distance away, and darkness was closing in. The Resolute would drift downwind swiftly, and they feared she would vanish from sight before they could start the chase, but they might just be able to rescue their exhausted friend. There was no doubt he'd soon tire; the water was freezing, and a short, choppy swell disturbed the bay. On top of that, the dire circumstances spurred them on. They faced being stranded without food or shelter on the barren island in harsh weather. They didn't even have a fishing line, and Bethune remembered he had only three or four matches loose in his pocket. He stumbled into a dip between two boulders, injuring his leg, but he got up quickly, rushing on with moran clattering a few steps behind. Thankfully, the tide had almost brought the dory to them when they reached it. They shoved it off, jumped in, and rowed with fierce determination, each man pulling an oar.

The small boat lifted its bow and surged forward with each powerful stroke, but an incoming swell started to push against the wind as the tide rose, checking its progress. Despite the sharp cold air, sweat trickled down the men's faces as they rowed, hearts pounding and breath coming laboriously. They kept glancing ahead, though spotting their friend in the choppy water was nearly impossible; a man's head is a small target in such conditions. The Resolute remained in view, not much farther offshore, giving them hope that Jimmy might have reached it. If so, they could still overtake the boat before the wind fully caught its sails. This thought energized them, compelling every muscle to propel their dory faster over the erratic swells.

When Jimmy plunged into the icy water, he gasped as the cold enveloped him, stealing his breath and paralyzing his limbs. An instinctive urge came over him to scramble back to safety, but this only lasted a moment. Before his feet could touch the bottom, he suppressed the impulse. Steeling himself, he thrust his left hand forward and struck out with vigorous strokes. Jimmy was practical rather than imaginative, endowed with spartan resolve. From his time on sailing ships, he had learned that necessity overcomes discomfort. Though he couldn't think in broad terms, he knew his mission: catch the sloop. Being the strongest swimmer of the group, he tackled the task with the unthinking stubbornness that defined him when effort was required. His focus zeroed in on his goal, not the peril he faced. After the initial shock subsided, his suffering dulled, but he realized with a dull awareness that he was making agonizingly slow progress.

Jimmy battled through the water, his clothes weighing him down, the waves pushing him back. The only thing working in his favor was the wind at his back, the ripples guiding him forward instead of crashing into his face. He swam with a powerful, determined stroke, but he knew the Resolute would drift away twice as fast unless he could catch her while she was still in the shallows. Whenever the swell lifted him up, he could see her, but he couldn't tell if he was closing the gap. She wasn't close, and every moment she kept moving farther away. He hoped the cable dragging along the uneven bottom might slow her down, but the reality grew grimmer with every stroke.

The cold bit into him, draining his energy. His legs started to cramp, his breath came short. Still, he pressed on. Turning back wasn't an option; he wouldn't make it to the beach before giving out. For a spell, he lost sight of the boat, his eyes stinging with seawater as the increasingly steep swells broke over his head. Dreading the distance left to cover, he barely looked up.

Then, he stopped for a brief moment, lifting his head. A glimmer of hope stirred within him; the Resolute was closer than he had imagined. This was his chance for one final, all-out push. As he neared, she had swung around, broadside to the wind. Mustering the last of his strength, Jimmy clutched the rail midship. Exhausted, he knew he faced another challenge: getting aboard.

As she drifted, his body dangled outward, unable to get his knees against the hull. Even if he could, he lacked the strength to haul himself on deck, and no ropes were there to grab onto. Then, a thought struck him: the wire bobstay, running from the bowsprit's end and fastening near the waterline. It was his only shot. With every last ounce of resolve, he struggled to reach it, knowing his survival depended on it.

He gingerly moved his hands along the rail, fully aware that if they slipped, he might lose his grip for good. Inch by painstaking inch, he moved forward, pausing now and then to attempt climbing up the shrouds. He slipped, leaving only three fingers clinging to the rail; the near miss left him shaken. He waited to regain his composure, then inched forward again, one hand over the other, slowly but surely.

As he progressed, the boat's bow rose sharply out of the water, making it harder to keep his grip as the weight on his arms increased. Finally, he managed to grab the bowsprit, splashing weakly as he sought the wire stay with his feet. Just as he neared safety, a surge of terror washed over him. He found the wire, nudged his foot along it, and heaved himself up onto the bowsprit, collapsing onto the deck, spent and motionless.

After a moment, he gathered enough strength to realize that staying prone would mean succumbing to the cold and his sheer exhaustion. Forcing himself up, he staggered aft and stumbled into the cabin. There was no liquor aboard, but he discovered some clothes that, while damp, were better than nothing. He rubbed himself down and dressed, chewing on a ship's biscuit as he did so.

Revitalized, albeit minimally, he ventured back on deck. The boat was drifting fast out to sea; he needed to get the anchor chain in and hoist some sail to regain control. Grabbing the chain, he was struck by how depleted he was from the swim. The chain was heavy, but he had managed it before, even with the anchor holding and the boat's resistance against him. This time, though, he was defeated after laboriously hauling a mere few feet. Determined, he tried again, lifting several more feet before he had to secure the chain around the bits with great effort.

He sat down to catch his breath and scanned the horizon for the dory. He spotted it, though it seemed quite a distance away. With the wind picking up, he wasn't sure if it could catch up to the sloop on its own. He considered setting sail since the foresail wouldn't be too hard to hoist, but the Resolute wouldn't sail effectively with the heavy cable dragging from her bow.

Jimmy recalled there was plenty of cable stored below deck—potentially enough to let several fathoms drop to the seabed. The added weight might serve as an anchor, slowing the sloop. It all hinged on the water depth. He released the chain and watched anxiously as it clanked out of the pipe. For a while, it just kept unraveling, but then he felt a jolt as the chain slowed. The lower end had found the bottom, but the ship might still lift a few fathoms before it could stop entirely.

The chain extended in a slanted line, and Jimmy noticed the absence of splashing at the bow—a sign the sloop was still adrift. Then the rattling of the cable started again, indicating more length was being deployed. Finally, she came to a slow stop. He felt a light tug and saw white ripples break angrily against the planking. Either she had stopped or was drifting very slowly now.

Jimmy climbed onto the cabin top, waving his jacket so his comrades in the dory would see he was on board. That done, he retreated below deck to escape the biting wind. There was nothing more he could do for now.

It was a while before the dory finally bumped against the side of the sloop, and moran clambered aboard, stepping into the cabin.

Jimmy couldn't see his face, but the man's gruff voice carried an unusual tone.

"that was one heck of a swim, buddy," he said. "i was afraid you wouldn't make it."

"me too," Jimmy replied with a tired smile. "i was too exhausted to throw the cable when i got on board."

"naturally," moran agreed sympathetically. "now just relax and let us handle things."

Bethune then came over and placed a hand on Jimmy's shoulder.

"thanks, my friend. Neither Hank nor i could have reached her."

None of them were the sentimental type, and Jimmy felt that enough had been said.

"i'm a bit worried about my heavy jacket and sea boots," he said. "i'll need them."

"right," said moran. "once we've got the sail up, we'll head back and look for them."

Jimmy protested. They were tired and hungry, and rowing back to the beach against the rising breeze would be tough. But moran just laughed, and Bethune insisted he stay put when Jimmy tried to get up to help them. He lit the stove, and when they called him, the reefed mainsail was flapping overhead. Bethune was in the dory, and moran, kneeling under the jib, was freeing a coil of chain from the anchor's fluke.

"i guess this caused the trouble," moran said. "we won't be long. Once you've made a few tacks, you can signal with a light."

He jumped into the dory, which vanished into the dark. Jimmy navigated the sloop ahead, close-hauled, until he could make out the boulders on a point. He then tacked and sailed along the shore, stopping briefly to light a lantern. Soon after, he heard a shout, and when he hove the boat to, there was the splash of oars. The dory emerged from the darkness, and moran, grabbing the rail, tossed a jacket and a pair of long boots onto the deck.

"got them all right," he said.

They were only a few feet from high tide; the beach was quite steep.

"i must have had the sense to toss them well out of the way, although i don't recall doing it," Jimmy replied with a laugh.

"we're about to have a better supper than i had expected not too long ago," Bethune noted as he hauled the dory ashore. Jimmy handed the helm to moran and went below deck to help prepare the meal.

CHAPTER TWENTY-EIGHT.

As Jimmy finally caught sight of the island where the wreck lay, a ghostly white glow shimmered among the dense mist clinging to the shore. Much of the landscape remained obscured, but the vapor's sharp outline hinted at something solid hidden behind it. The wind, though gentle, began to pick up as they sailed slowly forward. The fog receded just enough to reveal a broad, flat expanse glinting in the morning light. Closer to them, two tall, detached masses stood out, cold gray-white against a strip of deep indigo sea. Then, as the breeze faltered, the mist dropped again like a theatrical curtain.

"ice!" moran muttered. "looks like we got here too early."

"it seems to be piling up north of the point," Bethune noted, surveying the scene. "i think we'll be safe in the bay unless some of that thin, sharp ice starts drifting around."

Jimmy brought the boat to a halt and lit his pipe thoughtfully.

"we need to think this through, and we might as well wait for a clearer view," he said. "it doesn't look like we can start working just yet. If any large ice floes drifted across the shallows at high tide, we'd be in a tough spot in the bay. On the flip side, the ice will probably linger until a strong wind breaks it up, and i don't fancy being out at sea in wild weather with it nearby. Plus, the fog comes in thick, and the nights are still pretty dark."

The others agreed and fell into a brooding silence. No matter which decision they made, delays seemed inevitable. While it was a relief to know they had reached the island first, they were acutely aware that Clay couldn't be far behind them. The advantage of an early arrival could easily be lost if they didn't complete their task before he showed up.

The fog lingered all day and thickened as night descended. But with the red dawn came clearer air, hinting at a change. Jimmy maneuvered the boat toward the shore, his binoculars sweeping over the beach as they neared the sandy channel. This part of the island was free of ice, and after consulting one another, they chose to enter the bight. It seemed safer there, and they wanted to feel like their voyage was complete, ready to start their work.

By the afternoon, strong winds blew off the shore. The sloop rested in calm waters near the beach, but when night fell, the surf roared against the sands and the sound of cracking ice reached their ears. The noise was often terrifying but would fade away, and although they took turns keeping anchor watch, no ice floes troubled them. By dawn, most of the ice had vanished, leaving white patches shining far out at sea. Still, the wind blew too strongly for them to leave their shelter.

They waited two days, anxiously scanning for any sign of smoke on the horizon, but nothing broke the skyline. Finally, the wind died down. On a gray morning, they towed the Resolute out into a flat calm, although a steep swell and thin drizzle obscured the sea. The sloop plunged wildly over the long waves, jerking the dory back despite the crew's efforts at the oars. It was nearly noon when they managed to pick up their cross-bearings and anchored by the wreck.

No one mentioned stopping for lunch. Jimmy suited up in his diving gear as soon as he could. He found the wreck, which eased his anxiety, but had to resurface without entering the hold. The ship had shifted since he last saw it, now lying almost on its side with its upper works heavily damaged. The gap they had previously crawled through was now blocked by broken beams.

Jimmy figured the heavy ice, floating deep in the water, had grazed her upper parts as it drifted out to sea. Moran went down next and, on his return, reported that an entrance could be made, though it would take some effort. Bethune, armed with a crowbar, worked alongside. By nightfall, they had managed to remove several obstructing timbers and discovered a significant amount of sand that needed to be shifted. They devoured a hearty supper and went to sleep, exhausted.

The next day was more of the same. They started at first light, but by noon, it was clear they could only hope to clear the path for an entrance the following day. Everyone felt the effects of their hard labor and the strain of breathing compressed air. When it was Jimmy's turn to go down toward evening, he leaned on the coaming, hesitant to put on the diving gear.

"i'll be ready once i finish this pipe," he said. "you'd better tighten that pump-gland in the meantime. I didn't get enough air last time."

Moran got to work on it, and although every moment counted, Jimmy didn't rush him. He stood there, staring out at the sea with a sense of lethargy. A fine rain was falling, there was barely any wind, and belts of fog streaked the dim gray water between him and the horizon. He watched one of these fog belts when it seemed to part, and a blurred shape emerged. Startled, Jimmy dropped his pipe and scrambled to the cabin top. He could make out a patch of a white hull and a tall mast. As he called out to the others, a short funnel appeared, trailing a line of smoke along the edge of the fog.

"we don't need binoculars to know whose boat that is," he said harshly.

They recognized her immediately, and their expressions turned grim.

"Clay didn't waste any time," Bethune said. "looks like a showdown is inevitable. There's no point in fleeing now. We might as well stop diving until we figure out if continuing is worth it."

After securing the pumps and gear, they waited, eyes trained on the approaching yacht. It advanced at a steady pace, stopping about three or four hundred yards away. They watched the anchor drop and heard the chain rattle, but there was no further activity on the vessel.

"i bet Clay knows exactly who we are," moran said.

"absolutely," Bethune replied. "we'll hear from him soon enough, but he won't rush to send a boat over. As it's getting late, we should have supper."

As they finished eating, a sleek gig, manned by uniformed sailors, pulled alongside their sloop. The helmsman handed Jimmy two notes. In the cabin, Jimmy opened them, revealing two sheets of fine paper adorned with an embossed flag and the yacht's name. One note stated that Mr. Clay invited them to supper on his yacht. The other, longer note was from Aynsley, expressing his hope to see them despite uncertain past relations and urging them not to refuse his father's invitation.

"do you think Clay made him write this?" Jimmy asked.

"i doubt it," Bethune said. "i'd guess Aynsley sent it without Clay knowing. Aynsley has his reasons, but he's not part of clay's scheme."

"either way, i'm not going. I have no desire to dine with clay."

Bethune chuckled, gesturing to his pilot jacket, shriveled and stained from saltwater, and his old sea boots.

"our attire isn't exactly yacht-ready, and i have a feeling it might be smarter to stay put."

Despite the circumstances, we'll have to meet him eventually. You should write a polite refusal, though i doubt we can match his fancy stationery."

Jimmy tore a page from his notebook and scribbled for a moment with a pencil. Then he read it aloud:

"Mr. Farquhar and his friends regret that they can't leave their boat but would welcome Mr. Clay's visit."

"perfect!" exclaimed Bethune. "you've even sealed it with a thumbprint, and well, we don't have an envelope anyway."

With the crew rowing away with the note, the three men gathered in the cramped cabin.

"do you think he'll come?" moran asked.

"oh, definitely. But he'll probably eat first and take his time," Bethune replied. "i'm a bit concerned because if he doesn't show up, we should expect trouble."

"well, if he's looking for trouble, he'll find it," moran drawled from his spot on a locker. Jimmy sat in thoughtful silence, puffing on his cigarette. He knew Clay was shrewd and ruthless—if worse came to worst, they were cut off from any outside help by miles of empty sea. Clay had a strong crew, likely well-paid and loyal, for he wouldn't embark on such a mission with untrustworthy men. If Clay used force, they would be severely outnumbered, and seeking justice afterward would be tough. With Clay having numerous potential witnesses and them being only three, odds were against them. The situation required delicate handling, and Jimmy was relieved to have Bethune around. Still, if push came to shove, they wouldn't go down easily.

After a while, Jimmy stepped outside to check the weather. The rain had ceased, replaced by low-hanging mist, but a half-moon was rising through a clear patch in the sky. The gentle swell rolled beneath the sloop, lifting and lowering it in a steady rhythm.

Jimmy could see the yacht's anchor light not far away, its yellow glimmer seeping from the saloon windows. Despite the clear visibility, there were no sounds indicating a boat was being prepared to come over. The chill air in the cockpit drove him back into the cabin, where the others had lit the lamp. They sat in a heavy silence, their conversation sparse over the next hour. They could hear the halyards tapping against the mast, the ripple of water sloshing beneath the floorboards, and the gentle tide lapping against the hull. Moran suddenly raised his hand, the tension breaking as the rhythmic splash of oars reached their ears.

"that means he's ready to negotiate," Bethune remarked. Five minutes later, the yacht's boat pulled up alongside, and Clay climbed aboard.

"take a break ashore, guys, and come back when we signal," he told his crew, then turned to Jimmy. "i'm here for a talk."

"come below," Jimmy said, sliding the hatch open. "watch your step, it's cramped down there."

Clay bumped his head before finding a spot on a locker, where he sat, taking in the scene. The light from the bulkhead lamp cast a dim glow on the rough, utilitarian interior of the cabin. Moisture condensed on the low beams, the floorboards were damp and cluttered with coils of rope. A torn sail protruded from the forecastle door, and damp blankets were draped over lockers to dry near the rusty stove. The entire setting spoke of no-nonsense, practical frugality, matching the ragged, work-worn clothes of the men around him. Despite their attire, Clay could see the determination in their faces. They, in turn, observed that he appeared unwell, his face pale and puffy, with heavy shadows under his eyes.

"so, my invitation didn't entice you to come over," Clay said. "were you concerned i might whisk you away to sea?"

"not exactly," Bethune replied. "we figured you wouldn't resort to such a crude tactic. Consider it more a concern about a sudden shift in the wind."

"you see, it's a pretty vulnerable spot."

"that's true," Clay agreed. "you don't have any steam to help you weather a breeze. But let's get straight to the point. I offered you five thousand dollars for the first shot at salvaging this wreck. I'll up it to six thousand."

"that your final offer?"

"it is. No point in dragging this out. I've bid the maximum i think it's worth."

"and if we refuse?"

"it wouldn't be wise. You don't have a claim on this wreck; in a sense, i do. If we can't strike a deal, i'll start work immediately. My yacht can handle a storm, and our gear is robust enough to operate in rough conditions. You've got a small sailboat and mediocre equipment. As soon as the wind picks up, you'll have to call it quits."

"i imagine you haven't laid out all your advantages," Bethune said, his eyes narrowing.

Clay studied him, then smiled. "that's correct. I've been trying to be polite."

"so, you're holding back your strongest arguments. If we don't accept your offer, there's little chance we can recover anything from the wreck?"

"you've got it," Clay replied, his smile widening.

"the odds are against us. Perhaps i should be honest. The truth is, we've already recovered something valuable."

Clay's expression sharpened.

"then you're craftier than i thought, and you kept your cards close last time. But maybe it's time for full disclosure. What have you found?"

Bethune pulled out his notebook.

"first off, two bags of gold; the weight and markings, from what we could discern—"

"forget it," Clay cut in. "those don't count. You can keep your share of that. Get to the main point."

"one iron-clamped, sealed case. The stencil marks, though partially worn, seem to be d.o.c. In a circle; the impression on the seals matches the attached tracing."

Bethune paused, fixing his gaze on Clay with a steady intensity. "i suppose you know what these are?"

Clay retorted sharply, "and do you?"

"we opened the case."

A heavy silence settled over the room, and nobody moved. When Clay finally spoke, his voice betrayed a hint of unease.

"where is the case now?"

"it's not here," Bethune replied dryly. "if we don't show up to claim it soon, or if anyone else tries to take it, it'll go straight to the under-writers."

Clay raised an eyebrow. "you've taken precautions, i see."

"we did our best," Bethune said with modest pride.

"you thought you might sell me the box?"

Jimmy, brimming with tension, interjected sternly, "no! that wasn't our plan. When we let you make an offer for the wreck—"

Clay cut him off with a dismissive gesture. "it was to lure me in, no need to elaborate. Fine. I suggested laying down our cards, so now i'll tell you something unexpected. There's a duplicate box on board, and it has the gold."

Jimmy looked startled, moran furrowed his brow in confusion, while Bethune stared openly perplexed. Clay seemed quietly entertained by their reactions.

"you don't understand?" he asked. "no reason you should, but it's easily verified. Now, let me ask you straight—what do you plan to do with the gold once you get it?"

"deliver it to the underwriters and claim our salvage," Jimmy answered promptly.

"no other plans?"

"none."

"then i propose a trade. Give me the case you have, and i'll lead you to the one with the gold. You won't recover it without my help."

A weighty silence fell upon the room as the three partners exchanged puzzled glances. Clay remained calmly seated, offering no further explanation. The enigma of the situation eluded them, and Clay wasn't about to clarify. They were at a loss for what to do next.

"do you know where this other case is?" Bethune finally asked.

"i'm pretty sure i do," Clay replied.

"i suggest one of you come down to help me—preferably Mr. Farquhar."

"so, you're planning to go down there!" Jimmy exclaimed.

"i'm heading down first thing tomorrow morning, whether you join me or not. But what about my offer?" Clay inquired.

"we can't decide just yet," Bethune responded. "we need some time to think it over."

"alright," Clay conceded. "regardless, i have to start in the morning. If you prefer, we can shelve the discussion until we find the case." he paused and smiled at Jimmy. "you don't strike me as a nervous guy, and you don't need to worry. I've never put on a diving suit, while you have some experience. I'm also willing to use your boat and let your friends handle the pumps."

"i'm not scared," Jimmy shot back. "the real problem is that the path into the strong-room isn't cleared yet. It'll take at least a day to get rid of the sand that's piled up against the opening."

"then i suppose i'll have to wait. I'll send my diver over to help at dawn," Clay offered. "when everything is ready, just let me know. If there are no other suggestions, i think i'll head back now."

Moran signaled to the boat's crew, and once Clay had departed, the group sat thoughtfully in the cabin.

"i'll admit, this has taken an unexpected turn," Bethune said. "it's clear we're onto something significant, which might expose a clever fraud, but it's complicated by that genuine box of gold being shipped. I'm not sure how much it's our job to dig into this."

"you don't seem as quick to form theories as usual," Jimmy noted.

"i've come up with a couple, but they fall apart upon inspection. Given the possible risks of jumping to conclusions, i think we should hold off and see how things unfold. And since we're starting at dawn, it might be smart to get some sleep now."

CHAPTER TWENTY-NINE.

At dawn, the island still hung indistinct and shadowy across the dim waters as a gentle breeze stirred the air. The yacht's tender arrived, delivering clay's diver and a top-notch set of pumps. With the equipment assembled, the diver and moran joined the others below, each taking their shifts through the first half of the day to carve a path into the hold. They kept Clay updated on their progress, and by noon, aynsley was rowed over to the sloop.

"though you turned down my offer last night, i hope you'll join us on board for lunch," he said with a warm smile.

"we're swamped," Jimmy replied. "in fact, we're skipping meals entirely. The weather's unusually good, and we need access to the strong-room by sunset. It'll take us another three or four hours, minimum."

"that's a sensible excuse," Aynsley conceded. "honestly, i'm relieved you're too busy. My father is desperate to finish this job, and i don't want him fretting over delays." he paused, then continued candidly, "i need to ask a favor. He's not well. I understand there's some friction between you two, but could you try to keep things civil? stress isn't good for him."

"you have our word," Jimmy assured him. "it seems you're not entirely in the loop."

"not at all, and i prefer it that way."

"we wouldn't be able to share much even if you asked; but we noticed your father doesn't look well. Perhaps it's best if he stays topside."

"i wish i could," Aynsley said with a rueful smile. "but he's not one to be told what to do."

By evening, Clay came aboard. He settled in the cockpit, observing quietly as the men took turns working below, each driven by the promise of what lay hidden in the strong-room.

He asked a question every now and then, but mostly he waited quietly, watching the bubbles rise in a milky fizz. Finally, the diver surfaced, followed closely by Bethune, who was carrying a rope.

"the strong room's open," Bethune said excitedly. "pull on that line and see what you get!"

Moran pulled with all his might, feeling the resistance that fought back, while Jimmy leaned over in anticipation. When a sand-covered wooden case broke the surface, Jimmy grabbed it, nearly getting dragged overboard in the process. Bethune had to help him haul it onto the deck. Clay studied the case with a cool, analytical eye, examining the half-faded markings.

"you should get a good chunk for salvage on that, and i won't dispute your claim," he remarked. "keep it on board if you want; our diver's paid by the day. Now, if you're ready, we'll head down."

They carefully strapped him into his diving suit. When Bethune tried to give him a few pointers, Clay cut him off, saying his own man had briefed him thoroughly during the voyage. With a nod, Jimmy put on his helmet and descended the ladder, waiting at the bottom for clay. It felt surreal, walking along the ocean floor beside a man who had once been his adversary; now, he was in control. In fact, he had to assist Clay when they reached the entrance to the hold. Jimmy doubted Clay could have navigated the narrow passage between the shaft tunnel and the weed-covered wreck without help. Their lamps flickered weakly through the water that sucked in and out, and managing the signal-lines and air-pipes was no small feat. Despite his clumsiness and apparent frailty, Clay didn't lack nerve. When they finally crawled into the strong room, he stood still, moving his lamp in slow arcs. The pale light danced across the rough, iron-bound planks until it halted on one spot.

Clay waved Jimmy over, almost losing his balance as he stumbled and swayed awkwardly before steadying himself. Jimmy had his doubts, thinking Clay might be mistaken about the spot he indicated—a plank wedged between two iron plates on the deck of the wreck, now lying on its side instead of overhead. Jimmy shot Clay a questioning look, but the flashlight beam remained fixed on the plank. Trusting clay's intuition, Jimmy raised the crowbar and jammed it into a nearby joint at head level. Clay nodded, signaling that Jimmy was on the right track.

Jimmy knew they were racing against the clock. Clay was not in great health and had already been underwater for as long as was safe. If Clay collapsed, extracting him from the hold would be a monumental challenge. Still, Jimmy hesitated to abandon the search prematurely. Nightfall was approaching, the current was growing stronger, and it seemed unlikely they could make another dive that night. Jimmy was determined to finish what they had started.

The beam he worked on was decayed and soft, but two bolts and an iron strap reinforced its edge. Rotting wood peeled away in flakes, but dislodging a significant piece proved difficult, and the iron fixtures diverted his efforts. He checked on clay, who encouraged him with a nod, and then Jimmy resumed his work with renewed vigor. Minutes blurred into a single, relentless effort, only to be interrupted by a sudden shift in the water. He saw Clay swaying listlessly, as if about to collapse. Though his heavy boots and buoyant suit kept him upright, losing balance in a diving suit would be catastrophic. Jimmy had to get Clay out immediately.

Jimmy grabbed clay's arm and steered him towards the opening, pushing him along the side of the shaft tunnel. With immense relief, he managed to drag Clay out of the splintered beams at the entrance to the hold and stepped onto the seabed. No light filtered through the water, and even the silhouette of the sloop above had faded; but Jimmy had his signal line as a guide. He followed it, keeping his hand on clay's shoulder, until he felt the ripple of the tide around the ladder. He nudged Clay towards it and watched as he clumsily began to climb.

By the time Jimmy emerged on deck, Clay was already sitting there, slumping limply against the cabin top. As they removed his helmet, they could barely see in the near-darkness, but it was clear his lips were blue, and his pallid face was streaked with faint purple patches. He gasped and began fumbling awkwardly at the breast of his diving suit.

"i know what he needs!" Aynsley exclaimed. "get these things off him as quickly as you can! somebody get a spoon!"

They hurriedly stripped the canvas suit from the half-conscious man. Aynsley pulled a small bottle from his vest pocket and gave Clay a few drops of the liquid. Moments later, Clay feebly lifted himself.

"better now; not used to diving," he mumbled, turning to Jimmy as Aynsley and a seaman helped him into the waiting gig. "we'll get the case next time."

The gig rowed away, vanishing into the darkness. The three men on board watched it disappear.

"glad you managed to bring him up," Bethune remarked.

"i was terrified at first," Jimmy admitted. "maybe i should have surfaced sooner, but he was so determined to stay down."

"what about the case?"

"we didn't have enough time to reach it. It's not in the strong-room. He made me start cutting beneath the deck."

"the deck!" moran exclaimed. "then they must've hidden the stuff in the poop cabin!"

"i don't think so," Jimmy responded thoughtfully.

"i think there's a small space between the main beams and the cabin floor," Jimmy mused.

"and that's where the case is? that's quite puzzling," Bethune responded, intrigued.

"i suppose it is. The key point is that we should be able to reach the case within the hour."

"it's too dangerous. The tide's getting stronger, and it's going to be really dark. We've managed to avoid any serious trouble so far, and there hasn't been any sign of bad weather."

Reluctantly, Jimmy decided to wait until morning. Bethune went below deck to prepare supper. At dawn, Aynsley rowed over in the yacht's tiny dinghy. His anxious expression caught Jimmy's attention as he entered the cetacea's cabin, where Jimmy was cleaning some of the pump fittings by lamplight.

"how's Mr. Clay?" Jimmy asked.

"he looks very ill. I left him trying to get up and quietly rowed over to talk to you. Can you do anything to stop him from diving? i don't think he's fit for it."

"i'm afraid there's not much i can do. We're not on the best of terms, and if we argue, he'll get suspicious."

"couldn't you do something with the diving gear? the pressure and strain might be too much for him."

"we could disable our own pump, but we can't touch yours. He might insist on going alone."

"that wouldn't work," said Aynsley. "i wouldn't hesitate to sabotage our equipment, but he'd get so angry that the stress could be worse than the dive."

"then you've got to reason with him," Jimmy suggested.

Aynsley smiled wryly. "i've been trying to since we anchored, and it hasn't worked. You don't know my father." he gave Jimmy a serious look. "he intends for you to be his diving partner, and even though i have no right to ask, i'm pleading with you to look out for him."

Jimmy found it rather odd to be asked this favor; yet, he could see Aynsley's concern was genuine and felt a sense of responsibility towards him.

Clay had always been rough on them, but now he was sick and seemingly incapable of causing more harm.

"alright," he conceded. "i'll do what i can."

"thanks!" Aynsley responded, genuinely grateful. "i trust you, and i think my father feels safe with you too, even though he usually keeps his cards close to his chest."

"if you wait a moment, we can get you some coffee," Bethune offered.

"no, thanks," Aynsley replied. "i need to get back before anyone notices i'm gone. If my hot-headed father figures out why i'm here, things could get ugly."

He hopped into the dinghy and rowed silently into the fog that drifted between the vessels. Half an hour later, Clay arrived with the diver. His face was pale and strained, and Jimmy noticed he was laboring to breathe even after the minor effort of boarding the sloop.

"let me handle the rest of the job, sir," Jimmy suggested. "you'll be better off waiting here on deck until we bring up the case."

"i'm going down," Clay responded curtly. "you might need my help to get to it."

"at least wait until we break through the deck. That way, you'll spend less time underwater."

Clay hesitated but eventually agreed. He suggested moran and Bethune clear the area instead of his own diver, and within minutes, the two were underwater. They stayed down for a while; when they resurfaced and got out of their gear, Clay scrutinized Bethune.

"did you cut the hole?" he asked.

"yes," Bethune answered. "i think it's big enough."

"you didn't go through?"

"no, we'd been down long enough."

"hand me that brandy," Clay instructed a steward in the boat, and after downing a small glass, he turned to Jimmy. "let's get to work."

Jimmy descended the ladder, followed by clay, who walked steadily across the sand. The tide was low, the current barely moving, and the dim green water danced with strange refractions from the growing light above.

The sloop drifted above, casting a shadow like an opaque patch against the waters below, while the wreck loomed dark and formless before them. They reached it without trouble, and Jimmy flicked on his lamp, carefully clearing clay's air-pipe and line before crawling into the murky gap. Clay seemed to move with greater ease and confidence than the day before, and Jimmy felt a measure of reassurance as he guided him along the shaft tunnel. Gazing at the long strands of seaweed undulating mysteriously in the gloom, Jimmy recalled the fear he had overcome during his first dives. It looked like he needn't worry about his companion's nerve.

It was more challenging to get Clay into the strong-room, but eventually, they entered it safely. Jimmy noted that Bethune and moran had piled a bank of sand beneath the hole between the beams, which would make it easier to reach. As he prepared his air-pipe to enter, Clay made an insistent gesture. Jimmy was taken aback; the man clearly intended to go first. Climbing up after grabbing a timber wouldn't be too hard, but it did require some effort. Jimmy tried to convey this through gestures, but Clay dismissed his objections. Unable to properly communicate through silent gestures, and seeing clay's determination, Jimmy relented. Forcing him to stay might only arouse suspicion or lead to a confrontation.

Jimmy assisted him up, his concern mounting as clay's swollen legs and heavy boots disappeared through the opening. The space above was likely cramped and filled with wreckage, but the steady movement of clay's air-pipe and signal-line through the gap suggested he was moving without difficulty. Faint flashes of light, fragmented into wavering reflections, flickered out from the hole. Jimmy switched off his lamp to see them more clearly. Despite his resolve to keep his promise to Aynsley, he admitted that the tension he felt wasn't solely for clay's sake.

Recovering the case was crucial for their mission. If they failed now, deteriorating weather could thwart their next attempt or make the gold permanently unattainable. Jimmy started to worry that Clay should be coming out. Unaccustomed to diving and in fragile health, clay's chances of retrieving the case didn't seem promising. If Clay couldn't get it, Jimmy intended to dive in himself.

He tugged the line and got a signal back, nothing urgent—so he waited. Soon, the line and pipe began to move backward. Suddenly, a sharp flash of light warned him, and as he switched on his lamp, a dark, square object tumbled from the opening. It hit the sand and the impact murked up the water. A thrill of triumph surged through Jimmy. He shifted focus to help clay, who was emerging from the gap. But then, clay's legs slipped and he fell back. He didn't hit hard, just sort of sank until one foot touched the sand, writhing in odd spasms.

His buoyant suit kept him afloat, making him look awkward and ungainly. Yet, Jimmy felt a pang of alarm—this wasn't just clumsiness. Clay had lost control—too weak to balance the heavy helmet and weighted boots. Clearly helpless, it fell on Jimmy to rescue him from the wreck, a daunting task that required immediate action.

Jimmy hauled Clay through the opening into the hold, relieved to note that both air pipes were still running clear. Guiding him to the tunnel, he let Clay lean on it and gave him a push. Despite his bulk, clay's buoyant suit made him move like a floating object, though sometimes he drifted too far and veered off the tunnel.

Years later, Jimmy still remembered with a shiver the ordeal of reaching the outlet. He couldn't use his lamp, needing both hands free, and the fear of the pipes and lines tangling haunted him. He vaguely recalled pulling Clay down and dragging him through the water by his helmet, but the details were fuzzy. When they finally hit the level sand, Jimmy signaled urgently with his line and got a response. He looped a rope around clay's shoulders and held him steady as they were pulled toward the ladder. Moments later, Clay was hoisted onto the cetacea's deck, and Jimmy slumped down on the cabin top, feeling utterly drained. When someone removed his helmet, he saw Aynsley leaning over clay, trying to get him to drink something from a spoon. Jimmy wasn't sure Clay could take the restorative—his own exhaustion blurred his vision. Shortly after, Clay was moved into the gig, which set off for the yacht with the crew rowing hard. Jimmy turned to Bethune.

"i was scared i wouldn't get him up," he admitted, his voice weak. "he looks pretty bad."

"i think he is," Bethune replied, "and you're not looking too great yourself."

"the dizziness is the worst," Jimmy murmured. "i need to lie down. But wait—we found the case."

Bethune helped him into the cabin and settled him on a locker. Jimmy had a pounding headache and a sense of heaviness that only grew as the pain eased. Before long, he drifted into a deep sleep. While he slept, moran went below and brought up the case.

CHAPTER THIRTY.

When Jimmy woke up, the water was shrouded in thick fog. He slipped off the locker and, with his head brushing against the deck beams, turned to look at Bethune through bleary eyes.

"is it still dark?" he asked. "how long have i been out?"

"it's not dark yet. How are you feeling?"

"i think i'm okay. Did you manage to get the case?"

"sure did," Bethune grinned. "it's stashed safely beneath the floorboards, and it's hefty enough to make the salvage worthwhile. But i came down to give you this note from Aynsley. One of his crew delivered it, and his boat's waiting right alongside."

Jimmy unfolded the note, squinting to read it aloud in the cabin's dim light.

"i'd appreciate it if you could come over immediately. My father appears to be very ill, and he's insisting on seeing you."

"i think i should go," Jimmy said. "honestly, we couldn't have gotten the case without his help, and, in a way, i do feel sorry for him. He must've known he was taking a huge risk, but he was awfully brave."

"it probably won't hurt," Bethune agreed. "i have a feeling we've got nothing to worry about from him anymore. Still, i wish i could come along."

"i guess that wouldn't be appropriate," Jimmy said pensively.

"no, you can't bring your lawyer when visiting a sick man. But if he's not quite as bad off as Aynsley thinks, be cautious."

Jimmy climbed into the waiting boat, and the men began to row with a steady rhythm. A blanket of clammy fog lay on the rolling, slate-green sea. Moisture gathered on the boat's seats, and the planks were dotted with droplets. The air was chillingly raw, and the periodic crash of waves echoed from the concealed shore. Sometimes, the toll of a distant bell pierced the murmurs of the sea. When the yacht eventually loomed out of the fog, it appeared spectral and gray, its rigging dripping and deck slick. The sailors at the gangway looked listless and soaked.

Everything felt bleak and dismal as Aynsley hurried toward Jimmy, his expression tense.

"thanks for coming," he said, his voice filled with concern. "i hope you're okay."

"not too bad. I'm sorry your father had a rough trip, but i really did my best."

"i know you did," Aynsley replied sincerely. "he's waiting to see you."

Aynsley guided Jimmy into a finely crafted teak deckhouse situated between the masts. He opened a door to the owner's cabin, which spanned the full width of the structure. Inside, two electric lamps illuminated the space, with rich curtains drawn to block out the gloomy light outside. A fire crackled cheerfully in an open-fronted stove, adorned with decorated tiles. The brass pipe shimmered in the light, and the walls and ceiling were a pristine white, accented with color-coordinated moldings. Marine paintings adorned the cross bulkhead, adding a touch of elegance. To Jimmy, the cabin seemed luxurious compared to the cramped, damp quarters of the sloop. But his focus quickly shifted to the figure lying in the corner berth.

Clay had pushed away the covers and was propped up on a couple of large pillows. His silk pajamas revealed a stout neck and muscular chest and arms, but his face was pallid and lined, save for faint purple streaks. It was clear to Jimmy that Clay was very ill.

"i hear you got the case," Clay began, his voice strained as he motioned for Jimmy to sit down.

"yes. The others brought it up; i haven't had a chance to look at it yet."

"it'll be fine," Clay said with a weak smile. "i suppose you know there's another case and a couple of small packages still in the strong-room?"

"we heard about it."

"get them up; they're in the sand. You can use my diver, and it shouldn't take long. You're welcome to the salvage; it's not worth the hassle to dispute it. After that, there won't be anything left in her."

"i promise, you can leave whenever you like."

"none of us want to stay; we've had enough. I suppose you're not planning on heading back down?"

"no," Clay replied grimly. "that's not likely. I haven't thanked you yet for pulling me out." he turned to Aynsley. "Mr. Farquhar stayed with me when i was barely conscious and completely helpless. Please remember that. Now, i'd like a private word with him."

Aynsley exited, leaving Clay in silence for a moment. He laid back on the pillows, eyes closed. When he finally spoke, it seemed like it took all his effort.

"about the fake case. What's your plan for it?"

"we haven't had time to consider that. You mentioned an exchange, but we know it's not here."

"no," said clay. "your partner is smart. I'm sure it's safely locked away at one of the island ports. Odds are, you won't be able to hand it over to me."

Jimmy understood. Clay seemed aware of how gravely ill he was. He remained quiet again, as if talking drained him.

"it's been a fair fight on your side," Clay resumed after a short rest. "you might give that box to Osborne. You're decent men, despite the potential conflict it could cause. The thing's useless to you anyway. Do you know Osborne?"

"yes," Jimmy answered awkwardly, knowing what the question implied. Clay had rightly judged him; Jimmy had no intention of blackmailing anyone. He believed he could speak for his companions, though he wouldn't make a promise without their agreement.

"you know ruth Osborne?" Clay continued, watching Jimmy closely. Jimmy was a little taken aback, and Clay noticed his slight start and change in expression.

"i met miss Osborne on the empress," he replied cautiously.

Clay smiled.

"well," he said, "she's not the kind of girl you forget easily, and i have a feeling her personality is just as striking as her looks." he paused, reflecting for a moment. "anyway, she wouldn't have Aynsley."

Jimmy flushed. Clay's tone was suggestive but not unfriendly. Despite his illness, Jimmy sensed he was skillfully maneuvering, trying to convert his former adversary into an ally, possibly with a deeper purpose. Still, Jimmy believed clay's intentions were good.

"i shouldn't keep you talking too long," Jimmy said, keen to avoid a conversation about miss Osborne.

"i do get tired quickly these days, but there's something important
i need to address. You'll have the wreck cleared out in a few hours, and
then it might be best to blow it up. My diver can assist, and we have
some powerful explosives and the necessary ignition equipment."

"that does sound prudent. If it gets pushed closer to the bay, it could
become a real hazard. The island's charted, and ships do occasionally
come by."

Clay's eyes gleamed with a hint of mischief.

"indeed, we can agree it's a danger. I'll have my man give you whatever supplies you need, and you should try to finish up while the
weather holds."

With some effort, he extended his hand, signaling that their discussion was over. Jimmy took it without hesitation, feeling as if he
were making a pledge to his ailing adversary. Aynsley was waiting on
deck and insisted on Jimmy staying for dinner. Although impeccably
served, the meal had a somber air, and Jimmy felt an overwhelming
sense of isolation at the long table. Aynsley went out of his way to
ensure his comfort, attempting to keep the conversation flowing, but
his melancholy was palpable.

"what are your plans?" Aynsley asked.

"we start extracting the last of the gold at daybreak," Jimmy replied.
"with some luck, it should take only three or four hours."

"and after that?"

"i agreed with your father that it would be best to blow up the
wreck."

"you should aim to get that done before nightfall tomorrow."

"i think we can manage, as long as the sea remains calm."

"we should be done by the afternoon," Jimmy said confidently.

"that's a relief," Aynsley replied with a hint of urgency. "it's probably
not polite to say, but i honestly don't know—or want to know—what

business you have with my father. He's really sick, and we need to get him to a good doctor as soon as possible. The problem is, he won't leave until you've wrapped up whatever it is you're doing."

"we won't waste any time," Jimmy assured him. "the barometer's falling, but i don't think we'll get much wind yet."

"thanks," Aynsley said, visibly moved. "there's another thing: if the wind's light or against us, we'll start under steam. We can tow you south as long as the weather holds. It might save you a few days. You could stay with us if your friends can spare you. Honestly, it would be a great help to me. I'm worried and need someone to talk to."

Jimmy agreed, and soon after, he was rowed back to the sloop. By noon the next day, they had retrieved the last of the gold. After a quick lunch, they went down again, but the next task was more time-consuming. The diver insisted on securing the dynamite charges firmly to the main timbers, even boring holes in some. Then they had to run a series of wires below and connect them all. It was nearly dinner time when Jimmy surfaced from his final dive.

Anemic ripples disturbed the leaden water, too timid to break on the sloop's bow. The island lay shrouded in fog, and the swell was gentle, a muted whisper from the obscured beach. Out to sea, it was clearer. The yacht, a lengthy white shape, lifted her bow in a slow, rhythmic sway, a gray plume rising almost straight from her funnel. The sloop's anchor chain was drawn tight, and everything was set for departure.

The crew sat tensely in the cockpit, eyes fixed on the diver who was carefully connecting wires to the contact plug of the firing battery. Impatience buzzed through the group. They had weathered countless hardships in these desolate waters, and now, with their task complete, they longed to leave. The wreck carried its own enigma, one they had no desire to untangle. All they wanted was to see the end of it and escape the fog-shrouded island.

"we're ready," the diver announced finally. "double-check that nothing's loose; she'll shift some water."

He inserted the firing plug, and almost immediately, the sea erupted a short distance ahead, splitting to reveal shattered timbers churning in chaotic motion. A foaming wave surged from the chasm, hurling planks and massive beams skyward. They crashed back into the sea amid fountains of spray, and a white, ferocious wave raced toward the sloop. It broke before reaching her, but still, the yacht pitched violently, throwing her bows high as she dipped over the tumultuous swell, the deck awash with yeasty foam. Jimmy sprang forward, exhilarating in the destruction as he broke out the anchor—the powerful charge had obliterated the wreck. As the Resolute drifted gently on the current, the yacht's windlass clanked into action, and minutes later, she steamed toward a smaller vessel. Her gig ferried over a hawser and an invitation for Jimmy to come aboard. Once on deck, the gig was promptly hoisted to the davits and the engines revved faster. The sloop, now trailing behind, followed through the screw-cut waves, and soon, the fog surrounding the island vanished from sight. Jimmy, more relaxed, enjoyed dinner with Aynsley in the saloon.

The gloom that had weighed on them all seemed to lift with the disappearance of the wreck. Even Clay seemed brighter. He called for Jimmy to join him once dinner was over. When Jimmy stepped into the cabin, he saw Clay reclining in his berth, propped up comfortably by pillows. Clay greeted him with a friendly nod.

"it's gone? did you handle it well?"

"yes," Jimmy replied cheerfully. "we didn't hold back on the dynamite."

Clay motioned him closer and awkwardly reached for a glass of champagne on the small table by his berth. Another glass stood ready next to it.

"i'm not the best host and i tire easily, but Aynsley will take good care of you," he said warmly, smiling and raising his glass. "good luck to you; you're a good man!"

Jimmy finished his drink and took clay's empty glass from his trembling hand. When the older man thanked him with a slight gesture, Jimmy could tell he was too weak to speak further. Quietly, he left the cabin and joined Aynsley on deck. He stayed three days on the yacht as it sailed steadily south, but on the night of the fourth day, a steward woke him urgently.

"it's getting rough out there, sir," the steward said. "the captain thought you'd want to know your boat's towing wildly, and he can't hold on to it much longer."

Jimmy had anticipated this scenario and was on deck within five minutes, fully dressed in his sea-boots and slickers. Aynsley, also up, joined him in the shelter of the deckhouse, hastily throwing a pilot coat over his pajamas. The yacht's engines were turning slowly, and the way it heaved and sprayed showed that the sea was growing restless.

"they're launching the gig," Aynsley said. "i wish we could keep you here, but i guess your friends need your help?"

"thanks, but they wouldn't make it home without me."

Jimmy dashed to the rail and called out to the group of sailors:

"no need for that ladder, boys!"

A blue flare burst to life atop the deckhouse, illuminating the scene with a stark light. The gig bobbed wildly in the churning waters on the yacht's lee side.

Nearby, the Resolute surged through the waves with her staysail up, a lone figure on her deck signaling with a lantern. Jimmy shook hands with Aynsley and leapt onto the rail, gripping a davit-fall and sliding quickly down. A crewman released the tackle-hook, shoving the gig away; the oars splashed as the sea carried her away from the yacht. Within minutes, Jimmy boarded the sloop and assisted moran in casting off the hawser while the gig struggled back. Another flare illuminated the scene, revealing the boat being hoisted back on board. The light dwindled, and with a final whistle blast, the steamer faded into the darkness. Spray crashed against the rolling sloop, its low deck drenched by the relentless sea, ropes swinging damply from the mast.

"we've double-reefed the mainsail and rigged the storm-jib," moran yelled over the roaring sea. "she should handle that with the wind on her quarter."

"she should," replied Jimmy. "hoist the throat!"

In the darkness, they struggled to raise the flapping sail. When the Resolute heeled over, her rail slicing through the foam, Jimmy rushed aft to relieve Bethune at the helm.

"she'll make good time if this wind holds," he said, smiling. "i've had three nights of solid sleep; i'll take the first watch."

As the sloop careened southward before the tailwind, or tacked slowly with long turns when the breeze shifted and weakened, the yacht raced over the water at her top speed. One gray morning, she steamed up puget sound, her whistle sounding mournfully as she passed Osborne's house. Clay's journey had ended; she was bringing his lifeless body home.

CHAPTER THIRTY-ONE.

Jimmy and his friends sat on the balcony formed by the flat roof of the veranda in front of Jaques' store. The evening was pleasant, with a gentle breeze stirring up the dust in the streets of the wooden town. Beyond the plain, square buildings that extended down to the wharf, the waters shimmered in the twilight, and through a gap, the sloop was clearly visible, moored at the harbor's entrance. On the other side, a deep crimson blaze illuminated the hillcrest, casting the jagged pines into stark relief against the sky. The day's work was done, and clusters of men lounged in chairs outside the hotels, while scattered here and there, families sat on their stoops. Jimmy had given a brief account of their northern adventures but had yet to discuss their future plans. Now, Jaques and his wife awaited this discussion.

"Clay must have died shortly after you left the yacht," the storekeeper said. "since you believe his son is friendly, we don't have any opposition to worry about. We might as well decide on our next steps."

"Bethune is our business manager," Jimmy said. "perhaps he can give us his thoughts."

Bethune leaned forward, his expression thoughtful.

"firstly, it's not as straightforward as it seems. We don't know the full story behind the wreck, and frankly, i doubt we ever will. However, there's a lot we can infer, and it's possible to build a theory that's hard to dismiss. Honestly, if it weren't for some ethical concerns, i think there's money to be made."

"call them ethical concerns if you want," mrs. Jaques interjected. "but it would be wiser to stick to them."

"that might be true," Bethune conceded. "even so, we're in a rather delicate position."

"i'm a trader," Jaques remarked. "i aim for a fair profit on my investments, but that's where i draw the line."

"all the money i take is for the value i provide," said Jaques with a resolute tone, turning to face Jimmy.

"speaking of which, did you catch where Clay got that case?" Jaques asked him.

"not at all," Jimmy replied, shaking his head. "none of us did. We were far too engaged to look into where he holed up. My guess is there must have been some space between the top of the strong-room and the floor of the poop cabin."

Jaques frowned. "it's an odd spot to stash a box of gold. Placing a decoy in the strong-room makes sense if they wanted to scuttle the vessel. But why not transport the real cargo on another ship?"

"that's exactly where my theory hits a wall," Bethune said, smiling faintly. "the only reason i can think of is so implausible it seems absurd to even mention."

"let's not get bogged down in that," mrs. Jaques interrupted swiftly. "what's the plan for the gold you brought back?"

"we'll take it to the underwriters and push hard for the highest salvage we can muster. If they try to shortchange us, we'll drag them to court," Jaques said, his voice firm with intent.

"and what about the fake box? are you going to give it to them?"
mrs. Jaques's question hung in the air. Jimmy had anticipated this,
knowing he had to speak up. He was aware of a scam tied to the shipwreck, but delving into it wasn't his responsibility. Some might argue
against this view, but he was resolved even if it meant bending social
norms. Suspicion pointed at Osborne, but Jimmy was committed to
shielding ruth from any such disgrace. No shadow of sorrow or shame
would touch her, not if he could help it. Besides, he had promised Clay
something — the dying man's trust wasn't something he'd betray.

"i claim that case," Jimmy said quietly but resolutely. "i promised
Clay i'd give it to Osborne."

A silence fell over the room, thick with unspoken thoughts. Finally,
Jaques broke it.

"perhaps that's the best course of action," Jaques mused, looking
contemplative. "what do you think, Mr. Bethune?"

"on the whole, i concur," Bethune agreed.

"someone might've tried to sabotage the vessel, but we can't prove
it. And honestly, it's the gold that matters most to us, plus the underwriters get their money back. That should keep them happy, and
it saves us a lot of hassle." he grinned, adding, "it's probably the easiest
way out."

They decided to deposit the gold in the express company vaults in
Victoria, and then Bethune would start negotiations with the insurers.

"i think i could sell the Resolute for you at a decent price," Jaques
mentioned. "one of the guys here is thinking of starting in deep-water
fishing."

"i'd hate to let the boat go, but we really don't need her," Jimmy
admitted. "we're thinking if we get enough from the insurance, we
could get into towing and transport. A small wooden, propeller tug

wouldn't be too expensive; we might even start with a couple of large launches."

"that should work," Jaques agreed. "the coastal trade is booming; sometimes i have to wait ages to get my stuff moved."

"it's just the beginning," Bethune chimed in. "this province's coastline is barely touched. It's full of amazing natural harbors, and once the new railroads connect to the sea, trade will explode. The first guys in will profit. I see a future where these narrow waters are packed with steamboats, but for now, there's a living to be made towing timber for the sawmills and hauling small cargo between northern settlements."

He spoke with excitement, and Jaques looked eager.

"i think you're onto something. First, get the underwriters on board; then if you need some extra cash, let me know."

"i could help you in several ways."

They discussed the project in detail. Bethune and Jaques took the helm, while Jimmy, filled with a sense of quiet satisfaction, seated himself next to mrs. Jaques. After enduring immense hardship and effort, he had completed his mission, and now, the future looked promising. He trusted Bethune's judgment—this new path could very well lead to success. The thought of ruth Osborne urged Jimmy forward. He resolved that no obstacles would deter him. Though he lacked his partner's breadth of skills, he possessed a steady courage and a stubborn determination that promised to take him far. Mrs. Jaques gestured towards her husband and Bethune.

"they're getting quite enthusiastic, but i must say, tom rarely makes mistakes in business. He thinks your prospects are solid."

"we have to make them solid," Jimmy replied. "meeting your husband was a stroke of luck for us. We were in a really tight spot when he lent us a hand."

"i've often wondered why you didn't go back to sea when things got tough. It would've been an easy way out."

Jimmy leaned in, lowering his voice.

"there was a compelling reason for me to stay here."

"ah!" mrs. Jaques exclaimed, her eyes sparkling. "i see. I hope you've made a wise choice. Falling in love is quite serious. Is she pretty?"

"she's beautiful!"

Mrs. Jaques smiled warmly.

"so you stayed in Vancouver for her! naturally, she would want to keep you close."

"i have no reason to believe that," Jimmy admitted, his expression turning somber.

"you mean—" she prompted.

Jaques gave him a penetrating look before completing her thought: "...that you're not sure if she even likes you?"

Jimmy hesitated, feeling a flush creep onto his face as he recalled the night he had helped ruth out of the launch.

"it might be a long while before i find out," he admitted. "the problem is, she's a rich man's daughter."

"what's his name? your secret's safe with me."

"Osborne."

Mrs. Jaques raised an eyebrow in surprise, and Jimmy chuckled.

"oh, so now you think i'm crazy. Sometimes i think so myself."

She studied him quietly for a moment. He was strikingly handsome, with an amiable and honest face, yet there was an underlying determination too. He seemed dependable, someone you could trust, and mrs. Jaques had a warm affection for him.

"no," she said finally. "i don't think you're insane. Perhaps a bit rash, but you know, daring often trumps cautious timidity. It can take you much further. Sure, there'll be obstacles, but i wouldn't lose hope. This is a place where a bold man has plenty of opportunities."

"thank you," Jimmy murmured. "you've given me a bit of hope." he quickly looked up as Bethune spoke to him. "oh, yes," he said hastily. "quite so."

"quite so!" exclaimed Bethune, incredulous. "my guess is you didn't catch a single word i said."

"that's entirely possible," mrs. Jaques laughed. "but he has a good excuse. You can hardly fault him for talking to me."

The gathering dispersed soon after, and the next morning the sloop set sail for Victoria. Jimmy spent several anxious days in the city before he received a telegram from Bethune. They had struck a deal with the underwriters, more generous than Jimmy had anticipated, providing enough funds to start the new venture modestly. He instructed the express company to release the gold and then set off to visit Osborne. It was evening by the time he arrived. Entering the house, he was eager to see ruth and curious about her reaction, but also uneasy about his impending meeting with her father.

The butler led Jimmy straight to the library, where Osborne immediately stood to greet him.

"Aynsley Clay mentioned you'd drop by, and i'm glad you did," Osborne said warmly. "i hope you'll stay for a few days."

"thanks, but i can't," Jimmy replied. "i need to take care of some business. Clay insisted i deliver something to you. I left it in the hall."

Osborne rang the bell, and a square package, tightly wrapped in canvas, was brought in. Once they were alone, Jimmy placed it on the table and began cutting through the stitches.

"i'm not sure if this will surprise you," he remarked, revealing a rugged wooden box, still showing signs of prolonged exposure to water.

"that!" Osborne exclaimed, collapsing into the nearest chair. "who found this box?"

"i did, in the steamer's strong-room."

Sweat beads formed on Osborne's forehead, and his breath came in short, sharp gasps.

"do you know what's inside?" he managed to ask.

"yes," Jimmy said calmly. "it's not gold. Some of its contents are still there, but i removed the rest to make it lighter."

Osborne slumped back in his chair, overwhelmed.

"when did you discover it?" he questioned.

"about eight months ago, more or less."

"and Clay knew about it all this time?"

"no. We only told him a week before he died."

"that's unusual," Osborne said, eyeing Jimmy suspiciously. "why mention it after keeping silent for so long?"

"we anticipated trouble. Clay had the power to shut us down, so when he came aboard to discuss matters, we revealed the contents. Eventually, he lent us his diver and provided whatever help he could."

"and that was the only deal you struck with him?"

"yes," Jimmy replied, his face reddening. "it was all we asked for and all we got. It would make things simpler if you accepted that."

"don't you realize you settled too easily?" Osborne said with a sardonic edge to his voice.

Jimmy stayed silent.

"so, the case is mine to do with as i please?" Osborne asked.

"yes. Think of it as a gift from clay."

"who else knows about this?"

"my two partners, a storekeeper who financed us, and his wife. They're trustworthy. I can vouch for them."

"well," Osborne said softly, "i must say, you and your friends have behaved quite honorably. Clay sending me the case is typical of him, but i never expected you to feel obliged. If you don't mind, i'd like to thank you for your actions."

"i'm not done yet. You probably know we salvaged a lot of gold, but you won't have heard that we've accounted for every insured package."

Osborne looked perplexed, glancing at the box on the table.

"including this one?"

"no. We found a duplicate, containing gold of slightly more weight than declared, which the underwriters have compensated us for."

Osborne was stunned, his face showing sheer disbelief.

"but that sounds impossible! i can't grasp it."

"it's baffling," Jimmy agreed. "there's a mystery, but my partners and i decided not to dig into it."

"perhaps that's wise. Certainly considerate. But still, i don't get it. Did you find it in the strong-room?"

"not exactly. Clay showed me where to cut a hole in the roof. He crawled through and brought out the box. I assume it was hidden among the deck beams, but we didn't have time to inspect the place."

"ah!" Osborne exclaimed, a realization dawning as he remembered his partner's frantic effort to break through the cabin floor on the night of the wreck. "maybe you're right. So the insurance company paid your claim without questions. They were satisfied?"

"yes."

"i believe that settles the matter," Osborne said.

Relief washed over his face, and his previously tense posture sagged as he let out a breath. He stayed silent for a moment, then rose from his chair.

"Mr. Farquhar," he began, "you can't imagine the relief your news brings me. I need some time to process this. If you don't mind, my daughter and miss dexter can keep you company for a while."

"but i need to head back soon," Jimmy protested, feeling that staying any longer, as much as he wished to, would be awkward for both him and Osborne.

"you won't be able to leave until tomorrow," Osborne replied with a smile. "there's no night boat now, the launch is being repaired, and my car is in town. I'm afraid you'll have to accept our hospitality for the night."

Osborne rang the bell, and after Jimmy left the room, he sat down, his brow furrowed in thought. Where had Clay gotten that gold? his fist clenched involuntarily as he recalled the someone who had mined the alluvial gold before their arrival. This was suspicious, especially since the gold had been smuggled aboard without appearing on the ship's manifest. While the box of gold was intriguing, it wasn't the most pressing matter. On his deathbed, perhaps in an attempt at redemption, Clay had sent Osborne a gift that erased years of fear and anxiety. Whatever clay's past transgressions, Osborne could now forgive him. Finally, he was a free man; the only evidence against him was now in his possession, and he intended to destroy it immediately. After years of regretting his one grave mistake, his partner's final act had saved him from its repercussions.

CHAPTER THIRTY-TWO.

When Jimmy stepped into the spacious, cool living room, he felt an acute mix of satisfaction and the challenge of maintaining his composure. He had seen little of Osborne's home until now, and the room's beauty left a lasting impression on him. The blend of curtains, rugs, furniture, and artwork formed a symphony of soft colors and delicate designs—a setting perfectly suited to ruth.

Ruth wore an elegant evening dress tonight, a far cry from the casual attire Jimmy had seen her in before. He couldn't pinpoint the exact cut or shade of the dress, but he knew it was exactly what she should be wearing. The dress draped gracefully around her, hinting at her lithe figure and complementing the fairness of her complexion, accentuating the luster of her hair. The sight was both stunning and intimidating. Ruth appeared every bit the beautiful lady in her element, while Jimmy felt acutely rough and out of place.

As she moved toward him, Jimmy's heart pounded. He recalled their last encounter with a sense of unease, expecting a change in her demeanor that would push him away. Yet, there was no trace of that. It seemed she remembered how he had helped her out of the launch and had subtly acknowledged it and its implications. Though Jimmy wasn't skilled at deciphering others' thoughts, he sensed they were closer than ever before.

Ruth smiled up at him as she extended her hand, but her voice remained composed and factual.

"i'm glad you finally made it. It's nice to know you're back safely." she added with a playful pout, "i assume you had some business with my father, which explains your visit."

"it gave me a reason to do what i wanted," Jimmy confessed.

"did you need a reason? we gave you an open invitation."

"i felt like i did," Jimmy replied slowly, and ruth understood.

He was reserved yet proud, reluctant to join her circle just because of a favor. She hoped he'd see her, not as the heiress of wealth, but as an intriguing woman.

"you're too shy," she smiled at him. "but i won't start with criticisms. I want to hear about your thrilling adventures. Aynsley Clay was here, but he couldn't tell us much about you and he had his own issues."

"yes," Jimmy replied softly. "i feel for him. He's someone you quickly grow fond of; and there was much to respect in his father. We actually got quite close during the final days at the wreck."

Ruth paused for a moment, then said, "tell me about the wreck."

"it's a lengthy story, and you might find it dull."

"i asked you to tell it."

Jimmy welcomed the chance, determined to ensure she had no reason to doubt her father. Many things were still unclear, but she mustn't suspect this. It was unthinkable for her to be troubled by something he could shield her from. He knew he had to tread carefully, as there were delicate aspects to the tale. As he began the story, ruth watched him closely. His bronzed skin, steady eyes, and figure refined by hardship made him look striking and distinguished. He had evolved since their first meeting; this was no longer the amiable, carefree steamship officer. He was now alert and resolute, yet he had retained his earnestness. He was utterly trustworthy, and she realized she liked him even more than before.

His account of their northern ordeals captivated her, and she occasionally prodded him with questions, eager to uncover the truth about the wreck.

For months, she had been plagued by unsettling doubts.

"but despite everything, you found the gold!" ruth finally exclaimed.

"yes," Jimmy replied, seizing the moment he had been waiting for. "we retrieved it all."

"all of it!" ruth's relief was overwhelming, momentarily catching her off guard.

"i think so," Jimmy said. "we recovered every insured crate. The underwriters were completely satisfied."

A flush spread across ruth's face. All her fears had been baseless. Her father, whom she had doubted, was innocent. There was no hidden conspiracy behind the shipwreck, as she had unfairly imagined. Jimmy had dispelled her anxieties. The hardships he endured had freed her from her haunting suspicions. She realized he might be puzzled by her reaction, but that didn't matter. She was flooded with gratitude.

"thank you for telling me," she said, aware of how insufficient her words were. "it's a thrilling story."

"if you're pleased, that's all that matters."

"pleased! you have no idea how much."

"then i'm well-rewarded," said Jimmy boldly, losing his composure in the warmth of her gratitude. "finding the gold is secondary."

Ruth noticed his growing fervor and decided to give it one last push.

"and you must have been very determined to recover the gold, facing all those challenges."

"yes," Jimmy said, meeting her gaze steadily, "i wanted it badly, for a reason."

"didn't you want it just for the gold itself? that would be natural." ruth hesitated. "but you haven't shared your true reason."

He drew strength from her look, though she turned her head the next moment.

"i'm almost scared to say it, but you need to know. I was a steamboat mate without a ship, a laborer on the docks, and all the while i had this wild ambition locked in my heart."

My partner, Bethune, showed me a way to make it happen, and i seized the opportunity."

"it must have been a powerful ambition that drove you to face the harsh winds and ice."

"it was. Stronger than my better judgment. I knew it was nearly hopeless, but i couldn't let it go. You see, i had fallen in love."

"really? when did that happen? was it that night when you met the sound steamer with your launch?"

"oh, no; it started much earlier. It began one afternoon in yoko-hama, when a girl in a dust-veil and the most beautiful dress i had ever seen stepped onto the empress's gangway."

"so, it must have been an instant attraction," ruth replied, blushing and smiling. "the veil was pretty thick, and she didn't even speak to you."

"that didn't matter. She smiled her thanks when i moved a rope out of her way, and i've never seen a smile so sweet and gracious. After that, there were peaceful evenings when the empress gently rocked in the smooth seas, and she would leave her friends to walk the deck with me. I knew i was being foolish, but as soon as my watch was over, i'd wait with a hopeful heart, wishing she'd come."

"and sometimes she didn't."

"those were dark nights," said Jimmy. "while i waited, i tried to convince myself it would be better if i never saw her again. But i knew all along i couldn't bring myself to do it." he hesitated, reaching out as if begging for understanding. "ruth, haven't i said enough?"

"not quite. Did you think, when you went to find the wreck, that succeeding would make me look at you more favorably?"

"even if the wreck had been filled with gold, it wouldn't have made me your equal; but i knew what your friends would think."

"you shouldn't have needed to apologize on my behalf," Jimmy said, his voice earnest.

Ruth's smile lit up her face, sending a wave of warmth through him.

"ruth," he said suddenly, "you're the only thing that matters to me in this entire world."

She blushed and allowed herself to be gently pulled into his embrace. The little gilt clock on the mantel, crowned with a poised cupid, seemed to tick joyfully in the peaceful silence that filled the room. A half-hour slipped by before they heard footsteps in the hallway, and then Osborne entered. His eyes narrowed as he took in the scene; Jimmy's triumphant demeanor and ruth's flushed cheeks told him everything.

"well!" he said. "it appears you two have some news for me?"

"that's right," Jimmy affirmed, and ruth gave her father a confident smile.

"there's no reason for you to object, so don't act all huffy about it," she protested.

"i believe Mr. Farquhar and i need to have a conversation," Osborne said calmly. Once ruth left, he gestured for Jimmy to take a seat.

"now," Osborne began, "i'll admit i'm somewhat taken aback. Although from what i've seen and heard, i have no personal objections, there are some concerns."

"trust me, no one is more aware of the challenges ahead than i am," Jimmy said with a wry smile. "to be honest, they seemed daunting enough to make me think my hopes were impossible until just thirty minutes ago. My only defense is that i love your daughter."

"that's a strong point in your favor, but it doesn't solve every issue. May i ask about your plans for the future?"

"they're modest, but they have potential. My partners and i plan to start a small towing and transport business using the money from the salvage."

Intrigued, Osborne asked for more details. As Jimmy explained their venture, Osborne listened intently. The proposal was clearly well-conceived, and he felt it had a good chance of succeeding. Farquhar and his team had managed to pull off their salvage operations despite significant opposition from clay, which demonstrated their resourcefulness and tenacity.

Understanding the methods of his late partner, he could easily envision the challenges they had faced.

"i think you've chosen an opportune moment. The coastal trade seems poised for a significant expansion," he remarked. "however, the downside is you'll have to start small. I might be able to find you some additional capital."

"no, thanks!" Jimmy responded resolutely. "we've decided against borrowing."

Osborne flashed a knowing smile.

"am i to take that as you not wanting any assistance from me?"

Jimmy felt a twinge of discomfort. He couldn't shake the suspicion that Osborne had been involved in some shady scheme to profit unlawfully from the wreck. Any offer of help might be seen as a bribe.

"we think it's best to stand on our own two feet," he explained.

"perhaps you're right. Nonetheless, i hope you don't mind if i bring some business your way. That aside, what i wanted to discuss is different. I can't agree to anything now, but after you've been in business for a year, come see me again, and we'll review your progress."

"and in the meantime?" Jimmy asked, his concern evident.

"you're both free; there are no other conditions. If miss dexter approves, my door is open to you."

A few minutes later, Jimmy found ruth in the hall.

"well?" she inquired. "how did it go?"

"i think i got off easier than expected." Jimmy relayed Osborne's conditions to her.

"so, you're free for another year! are you sure you won't change your mind?"

"i'm committed forever! and i'm more than happy with that. But your father suggested i'd need your aunt's approval to see you."

"that won't be difficult," ruth laughed. "if you don't trust your own merits, leave it to me."

"maybe it's time you came to see her."

Miss dexter spent a considerable amount of time questioning Jimmy, her direct inquiries making him uncomfortable. Later, she remarked to her niece, "i like your sailor. He seems honest, and that's crucial. Still, i can't help but feel a bit disappointed you didn't choose Aynsley, whom i've always been fond of. It's odd how different he is from his father."

"Clay had his good traits," ruth replied warmly. "he was incredibly generous, and though i don't fully grasp the details, i believe he lost his life trying to clear his name for his son's sake."

"maybe. There was something strange about that wreck. Clay was a pirate, my dear—perhaps a noble and magnanimous one—but still a pirate."

Osborne had quietly entered the room during their conversation.

"i owe Clay a lot; he deserved more sympathy than he received," he said. "he had his critics, but often those who judged him harshest were not without their own flaws."

"you're all pirates at heart," miss dexter declared.

"there's probably some truth to that," Osborne admitted with a smile. The next morning, Jimmy left the house, and not long after, he opened his modest office in Vancouver. Shortly thereafter, Aynsley paid him a visit.

"first of all, congratulations," Aynsley began. "you must know you're exceptionally fortunate."

"i'm well aware," Jimmy replied. "but in some sense, you're a bit early; i'm still on probation."

He felt a bit awkward, knowing from Clay about Aynsley's feelings for ruth.

"there's another reason for my visit. We often raft substantial amounts of lumber to the sea for shipment and sometimes purchase high-quality logs from the coast. I don't see why you shouldn't handle our towing for us."

"are you open for business?" Jimmy asked, peering around the office.

"absolutely," Aynsley replied, meeting his gaze. "thanks for giving me a lift."

A brief silence fell between them before Aynsley finally smiled. "i'll admit, if i'd had the chance before you came along, i might have felt some resentment. But i knew from the beginning it wasn't in the cards for me. Ruth chose you, and i'm honestly trying to wish you both happiness. Truthfully, she could have picked worse."

"thanks," Jimmy acknowledged, his tone sincere.

"anyway, let's move on. My father mentioned being grateful to you. Said you'd taken a load off his mind. I owe you for that. Plus, i think it could benefit us both if you handled our towing. What do you say we explore this as a business opportunity?"

They struck a deal that day, and within weeks, work flooded in for the new firm, more than they could manage comfortably. Just a few months later, they decided to invest in a large, albeit rundown, tug. After refurbishing it, they found ample work to keep the vessel occupied. Their reputation solidified when they successfully towed several massive log booms down the coast during stormy weather. Jimmy personally managed the tougher jobs with moran's assistance, while Bethune managed the office and secured client trust.

Their real breakthrough came the following year. A large american collier had run aground near the wellington mines. Damaged and stranded, the owners opted to send her back to portland for repairs, seeking bids for the tow. Jimmy played a crucial role in the salvage effort and won their trust.

Picking up on the captain's subtle cue, Jimmy quickly reconvened with his team for a strategic huddle.

"we have to clinch this deal, even if it means no profit for us," Bethune asserted. "it's our breakthrough chance and a prime opportunity to prove our capabilities. Are you confident about handling the trip down the coast?"

"it's a tall order. The vessel's propeller is gone, and her stern-frame is in shambles. The makeshift rudder they've jerry-rigged won't steer for beans, and i'm doubtful the bolted plates will keep much water out if she starts straining. Still, i'll give it a shot if you can secure another tug. One boat won't cut it for this load."

"the old guillemot is an option. We could get her on a short-term lease for a reasonable price."

Jimmy nodded. "see what you can negotiate," he replied, and the next day, Bethune dispatched a formal proposal. Upon receiving it, the managing owner of the collier crossed over to discuss matters with the captain.

"i'm inclined to award the contract to the san francisco team," he said. "they've got vast experience with these operations, and their vessels are top-notch on the pacific. Their bid is steep, but i trust their reliability."

"you're in good hands with Farquhar. The salvage team only got her free because of him."

"i hear his firm is small. His bid is low, but he claims he can tow her down."

"then take his offer," the captain advised. "what that man promises, he delivers. I've seen him in action."

With the captain further reinforcing Farquhar's competency, Bethune secured the contract. Jimmy and his crew promptly departed Vancouver with two tugs in tow. They navigated past Victoria with the crippled vessel in calm conditions. However, by nightfall, the weather turned, and a gale brewed. It raged for two weeks, hammering in from the pacific and whipping the coast with a relentless, furious surf.

Three days after Jimmy had navigated the strait, the chartered tug returned, its engines crippled and hull battered by the ferocious storm. The skipper reported leaving Jimmy with a snapped towline, clinging to the collier, which was being dragged dangerously close to the treacherous coastline. An incoming steamer later mentioned sighting a disabled vessel with a tug nearby in the heart of the tempest, but the violent weather made it impossible to render aid and no distress signals were visible. Days passed with no updates. The lack of news prompted an assessment of reinsurance for the collier, which summonsed Bethune to Osborne's home. Bethune struggled to offer any optimism, and ruth's worried expression lingered in his mind long after their meeting. As public curiosity about the missing vessel grew, newspapers started running stories about her. Some speculated that the collier and the tug had sunk in deep waters since no debris had washed ashore.

Finally, when hope was nearly extinguished, the vessel limped into harbor across the turbulent columbia bar on a stormy morning, led by her tug, with Jimmy at the helm. He became an overnight sensation, though he swiftly dodged reporters and went in search of coal, setting back to sea as soon as he could. However, the grateful captain spoke freely, and the media turned the ordeal into a dramatic tale of perseverance. According to the accounts, Jimmy had smashed two lifeboats while replacing broken towlines amidst perilous seas, holding onto the crippled vessel as it was pushed to the edge of the breakers against a rocky shore. A sudden shift in the wind saved them, but the next night the collier broke free again. For two relentless days, Jimmy searched through a haze of spray and distant fog. He found her, once more teetering on the brink, and managed to secure her again, battling a fierce, almost hopeless fight against the raging ocean.

Jimmy reached Vancouver early one morning and made his way to Osborne's house by the afternoon, looking noticeably thin and tired. Osborne greeted him warmly in the hallway, extending a friendly hand.

"congratulations are in order," Osborne said, his voice filled with admiration. "you've propelled your company to the forefront with one bold move. If you let your friends support you, there's a tremendous opportunity ahead to expand your business."

"that's not what matters most to me," Jimmy replied with a meaningful intensity.

"well," Osborne said with a knowing smile, "i believe i can trust ruth to you. Even though the year isn't up yet, you've proved yourself."

As ruth stepped forward, Osborne discreetly moved away. Her eyes shone as she gazed at Jimmy, and she eagerly embraced him.

"i've heard amazing stories about your achievements, dear. But deep down, i always knew what you were capable of. Now, all that matters is that you're back safely with me," she said.

The end.

Printed in Great Britain
by Amazon

58940246R00170